Desmond Bagley was born in 1923 in England's Lake District and emigrated to Africa after the war. He held a number of jobs in Nairobi, Rhodesia and South Africa, and then became a journalist there. In 1962 he began to write a novel, *The Golden Keel*; after its successful publication in 1963, he and his wife returned to England, and he has been a full-time novelist ever since. He now lives in Guernsey.

Desmond Bagley has now written eleven highly-praised novels, each more successful than the last: all have been bestsellers in England and America, and they have now been translated into nineteen foreign languages. William Collins published his most recent book, *Flyaway*, in 1978.

DESMOND BAGLEY

Running Blind

FONTANA/Collins

First published in 1970 by William Collins Sons & Co Ltd
First issued in Fontana Books 1972
Twentieth Impression January 1980

© L. J. Jersey Ltd 1970

Made and printed in Great Britain by
William Collins Sons & Co Ltd, Glasgow

To: Torfi, Gudjon Helga, Gisli, Herdis,
Valtýr, Gudmundur, Teitur, Siggi and all
the other Icelanders.
Thanks for lending me your country.

CHAPTER ONE

I

To be encumbered with a corpse is to be in a difficult position, especially when the corpse is without benefit of death certificate. True, any doctor, even one just hatched from medical school, would have been able to diagnose the cause of death. The man had died of heart failure or what the medical boys pompously call cardiac arrest.

The proximate cause of his pumper having stopped pumping was that someone had slid a sharp sliver of steel between his ribs just far enough to penetrate the great muscle of the heart and to cause a serious and irreversible leakage of blood so that it stopped beating. Cardiac arrest, as I said.

I wasn't too anxious to find a doctor because the knife was mine and the hilt had been in my hand when the point pricked out his life. I stood on the open road with the body at my feet and I was scared, so scared that my bowels loosened and the nausea rose in my throat to choke me. I don't know which is the worse—to kill someone you know or to kill a stranger. This particular body had been a stranger—in fact, he still was—I had never seen him before in my life.

And this was the way it happened.

Less than two hours previously the airliner had slid beneath the clouds and I saw the familiar, grim landscape of Southern Iceland. The aircraft lost height over the Reykjanes Peninsula and landed dead on time at Keflavik International Airport, where it was raining, a thin drizzle weeping from an iron grey sky.

I was unarmed, if you except the *sgian dubh*. Customs officers don't like guns so I didn't carry a pistol, and Slade said it wasn't necessary. The *sgian dubh*—the black knife of the Highlander—is a much underrated weapon if, these days, it is ever regarded as a weapon at all. One sees it in the stocking tops of sober Scotsmen when they are in the glory of national dress and it is just another piece of masculine costume jewellery.

Mine was more functional. It had been given to me by my grandfather who had it of his grandfather, so that made it at least a hundred and fifty years old. Like any good piece of killing equipment it had no unnecessary trimmings—even the apparent decorations had a function. The ebony haft was ribbed on one side in the classic Celtic basket-weave pattern to give a good grip when drawing, but smooth on the other side so it would draw clear without catching; the blade was less than four inches long, but long enough to reach a vital organ; even the gaudy cairngorm stone set in the pommel had its use—it balanced the knife so that it made a superlative throwing weapon.

It lived in a flat sheath in my left stocking top. Where else would you expect to keep a *sgian dubh*? The obvious way is often the best because most people don't see the obvious. The Customs officer didn't even look, not into my luggage and certainly not into the more intimate realms of my person. I had been in and out of the country so often that I am tolerably well known, and the fact I speak the language was a help—there are only 20,000 people who speak Icelandic and the Icelanders have a comical air of pleased surprise when they encounter a foreigner who has taken the trouble to learn it.

'Will you be fishing again, Mr Stewart?' asked the Customs officer.

I nodded. 'Yes, I hope to kill a few of your salmon. I've had my gear sterilized—here's the certificate.' The Icelanders are trying to keep out the salmon disease which has attacked the fish in British rivers.

He took the certificate and waved me through the barrier. 'The best of luck,' he said.

I smiled at him and passed through into the concourse and went into the coffee shop in accordance with the instructions Slade had given me. I ordered coffee and presently someone sat next to me and laid down a copy of the *New York Times*. 'Gee!' he said. 'It's colder here than in the States.'

'It's even colder in Birmingham,' I said solemnly, and then, the silly business of the passwords over, we got down to business.

'It's wrapped in the newspaper,' he said.

He was a short, balding man with the worried look of the

ulcered executive. I tapped the newspaper. 'What is it?' I asked.

'I don't know. You know where to take it?'

'Akureyri,' I said. 'But why me? Why can't you take it?'

'Not me,' he said definitely. 'I take the next flight out to the States.' He seemed relieved at that simple fact.

'Let's be normal,' I said. 'I'll buy you a coffee.' I caught the eye of a waitress.

'Thanks,' he said, and laid down a key-ring. 'There's a car in the parking lot outside—the registration number is written alongside the mast head of *The Times* there.'

'Most obliging of you,' I said. 'I was going to take a taxi.'

'I don't do things to be obliging,' he said shortly. 'I do things because I'm told to do them, just like you—and right now I'm doing the telling and you're doing the doing. You don't drive along the main road to Reykjavik; you go by way of Krysuvik and Kleifavatn.'

I was sipping coffee when he said that and I spluttered. When I came to the surface and got my breath back I said, 'Why the hell should I do that? It's double the distance and along lousy roads.'

'I don't know,' he said. 'I'm just the guy who passes the word. But it was a last-minute instruction so maybe someone's got wind that maybe someone else is laying for you somewhere on the main road. I wouldn't know.'

'You don't know much, do you?' I said acidly, and tapped the newspaper. 'You don't know what's in here; you don't know why I should waste the afternoon in driving around the Reykjanes Peninsula. If I asked you the time of day I doubt if you'd tell me.'

He gave me a sly, sideways grin. 'I bet one thing,' he said. 'I bet I know more than you do.'

'That wouldn't be too difficult,' I said grumpily. It was all of a piece with everything Slade did; he worked on the 'need to know' principle and what you didn't know wouldn't hurt him.

He finished his coffee. 'That's it, buster—except for one thing. When you get to Reykjavik leave the car parked outside the Hotel Saga and just walk away from it. It'll be taken care of.'

He got up without another word and walked away, seemingly in a hurry to get away from me. All during our brief conversation he had seemed jittery, which worried me because it didn't square with Slade's description of the job. 'It'll be simple,' Slade had said. 'You're just a messenger boy.' The twist of his lips had added the implied sneer that it was all I was good for.

I stood and jammed the newspaper under my arm. The concealed package was moderately heavy but not obtrusive. I picked up my gear and went outside to look for the car; it proved to be a Ford Cortina, and minutes later I was on my way out of Keflavik and going south—away from Reykjavik. I wished I knew the idiot who said, 'The longest way round is the shortest way there.'

When I found a quiet piece of road I pulled on to the shoulder and picked up the newspaper from the seat where I had tossed it. The package was as Slade had described it —small and heavier than one would have expected. It was covered in brown hessian, neatly stitched up, and looked completely anonymous. Careful tapping seemed to indicate that under the hessian was a metal box, and there were no rattles when it was shaken.

I regarded it thoughtfully but that didn't give me any clue, so I wrapped it in the newspaper again, dropped it on the back seat, and drove on. It had stopped raining and driving conditions weren't too bad—for Iceland. The average Icelandic road makes an English farm track look like a super-highway. Where there are roads, that is. In the interior, which Icelanders know as the *Óbyggdir*, there are no roads and in winter the *Óbyggdir* is pretty near as inaccessible as the moon unless you're the hearty explorer type. It looks very much like the moon, too; Neil Armstrong practised his moon-walk there.

I drove on and, at Krysuvik, I turned inland, past the distant vapour-covered slopes where super-heated steam boils from the guts of the earth. Not far short of the lake of Kleifavatn I saw a car ahead, pulled off the road, and a man waving the universally recognized distress signal of the stranded motorist.

We were both damned fools; I because I stopped and he because he was alone. He spoke to me in bad Danish and then in good Swedish, both of which I understand. It turned out, quite naturally, that there was something wrong with his car and he couldn't get it to move.

I got out of the Cortina. 'Lindholm,' he said in the formal Swedish manner, and stuck out his hand which

I pumped up and down once in the way which protocol dictates.

'I'm Stewart,' I said, and walked over to his Volkswagen and peered at the exposed rear engine.

I don't think he wanted to kill me at first or he would have used the gun straight away. As it was he took a swipe at me with a very professionally designed lead-loaded cosh. I think it was when he got behind me that I realized I was being a flaming idiot—that's a result of being out of practice. I turned my head and saw his upraised arm and dodged sideways. If the cosh had connected with my skull it would have jarred my brains loose; instead it hit my shoulder and my whole arm went numb.

I gave him the boot in the shin, raking down from knee to ankle, and he yelped and hopped back, which gave me time to put the car between us, and groped for the *sgian dubh* as I went. Fortunately it's a left-handed weapon which was just as well because my right arm wasn't going to be of use.

He came for me again but when he saw the knife he hesitated, his lips curling away from his teeth. He dropped the cosh and dipped his hand beneath his jacket and it was my turn to hesitate. But his cosh was *too* well designed; it had a leather wrist loop and the dangling weapon impeded his draw and I jumped him just as the pistol came out.

I didn't stab him. He swung around and ran straight into the blade. There was a gush of blood over my hand and he sagged against me with a ludicrous look of surprise on his face. Then he went down at my feet and the knife came free and blood pulsed from his chest into the lava dust.

So there I was on a lonely road in Southern Iceland with a newly created corpse at my feet and a bloody knife in my hand, the taste of raw bile in my throat and a frozen brain. From the time I had got out of the Cortina to the moment of death had been less than two minutes.

I don't think I consciously thought of what I did next; I think that rigorous training took over. I jumped for the Cortina and ran it forward a little so that it covered the body. Lonely though the road might be that didn't mean a car couldn't pass at any time and a body in plain sight would take a hell of a lot of explaining away.

Then I took the *New York Times* which, its other virtues apart, contains more newsprint than practically any other newspaper in the world, and used it to line the boot of the car. That done, I reversed again, picked up the body and dumped it into the boot and slammed the lid down quickly. Lindholm—if that was his name—was now out of sight if not out of mind.

He had bled like a cow in a Moslem slaughter-house and there was a great pool of blood by the side of the road. My jacket and trousers were also liberally bedaubed. I couldn't do much about my clothing right then but I covered the blood pool with handfuls of lava dust. I closed the engine compartment of the Volkswagen, got behind the wheel and switched on. Lindholm had not only been an attempted murderer—he had also been a liar because the engine caught immediately. I reversed the car over the bloody bit of ground and left it there. It was too much to hope that the blood wouldn't be noticed when the car was taken away but I had to do what I could.

I got back into the Cortina after one last look at the scene of the crime and drove away, and it was then I began to think consciously. First I thought of Slade and damned his soul to hell and then I moved into more practicable channels of thought such as how to get rid of Lindholm. You'd think that in a country four-fifths the size of England with a population less than half of, say Plymouth, there'd be wide open spaces with enough nooks and crannies to hide an inconvenient body. True enough, but this particular bit of Iceland—the south-west—was also the most heavily populated and it wasn't going to be particularly easy.

Still, I knew the country and, after a little while, I began to get ideas. I checked the petrol gauge and settled down for a long drive, hoping that the car was in good trim. To stop and be found with a blood-smeared jacket would cause the asking of pointed questions. I had another outfit in my suitcase but all at once there were too many cars about and I preferred to change discreetly.

Most of Iceland is volcanic and the south-west is particularly so with bleak vistas of lava fields, ash cones and shield volcanoes, some of them extinct, some not. In my travels I had once come across a gas vent which now seemed an ideal place for the last repose of Lindholm, and it was there I was heading.

It was a two-hour drive and, towards the end, I had to leave the road and take to the open country, bouncing across a waste of volcanic ash and scoria which did the Cortina no good. The last time I had been that way I had driven my Land-Rover which is made for that sort of country.

The place was exactly as I remembered it. There was an extinct crater with a riven side so that one could drive right into the caldera and in the middle was a rocky pustule with a hole in it through which the hot volcanic gases had driven in some long-gone eruption. The only sign that any other human being had been there since the creation of the world was the mark of tyre tracks driving up towards the lip of the crater. The Icelanders have their own peculiar form of motor sport; they drive into a crater and try to get out the hard way. I've never known anyone break his neck at this hazardous game but it's not for want of trying.

I drove the car as near to the gas vent as I could and then went forward on foot until I could look into the impenetrable darkness of the hole. I dropped a stone into it and there was a receding clatter which went on for a long time. Verne's hero who went to the centre of the earth might have had an easier time if he had picked this hole instead of Snaefellsjökull.

Before I popped Lindholm into his final resting-place I searched him. It was a messy business because the blood was still sticky and it was lucky I had not yet changed my suit. He had a Swedish passport made out in the name of Axel Lindholm, but that didn't mean a thing—passports are easy to come by. There were a few more bits and pieces but nothing of importance, and all I retained were the cosh and the pistol, a Smith & Wesson .38.

Then I carried him up to the vent and dropped him into it. There were a few soggy thumps and then silence—a silence I hoped would be eternal. I went back to the car and changed into a clean suit and pulled the stained clothing inside out so that the blood would not touch the inside of my suitcase. The cosh, the pistol and Slade's damned package I also tossed into the suitcase before I closed it, and then I set off on the wearisome way to Reykjavik.

I was very tired.

II

It was late evening when I pulled up in front of the Hotel Saga, although it was still light with the brightness of the northern summer. My eyes were sore because I had been driving right into the western sun and I stayed in the car for a moment to rest them. If I had stayed in the car two minutes more the next fateful thing would not have happened, but I didn't; I got out and was just extracting the suitcase when a tall man came out of the hotel, paused, and hailed me. 'Alan Stewart!'

I looked up and cursed under my breath because the man in the uniform of an Icelandair pilot was the last man I wanted to see—Bjarni Ragnarsson. 'Hello, Bjarni,' I said.

We shook hands. 'Elin didn't tell me you were coming.'

'She didn't know,' I said. 'It was a last-minute decision; I didn't even have time to telephone.'

He looked at my suitcase resting on the pavement. 'You're not staying at the Saga!' he said in surprise.

It was a snap judgment and I had to make it fast. 'No,' I said. 'I'll be going to the apartment.' I didn't want to bring Elin into this but now her brother knew I was in Reykjavik he would be sure to tell her and I didn't want her to be hurt in that way. Elin was very special.

I saw Bjarni looking at the car. 'I'll leave it here,' I said lightly. 'It's just a delivery job for a friend. I'll take a taxi to the apartment.'

He accepted that, and said, 'Staying long?'

'For the rest of the summer, as usual,' I said easily.

'We must go fishing,' he said.

I agreed. 'Have you become a father yet?'

'Another month,' he said glumly. 'I'm dreading it.'

I laughed. 'I should think that's Kristin's worry; you aren't even in the country half the time. No nappy-changing for you.'

We spent another few minutes in the usual idle-small-talk of old friends just met and then he glanced at his watch. 'I have a flight to Greenland,' he said. 'I must go. I'll ring you in a couple of days.'

'Do that.' I watched him go and then captured a taxi which had just dropped a fare at the hotel and told the driver where to go. Outside the building I paid him off and then stood uncertainly on the pavement wondering whether I was doing the right thing.

Elin Ragnarsdottir was someone very special.

She was a schoolteacher but, like many other Icelanders of her type, she held down two jobs. There are certain factors about Iceland—the smallness of population, the size of the country and its situation in high northern latitudes—which result in a social system which outsiders are apt to find weird. But since the system is designed to suit Icelanders they don't give a damn what outsiders think, which is just as it should be.

One result of this social system is that all the schools close down for four months in the summer and a lot of them are used as hotels. The teachers thus have a lot of spare time and many of them have quite a different summer occupation. When I first met her three years earlier, Elin had been a courier for *Ferdaskrifstofaa Nordri*, a travel agency in Reykjavik, and had shown visitors around the country.

A couple of seasons before, I had persuaded her to become my personal courier on a full-time summer basis. I had been afraid that her brother, Bjarni, might have thought that a touch irregular and put in an objection, but he didn't—presumably he thought his sister to be grown-up enough to handle her own affairs. She was an undemanding person and it was an easy relationship, but obviously it couldn't go on like that for ever and I intended to do something about it, but I doubted if this was the appropriate time—it takes someone with a stronger stomach than mine to propose marriage on the same day one has dropped a body down a hole.

I went up to the apartment and, although I had a key, I didn't use it; instead I knocked on the door. Elin opened it and looked at me with an expression of surprise changing to delight, and something in me jumped at the sight of her trim figure and corn-coloured hair. 'Alan!' she said. 'Why didn't you tell me you were coming?'

'A quick decision,' I said, and held up the cased fishing-rod. 'I've got a new one.'

Her lips curved down in mock glumness. 'That makes six,' she said severely, and held the door wide. 'Oh, come in, darling!'

I went in, dropped the suitcase and the rod, and took her in my arms. She held me closely and said, with her head against my chest, 'You didn't write, and I thought . . .'

'You thought I wasn't coming.' The reason I hadn't written was because of something Slade had said, but I couldn't tell her that. I said, 'I've been very busy, Elin.'

She drew back her head and looked at me intently. 'Yes, your face is drawn; you look tired.'

I smiled. 'But I feel hungry.'

She kissed me. 'I'll prepare something.' She broke away. 'Don't worry about unpacking your bag; I'll do it after supper.'

I thought of the bloody suit. 'Not to worry,' I said. 'I can do it.' I picked up the suitcase and the rod and took them into my room. I call it my room because it was the place where my gear was stored. Actually, the whole apartment was mine because, although it was in Elin's name, I paid the rent. Spending one-third of every year in Iceland, it was convenient to have a *pied-à-terre*.

I put the rod with the others and laid down the suitcase, wondering what to do with the suit. Until that moment I had never had any secrets I wanted to keep from Elin—with the one important exception—and there wasn't a lockable cupboard or drawer in the place. I opened the wardrobe and surveyed the line of suits and jackets, each on its hanger and neatly encased in its zippered plastic bag. It would be very risky to let the suit take its place in that line; Elin was meticulous in the care of my clothes and would be certain to find it.

In the end I emptied the suitcase of everything but the suit and the weapons, locked it, and heaved it on top of the wardrobe where it usually lived when not in use. It was unlikely that Elin would pull it down and even then it was locked, although that was not usual.

I took off my shirt and examined it closely and discovered a spot of blood on the front so I took it into the bathroom and cleaned it under the cold tap. Then I scrubbed my face in cold water and felt better for it. By the time Elin called that supper was ready I was cleaned up and already in the living-room looking through the window.

I was about to turn away when my attention was caught by a flicker of movement. On the other side of the street there was an alley between two buildings and it had seemed that someone had moved quickly out of sight when I twitched the curtains. I stared across the street but saw nothing more, but when Elin called again I was thoughtful as I turned to her.

Over supper I said, 'How's the Land-Rover?'

'I didn't know when you were coming but I had a complete overhaul done last week. It's ready for anything.'

Icelandic roads being what they are, Land-Rovers are as thick as fleas on a dog. The Icelanders prefer the short wheelbase Land-Rover, but ours was the long wheelbase job, fitted out as a camping van. When we travelled we were self-contained and could, and did, spend many weeks away from civilization, only being driven into a town by running out of food. There were worse ways of spending a summer than to be alone for weeks on end with Elin Ragnarsdottir.

In other summers we had left as soon as I arrived in Reykjavik, but this time it had to be different because of Slade's package, and I wondered how I was to get to Akureyri 'alone without arousing her suspicions. Slade had said the job was going to be easy but the late Mr Lindholm made all the difference and I didn't want Elin involved in any part of it. Still, all I had to do was to deliver the package and the job would be over and the summer would be like all the other summers. It didn't seem too difficult.

I was mulling this over when Elin said, 'You really do look tired. You must have been overworking.'

I managed a smile. 'An exhausting winter. There was too much snow on the hills—I lost a lot of stock.' Suddenly I remembered. 'You wanted to see what the glen was like; I brought you some photographs.'

I went and got the photographs and we pored over them. I pointed out Bheinn Fhada and Sgurr Dearg, but Elin was more interested in the river and the trees. 'All those trees,' she said luxuriously. 'Scotland must be beautiful.' That was an expected reaction from an Icelander; the island is virtually treeless. 'Are there salmon in your river?'

'Just trout,' I said. 'I come to Iceland for salmon.'

She picked up another photograph—a wide landscape. 'What on here is yours?'

I looked at it and grinned. 'All you can see.'

'Oh!' She was silent for a while, then said a little shyly, 'I've never really thought about it, Alan; but you must be rich.'

'I'm no Croesus,' I said. 'But I get by. Three thousand acres of heather isn't very productive, but sheep on the hills and forestry in the glen bring in the bread, and Americans who come to shoot the deer put butter on the bread.' I stroked her arm. 'You'll have to come to Scotland.'

'I'd like that,' she said simply.

I put it to her fast. 'I have to see a man in Akureyri tomorrow—it's a favour I'm doing for a friend. That means I'll have to fly. Why don't you take up the Land-Rover and meet me there? Or would it be too much for you to drive all that way?'

She laughed at me. 'I can drive the Land-Rover better than you.' She began to calculate. 'It's 450 kilometres; I wouldn't want to do that in one day so I'd stop somewhere near Hvammstangi. I could be in Akureyri at mid-morning the next day.'

'No need to break your neck,' I said casually. I was relieved; I could fly to Akureyri, get rid of the package before Elin got there and all would be well. There was no need to involve her at all. I said, 'I'll probably stay at the Hotel Vardborg. You can telephone me there.'

But when we went to bed I found I was strung up with unrelieved tensions and I could do nothing for her. While holding Elin in the darkness, Lindholm's face hovered ghost-like in my inner vision and again I tasted the nausea in my throat. I choked a little, and said, 'I'm sorry.'

'It doesn't matter, darling,' she said quietly. 'You're tired. Just go to sleep.'

But I couldn't. I lay on my back and reviewed the whole of an unpleasant day. I went over every word that had been said by my uncommunicative contact at Keflavik airport, the man whom Slade had said would pass me the package. *'Don't take the main road to Reykjavik,'* he had said. *'Go by Krysuvik.'*

So I had gone by Krysuvik and come within an ace of being killed. Chance or design? Would the same thing have happened had I gone by the main road? Had I been set up as a patsy deliberately?

The man at the airport had been Slade's man, or at least he had the password that Slade had arranged. But supposing he wasn't Slade's man and still had the password —it wasn't too hard to think up ways and means of that coming about. Then why had he set me up for Lindholm? Certainly not for the package—he already had the package! Scratch that one and start again.

Supposing he *had* been Slade's man and had still set me up for Lindholm—that made less sense. And, again, it couldn't have been for the package; he needn't have given it to me in the first place. It all boiled down to the fact that the man at the airport and Lindholm had nothing to do with each other.

But Lindholm had definitely been waiting for me. He had even made sure of my name before attacking. So how in hell did he know I'd be on the Krysuvik road? That was one I couldn't answer.

Presently, when I was sure Elin was sound asleep, I got out of bed quietly and went into the kitchen, not bothering to turn on a light. I opened the refrigerator and poured myself a glass of milk, then wandered into the living-room and sat by the window. The short northern night was almost over but it was still dark enough to see the sudden glow from the alley across the street as the watching man drew on a cigarette.

He worried me because I was no longer certain Elin was safe.

III

We were both up early, Elin because she wanted to make a quick start for Akureyri, and I because I wanted to get at the Land-Rover before Elin did. I had some things to stow in the Land-Rover that I didn't want Elin to know about; Lindholm's gun, for instance. I taped it securely to one of the main chassis girders and well out of sight. His cosh I put in my pocket. It had occurred to me that if things did not go well I might be in need of weaponry in Akureyri.

I didn't have to go out of the front door to get at the Land-Rover because the garage was at the back, and so the watcher in the alley got no sight of me. But I saw him because the next thing I did was to take a pair of field glasses one flight up to a landing where there was a window overlooking the street.

He was a tall, lean man with a neat moustache and he looked cold. If he had been there all night without a break he would be not only frozen to the marrow but starving. I made sure I would know him again if I saw him and lowered the glasses just as someone came downstairs from an upstairs flat. It was a middle-aged grey-haired woman who looked at me and then at the glasses and gave a meaningful sniff.

I grinned. It was the first time I had been suspected of voyeurism.

I enjoyed breakfast all the more because of my hungry friend across the street. 'You're looking more cheerful,' said Elin.

'It's your cooking,' I said.

She looked at the herring, the cheese, the bread and the eggs. 'What cooking? Anyone can boil an egg.'

'Not like you,' I assured her.

But I *was* more cheerful. The dark thoughts of the night had gone and in spite of all the unanswered questions the death of Lindholm no longer oppressed me. He had tried to kill me and failed, and had suffered the penalty for failure. The fact that I had killed him didn't weigh too heavily upon my conscience. My only lingering worry was for Elin.

I said, 'There's a flight for Akureyri from Reykjavik City Airport at eleven.'

'You'll have lunch there,' said Elin. 'Spare a thought for me bouncing about down in Kaldidalur.' She swallowed hot coffee hastily. 'I'd like to leave as soon as possible.'

I waved at the laden table. 'I'll clean up here.'

She got ready to leave, then picked up the binoculars. 'I thought these were in the Land-Rover.'

'I was just checking them,' I said. 'They seemed a bit out of focus last time I used them. They're all right, though.'

'Then I'll take them,' she said.

I went with her down to the garage and kissed her goodbye. She looked at me closely, and said, 'Everything *is* all right, isn't it, Alan?'

'Of course; why do you ask?'

'I don't really know. I'm just being feminine, I suppose. See you in Akureyri.'

I waved her off and watched as she drove away. Nobody seemed to bother; no heads popped around corners and no one followed in hot pursuit. I went back into the flat and checked on the watcher in the alley. He wasn't to be seen, so I made a mad dash for the upstairs landing from where I could get a better view and I breathed easier when I saw him leaning against the wall, beating his hands against his arms.

It would seem that he was not aware that Elin had left or, if he was, he didn't care. It lifted a considerable load off my mind.

I washed the breakfast crockery and then went to my room where I took a camera bag and emptied it of its contents. Then I took the hessian-covered steel box and found that it fitted neatly into the leather bag. From now on it was not going to leave my person until I handed it over in Akureyri.

At ten o'clock I rang for a taxi and left for the airport, a move which resulted in some action. I looked back along the street and saw a car draw up near the alley into which my watcher jumped. The car followed the taxi all the way to the airport, keeping a discreet distance.

On arrival I went to the reservation counter. 'I have a reservation on the flight to Akureyri. My name is Stewart.'

The receptionist checked a list. 'Oh, yes; Mr Stewart.' She looked at the clock. 'But you're early.'

'I'll have a coffee,' I said. 'It passes the time.'

She gave me the ticket and I paid for it, then she said, 'Your luggage is weighed over there.'

I touched the camera case. 'This is all I have. I travel light.'

She laughed. 'So I see, Mr Stewart. And may I compliment you on how you speak our language.'

'Thank you.' I turned and saw a recognized face lurking close by—my watcher was still watching. I ignored him and headed for the coffee-counter where I bought a newspaper and settled down to wait.

My man had a hurried conversation at the reservation counter, bought a ticket, and then came my way and both of us ignored each other completely. He ordered a late breakfast and ate ravenously, his eyes flicking in my direction infrequently. Presently I had a stroke of luck; the announcement loudspeaker cleared its throat and said in Icelandic, 'Mr Buchner is wanted on the telephone.' When it repeated this in fluent German my man looked up, got to his feet, and went to answer the call.

At least I could now put a name to him, and whether

the name was accurate or not was really immaterial.

He could see me from the telephone-box and spoke facing outwards as though he expected me to make a break for it. I disappointed him by languidly ordering another coffee and becoming immersed in a newspaper account of how many salmon Bing Crosby had caught on his latest visit to Iceland.

In airport waiting lounges time seems to stretch interminably and it was a couple of eons before the flight to Akureyri was announced. Herr Buchner was close behind me in the queue and in the stroll across the apron towards the aircraft, and he chose a seat on the aisle just behind me.

We took off and flew across Iceland, over the cold glaciers of Langjökull and Hofsjökull, and soon enough we were circling over Eyjafjördur preparatory to landing at Akureyri, a city of fully ten thousand souls, the metropolis of Northern Iceland. The aircraft lurched to a halt and I undid my seat-belt, hearing the answering click as Buchner, behind me, did the same.

The attack, when it came, was made with smoothness and efficiency. I left the airport building and was walking towards the taxi rank when suddenly they were all about me—four of them. One stood in front of me and grabbed my right hand, pumping it up and down while babbling in a loud voice about how good it was to see me again and the enormous pleasure it would give him to show me the marvels of Akureyri.

The man on my left crowded hard and pinned my left arm. He put his mouth close to my ear, and said in Swedish, 'Don't make trouble, Herr Stewartsen; or you will be dead.' I could believe him because the man behind me had a gun in my back.

I heard a snip and turned my head just as the man on my right cut through the shoulder-strap of the camera case with a small pair of shears. I felt the strap snake loose and then he was gone and the camera case with him, while the man behind me took his place with one arm thrown carelessly over my shoulder and the other digging the gun into my ribs.

I could see Buchner standing by a taxi about ten yards away. He looked at me with a blank face and then turned and bent to get into the car. It drove away and I saw the white smudge of his face as he looked through the back window.

They kept up the act for two minutes more to give the man with the camera case time to get clear, and the man on my left said, again in Swedish, 'Herr Stewartsen: we're going to let you go now, but I wouldn't do anything foolish if I were you.'

They released me and each took a step away, their faces hard and their eyes watchful. There were no guns in sight but that didn't mean a damn thing. Not that I intended to start anything; the camera case was gone and the odds were too great anyway. As though someone had given a signal they all turned and walked away, each in a different direction, and left me standing there. There was quite a few people around but not one of the good people of Akureyri had any idea that anything untoward had just happened in their line of sight.

I felt ruffled so I straightened my jacket and then took a taxi to the Hotel Vardborg. There wasn't anything else to do.

IV

Elin had been right; I was in time to lunch at the Vardborg. I had just stuck my fork into the mutton when Herr Buchner walked in, looked around and spotted me, and headed in my direction. He stood on the other side of the table, twitched his moustache, and said, 'Mr Stewart?'

I leaned back. 'Well, if it isn't Herr Buchner! What can I do for you?'

'My name is Graham,' he said coldly. 'And I'd like to talk to you.'

'You were Buchner this morning,' I said. 'But if I had a name like that I'd want to change it, too.' I waved him towards a chair. 'Be my guest—I can recommend the soup.'

He sat down stiffly. 'I'm not in the mood for acting straight man to your comedian,' he said, extracting his wallet from his pocket. 'My credentials.' He pushed a scrap of paper across the table.

I unfolded it to find the left half of a 100-kronur banknote. When I matched it against the other half from my own wallet the two halves fitted perfectly. I looked up at him. 'Well, Mr Graham; that seems to be in order. What can I do for you?'

'You can give me the package,' he said. 'That's all I want.'

I shook my head regretfully. 'You know better than that.'

He frowned. 'What do you mean?'

'I mean that I can't give you the package because I haven't got it.'

His moustache twitched again and his eyes turned cold. 'Let's have no games, Stewart. The package.' He held out his hand.

'Damn it!' I said. 'You were there—you know what happened.'

'I don't know what you're talking about. I was where?'

'Outside Akureyri Airport. You were taking a taxi.'

His eyes flickered. 'Was I?' he said colourlessly. 'Go on!'

'They grabbed me before I knew what was happening, and they got clean away with the package. It was in my camera case.'

His voice cracked. 'You mean you haven't got it!'

I said sardonically, 'If you were supposed to be my body-guard you did a bloody awful job. Slade isn't going to like it.'

'By God, he's not!' said Graham with feeling. A tic pulsed under his right eye. 'So it was in the camera case.'

'Where else would it be? It was the only luggage I carried. You ought to know that—you were standing right behind me with your big ears flapping when I checked in at Reykjavik airport.'

He gave me a look of dislike. 'You think you're clever, don't you?' He leaned forward. 'There's going to be a Godawful row about this. You'd better stay available, Stewart; you'd better be easy to find when I come back.'

I shrugged. 'Where would I go? Besides, I have the Scottish sense of thrift, and my room here is paid for.'

'You take this damned coolly.'

'What do you expect me to do? Burst into tears?' I laughed in his face. 'Grow up, Graham.'

His face tightened but he said nothing; instead he stood up and walked away. I put in fifteen minutes of deep thought while polishing off the mutton and at the end of that time I came to a decision, and the decision was that I could do with a drink, so I went to find one.

As I walked through the hotel foyer I saw Buchner-Graham hard at work in a telephone-box. Although it wasn't particularly warm he was sweating.

V

I came out of a dreamless sleep because someone was shaking me and hissing, 'Stewart, wake up!' I opened my eyes and found Graham leaning over me.

I blinked at him. 'Funny! I was under the impression I locked my door.'

He grinned humourlessly. 'You did. Wake up—you're going to be interviewed. You'd better have your wits sharpened.'

'What time is it?'

'Five a.m.'

I smiled. 'Gestapo technique, eh! Oh, well: I suppose I'll feel better when I've shaved.'

Graham seemed nervous. 'You'd better hurry. He'll be here in five minutes.'

'Who will?'

'You'll see.'

I ran hot water into the basin and began to lather my face. 'What *was* your function on this particular exercise, Graham? As a bodyguard you're a dead loss, so it can't have been that.'

'You'd better stop thinking about me and start to think about yourself,' he said. 'You have a lot of explaining to do.'

'True,' I said, and put down the brush and picked up the razor. The act of scraping one's face with a sliver of sharp metal always seems futile and a little depressing; I would have been happier in one of the hairier ages—counter-espionage agent by appointment to Her Majesty Queen Victoria would have been the ideal ticket.

I must have been more nervous than I thought because I shaved myself down to the blood on the first pass. Then someone knocked perfunctorily on the door and Slade came into the room. He kicked the door shut with his foot and glowered at me with a scowl on his jowly face, his hands thrust deep into his overcoat pockets. Without an overture he said briefly, 'What's the story, Stewart?'

There's nothing more calculated to put a man off his stroke than having to embark on complicated explanations with a face full of drying lather. I turned back to the mirror and continued to shave—in silence.

Slade made one of those unspellable noises—an explosive outrush of air expelled through mouth and nose. He sat on the bed and the springs creaked in protest at the excessive weight. 'It had better be good,' he said. 'I dislike being hauled out of bed and flown to the frozen north.'

I continued to shave, thinking that whatever could bring Slade from London to Akureyri must be important. After the last tricky bit around the Adam's apple, I said, 'The package must have been more important than you told me.' I turned on the cold tap and rinsed the soap from my face.

'. . . that bloody package,' he said.

'I'm sorry,' I apologized. 'I didn't hear that. I had water in my ears.'

He contained himself with difficulty. 'Where's the package?' he asked with synthetic patience.

'As of this moment I couldn't tell you.' I dried my face vigorously. 'It was taken from me at midday yesterday by four unknown males—but you know that already from Graham.'

His voice rose. 'And you let them take it—just like that!'

'There wasn't much I could do about it at the time,' I said equably. 'I had a gun in my kidneys.' I nodded towards Graham. 'What was he supposed to be doing about it—if it isn't a rude answer?'

Slade folded his hands together across his stomach. 'We thought they'd tagged Graham—that's why we brought you in. We thought they'd tackle Graham and give you a free run to the goal line.'

I didn't think much of that one. If they—whoever they were—had tagged Graham, then it wasn't at all standard procedure for him to draw attention to me by lurking outside my flat. But I let it go because Slade always had been a slippery customer and I wanted to keep something in reserve.

Instead, I said, 'They didn't tackle Graham—they tackled me. But perhaps they don't know the rules of rugby football; it's not a game they go for in Sweden.' I gave myself a last dab behind the ears and dropped the towel. 'Or in Russia,' I added as an afterthought.

Slade looked up. 'And what makes you think of Russians?'

I grinned at him. 'I always think of Russians,' I said drily. 'Like the Frenchman who always thought of sex.'

I leaned over him and picked up my cigarettes. 'Besides, they called me Stewartsen.'

'So?'

'So they knew who I was—not who I am now, but what I was once. There's a distinction.'

Slade shifted his eyes to Graham and said curtly, 'Wait outside.'

Graham looked hurt but obediently went to the door. When he'd closed it I said, 'Oh, goody; now the children are out of the room we can have a grown-up conversation. And where, for Christ's sake, did you get that one? I told you I wouldn't stand for trainees on the operation.'

'What makes you think he's a trainee?'

'Come, now; he's still wet behind the ears.'

'He's a good man,' said Slade, and shifted restlessly on the bed. He was silent for a while, then he said, 'Well, you've really cocked this one up, haven't you? Just a simple matter of carrying a small parcel from A to B and you fall down on it. I knew you were past it but, by God, I didn't think you were so bloody decrepit.' He wagged his finger. 'And they called you Stewartsen! You know what that means?'

'Kennikin,' I said, not relishing the thought. 'Is he here—in Iceland?'

Slade hunched his shoulders. 'Not that I know of.' He looked at me sideways. 'When you were contacted in Reykjavik what were you told?'

I shrugged. 'Not much. There was a car provided which I had to drive to Reykjavik by way of Krysuvik and leave parked outside the Saga. I did all that.'

Slade grunted in his throat. 'Run into any trouble?'

'Was I supposed to?' I asked blandly.

He shook his head irritably. 'We had word that something might happen. It seemed best to re-route you.' He stood up with a dissatisfied look on his face and went to the door. 'Graham!'

I said, 'I'm sorry about all this, Slade; I really am.'

'Being sorry butters no bloody parsnips. We'll just have to see what we can salvage from this mess. Hell, I brought you in because the Department is short-handed—and now we have a whole country to seal off because of your stupidity.' He turned to Graham. 'Put a call through to the Department in London; I'll take it downstairs. And talk to Captain Lee at the airport; I want that plane to be ready to take off at five minutes' notice. We may have to move fast.'

I coughed delicately. 'Me, too?'

Slade looked at me malevolently. 'You! You've caused enough of a shambles on this operation.'

'Well, what do I do?'

'You can go to hell for all I care,' he said. 'Go back to Reykjavik and shack up with your girl-friend for the rest of the summer.' He turned and bumped into Graham. 'What the hell are you waiting for?' he snarled, and Graham fled.

Slade paused at the door and said without turning, 'But you'd better watch out for Kennikin because I'll not lift a finger to stop him. By God, I hope he *does* nail you!'

The door slammed and I sat on the bed and brooded. I knew that if ever I met Kennikin again I would be meeting death.

CHAPTER TWO

I

Elin rang up as I was finishing breakfast. From the static and the slight fading I could tell she was using the radio-telephone in the Land-Rover. Most vehicles travelling long distances in Iceland are fitted with radio-telephones, a safety measure called for by the difficult nature of the terrain. That's the standard explanation, but not the whole truth. The fact is that Icelanders *like* telephoning and constitute one of the gabbiest nations on earth, coming just after the United States and Canada in the number of calls per head.

She asked if I had slept well and I assured her I had, then I said, 'When will you get here?'

'About eleven-thirty.'

'I'll meet you at the camp site,' I said.

That gave me two hours which I spent in walking around Akureyri like a tourist, ducking in and out of shops, unexpectedly retracing my steps and, in general acting the fool. But when I joined Elin at the camp site I was absolutely sure that I didn't have a tail. It seemed as though Slade had been telling the truth when he said he had no further use for me.

I opened the door of the Land-Rover, and said, 'Move over; I'll drive.'

Elin looked at me in surprise. 'Aren't we staying?'

'We'll drive a little way out of town and then have lunch. There's something I want to talk to you about.'

I drove along the north road by the coast, moving fast and keeping a close check behind. As it became clear that no one was following I began to relax, although not so much as to take the worry from Elin's eyes. She could see I was preoccupied and tactfully kept silent, but at last she said, 'There's something wrong, isn't there?'

'You're so damn right,' I said. 'That's what I want to discuss.'

Back in Scotland Slade had warned me about involving Elin in the operation; he had also invoked the Official

Secrets Act with its penalties for blabbermouths. But if my future life with Elin was going to mean anything at all I had to tell her the truth and to hell with Slade and to hell with the Official Secrets Act.

I slowed down and left the road to bump over turf, and stopped overlooking the sea. The land fell away in a rumble of boulders to the grey water and in the distance the island of Grimsey loomed hazily through the mist. Apart from the scrap of land there wasn't a damned thing between us and the North Pole. This was the Arctic Ocean.

I said, 'What do you know about me, Elin?'

'That's a strange question. You're Alan Stewart—whom I like very much.'

'Is that all?'

She shrugged. 'What else do I need to know?'

I smiled. 'No curiosity, Elin?'

'Oh, I have my curiosity but I keep it under control. If you want me to know anything, you'll tell me,' she said tranquilly, then hesitated. 'I do know one thing about you.'

'What's that?'

She turned to face me. 'I know that you have been hurt, and it happened not long before we met. That is why I keep my questions to myself—I don't want to bring the hurt back.'

'You're very perceptive,' I said. 'I didn't think it showed. Would it surprise you to know I was once a British agent —a spy?'

She regarded me curiously. 'A spy,' she said slowly, as though rolling the word about her mouth to taste it. 'Yes, it surprises me very much. It is not a very honourable occupation—you are not the type.'

'So someone else told me recently,' I said sardonically. 'Nevertheless, it is true.'

She was silent for a while, then she said, 'You *were* a spy. Alan, what you were in the past doesn't matter. I know you as you are now.'

'Sometimes the past catches up with you,' I said. 'It did with me. There's a man called Slade . . .' I stopped, wondering if I was doing the right thing.

'Yes?' she prompted me.

'He came to see me in Scotland. I'll tell you about that— about Slade in Scotland.'

The shooting was bad that day. Something had disturbed
the deer during the night because they had left the valley
where my calculations had placed them and had drifted
up the steep slopes of Bheinn Fhada. I could see them
through the telescopic sight—pale grey-brown shapes graz-
ing among the heather. The way the wind was blowing
the only chance I had of getting near them was by sprout-
ing wings and so, since it was the last day of the season,
the deer were safe from Stewart for the rest of the
summer.

At three in the afternoon I packed up and went home
and was scrambling down Sgurr Mor when I saw the car
parked outside the cottage and the minuscule figure of a
man pacing up and down. The cottage is hard to get to—
the rough track from the clachan discourages casual
tourists—and so anyone who arrives usually wants to see
me very much. The reverse doesn't always apply; I'm of
a retiring nature and I don't encourage visitors.

So I was very careful as I approached and stopped
under cover of the rocks by the burn. I unslung the rifle,
checked it again to make sure it was unloaded, and set
it to my shoulder. Through the telescopic sight the man
sprang plainly to view. He had his back to me but when he
turned I saw it was Slade.

I centred the cross-hairs on his large pallid face and
gently squeezed the trigger, and the hammer snapped home
with a harmless click. I wondered if I would have done the
same had there been a bullet up the spout. The world
would be a better place without men like Slade. But to
load was too deliberate an act, so I put up the gun and
walked towards the cottage. I should have loaded the gun.

As I approached he turned and waved. 'Good afternoon,' he called, as coolly as though he were a regular
and welcome guest.

I stepped up to him. 'How did you find me?'

He shrugged. 'It wasn't too hard. You know my
methods.'

I knew them and I didn't like them. I said, 'Quit playing
Sherlock. What do you want?'

He waved towards the door of the cottage. 'Aren't you

going to invite me inside?'

'Knowing you, I'll bet you've searched the place already.'

He held up his hands in mock horror. 'On my word of honour, I haven't.'

I nearly laughed in his face because the man had no honour. I turned from him and pushed open the door and he followed me inside, clicking his tongue deprecatingly. 'Not locked? You're very trusting.'

'There's nothing here worth stealing,' I said indifferently.

'Just your life,' he said, and looked at me sharply.

I let that statement lie and put up the rifle on its rack. Slade looked about him curiously. 'Primitive—but comfortable,' he remarked. 'But I don't see why you don't live in the big house.'

'It happens to be none of your business.'

'Perhaps,' he said, and sat down. 'So you hid yourself in Scotland and didn't expect to be found. Protective coloration, eh? A Stewart hiding among a lot of Stewarts. You've caused us some little difficulty.'

'Who said I was hiding? I am a Scot, you know.'

He smiled fatly. 'Of a sort. Just by your paternal grandfather. It's not long since you were a Swede—and before that you were Finnish. You were Stewartsen then, of course.'

'Have you travelled five hundred miles just to talk of old times?' I asked tiredly.

'You're looking very fit,' he said.

'I can't say the same for you; you're out of condition and running to fat,' I said cruelly.

He chuckled. 'The fleshpots, dear boy; the fleshpots—all those lunches at the expense of Her Majesty's Government.' He waved a pudgy hand. 'But let's get down to it, Alan.'

'To you I'm Mr Stewart,' I said deliberately.

'Oh, you don't like me,' he said in a hurt voice. 'But no matter—it makes no difference in the end. I . . . we . . . want you to do a job for us. Nothing too difficult, you understand.'

'You must be out of your mind,' I said.

'I know how you must feel, but . . .'

'You don't know a damn thing,' I said sharply. 'If you expect me to work for you after what happened then you're crazier than I thought.'

I was wrong, of course; Slade knew perfectly well how I

felt—it was his business to know men and to use them like tools. I waited for him to put on the pressure and, sure enough, it came, but in his usual oblique manner.

'So let's talk of old times,' he said. 'You must remember Kennikin.'

I remembered—I'd have to have total amnesia to forget Kennikin. A vision of his face swam before me as I had last seen him; eyes like grey pebbles set above high Slavic cheekbones, and the scar ran from his right temple to the corner of his mouth standing out lividly against the suddenly pale skin. He had been angry enough to kill me at that moment.

'What about Kennikin?' I said slowly.

'Just that I hear he's been looking for you, too. You made a fool of him and he didn't like it. He wants to have you . . .' Slade paused as though groping for a thought. 'What's that delicate phrase our American colleagues of the CIA use? Oh, yes—Kennikin wants to have you "terminated with extreme prejudice." Although I daresay the KGB don't employ that exact wording.'

A damned nice term for a bullet in the back of the head one dark night. 'So?' I said.

'He's still looking for you,' Slade pointed out.

'Why?' I asked. 'I'm no longer with the Department.'

'Ah, but Kennikin doesn't know that.' Slade examined his fingernails. 'We've kept the information from him —quite successfully, I believe. It seemed useful to do so.'

I saw what was coming but I wanted to make Slade come right out with it, to commit himself in plain language —something he abhorred. 'But he doesn't know where I am.'

'Quite right, dear boy—but what if someone should tell him?'

I leaned forward and looked closely at Slade. 'And who would tell him?'

'I would,' he said blandly. 'If I thought it necessary. I'd have to do it tactfully and through a third party, of course; but it could be arranged.'

So there it was—the threat of betrayal. Nothing new for Slade; he made a life's work out of corruption and betrayal. Not that I was one to throw stones; it had been my work too, once. But the difference between us was that Slade liked his work.

I let him waffle on, driving home the point unnecessarily.

'Kennikin runs a very efficient *Mordgruppe*, as we know to our cost, don't we? Several members of the Department have been . . . er . . . terminated by Kennikin's men.'

'Why don't you just say murdered?'

He frowned and his piggy eyes sank deeper into the rolls of fat that larded his face. 'You always were blunt, Stewart; perhaps too blunt for your own good. I haven't forgotten the time you tried to get me in trouble with Taggart. I remember you mentioned that word then.'

'I'll mention it again,' I said. 'You murdered Jimmy Birkby.'

'Did I?' Slade asked softly. 'Who put the gelignite in his car? Who carefully connected the wire from the detonator to the ignition system? You did!' He cut me off with a chopping motion of his hand. 'And it was only that which got you next to Kennikin, only that induced Kennikin to trust you enough so that we could break him. You did very well, Stewart—all things considered.'

'Yes, you used me,' I said.

'And I'll use you again,' he said brutally. 'Or would you rather be thrown to Kennikin?' He laughed suddenly. 'You know, I don't think Kennikin gives a damn if you're with the Department or not. He wants you for your own sweet self.'

I stared at him. 'And what do you mean by that?'

'Didn't you know that Kennikin is impotent now?' Slade said in surprise. 'I know you intended to kill him with that last shot, but the light was bad and you thought you'd merely wounded him. Indeed you had, but not merely—you castrated the poor man.' His hands, which were folded across his belly, shook with his sniggers. 'To put it crudely—or bluntly, if you like, dear boy—you shot his balls off. Can you imagine what he'll do to you if—and when—he catches up with you?'

I felt cold and there was a yawning emptiness in the pit of my stomach. 'There's only one way of opting out of the world and that's by dying,' said Slade with phoney philosophy. 'You tried your way and it doesn't work.'

He was right; I shouldn't have expected otherwise. 'What it comes to is this,' I said. 'You want me to do a job. If I don't do it, you'll tip off the opposition and the opposition will knock me off—and your hands will be theoretically clean.'

'Very succinctly put,' said Slade. 'You always did write good, clear reports.' He sounded like a schoolmaster complimenting a boy on a good essay.

'What's the job?'

'Now you're being sensible,' he said approvingly. He produced a sheet of paper and consulted it. 'We know you are in the habit of taking an annual holiday in Iceland.' He looked up. 'Still sticking to your northern heritage, I see. You couldn't very well go back to Sweden—and Finland would be even more risky. Too close to the Russian border for comfort.' He spread his hands. 'But who goes to Iceland?'

'So the job is in Iceland?'

'Indeed it is.' He tapped the paper with his fingernail. 'You take long holidays—three and four months at a time. What it is to have a private income—the Department did very well by you.'

'The Department gave me nothing that wasn't mine,' I said shortly.

He ignored that. 'I note you've been doing very well for yourself in Iceland. All the home comforts down to a love-nest. A young lady, I believe, is . . .'

'We'll leave her out of it.'

'Just the point I'm making, dear boy. It would be most unwise if she became involved. It could be most dangerous for her, don't you think? I wouldn't tell her anything about it.' His voice was kindly.

Slade had certainly done his homework. If he knew about Elin then he must have tapped me a long time before. All the time I thought I was in cover I'd been under a microscope.

'Come to the job.'

'You will collect a package at Keflavik International Airport.' He sketched dimensions with his hands. 'About eight inches by four inches by two inches. You will deliver it to a man in Akureyri—you know where that is?'

'I know,' I said, and waited for him to continue, but he didn't. 'That's all?' I asked.

'That's all; I'm sure you will be able to accomplish it quite easily.'

I stared at him incredulously. 'Have you gone through all this rigmarole of blackmail just to give me a messenger boy's job?'

'I wish you wouldn't use such crude language,' he said

peevishly. 'It's a job suitable for one who is out of practice, such as yourself. It's important enough and you were to hand, so we're using you.'

'This is something that's blown up quite quickly, isn't it?' I hazarded. 'You're forced to use me.'

Slade waggled his hand. 'We're a bit stretched for manpower, that's all. Don't get delusions of grandeur—in using you I'm scraping the bottom of the barrel.'

Slade could be blunt enough when it suited his purpose. I shrugged, and said, 'Who is the man in Akureyri?'

'He'll make himself known,' Slade took a slip of paper from his wallet and tore it jaggedly across. One piece he passed to me and it proved to be half of a 100-kronur banknote. 'He'll have the other half. Old ways are best, don't you think? Effective and uncomplicated.'

I looked at the ruined Icelandic currency in my hand and said ironically, 'I don't suppose I'll be paid for this enterprise?'

'Of course you will, dear boy. Her Majesty's Government is never niggardly when it comes to valuable services rendered. Shall we say two hundred pounds?'

'Send it to Oxfam, you bastard.'

He shook his head deprecatingly. 'Such language—but I shall do as you say. You may depend on it.'

I studied Slade and he looked back at me with eyes as candid as those of a baby. I didn't like the smell of this operation—it sounded too damned phoney. It occurred to me that perhaps he was setting up a training exercise with me as the guinea pig. The Department frequently ran games of that sort to train the new boys, but all the participants usually knew the score. If Slade was ringing me into a training scheme without telling me I'd strangle the sadistic bastard.

To test him, I said, 'Slade, if you're using me as the football in a training game it could be dangerous. You could lose some of your budding spies that way.'

He looked shocked. 'Oh, I wouldn't do that to you.'

'All right; what do I do if someone tries to take the package?'

'Stop him,' he said succinctly.

'At any cost?'

He smiled. 'You mean—should you kill? Do it any way you want. Just deliver the package to Akureyri.' His paunch shook with amusement. 'Killer Stewart!' he mocked gently. 'Well, well!'

I nodded. 'I just wanted to know. I'd hate to make your manpower problems more difficult. After Akureyri —what happens then?'

'Then you may go on your way rejoicing. Complete your holiday. Enjoy the company of your lady friend. Feel free as air.'

'Until the next time you drop by.'

'That is a highly unlikely eventuality,' said Slade decisively. 'The world has passed you by. Things are not the same in the Department as they were—techniques are different—many changes you would not understand. You would be quite useless, Stewart, in any real work; but this job is simple and you're just a messenger boy.' He looked around the room a little disdainfully. 'No, you may come back here and rusticate peacefully.'

'And Kennikin?'

'Ah, I make no promises there. He may find you—he may not; but if he does it will not be because of my doing, I assure you.'

'That's not good enough,' I said. 'You'll tell him I haven't been a member of the Department for four years?'

'I may,' he said carelessly. 'I may.' He stood and buttoned his coat. 'Of course, whether he would believe it is one thing, and whether it would make any difference is yet another. He has his own, strictly unprofessional, reasons for wanting to find you, and I'm inclined to think that he'll want to operate on you with a sharp knife rather than to ask you to share his bottle of Calvados.'

He picked up his hat and moved over to the door. 'You will receive further instructions about picking up the package before you leave. It's been nice to see you again, Mr Stewart.'

'I wish I could say the same,' I said, and he laughed jollily.

I walked with him to his car and pointed to the rocks from where I had watched him waiting outside the cottage. 'I had you in rifle sights from up there. I even squeezed the trigger. Unfortunately the rifle wasn't loaded.'

He looked at me, his face full of confidence. 'If it had been loaded you wouldn't have pulled the trigger. You're a civilized man, Stewart; too civilized. I sometimes wonder how you lasted so long in the Department—you were always a little too soft-centred for the big jobs. If it had been my decision you'd have been out long before you decided to . . . er . . . retire.'

I looked into his pale cold eyes and knew that if it *had* been his decision I would never have been allowed to retire. He said, 'I trust you remember the terms of the Official Secrets Act.' Then he smiled. 'But, of course, you remember.'

I said, 'Where are you in the hierarchy now, Slade?'

'Quite close to the top, as a matter of fact,' he said cheerfully. 'Right next to Taggart. I *do* make the decisions now. I get to have lunch with the Prime Minister from time to time.' He gave a self-satisfied laugh and got into the car. He rolled down the window, and said, 'There's just one thing. That package—don't open it, dear boy. Remember what curiosity did to the cat.'

He drove away, bumping down the track, and when he had disappeared the glen seemed cleaner. I looked up at Sgurr Mor and at Sgurr Dearg beyond and felt depressed. In less than twenty minutes my world had been smashed to pieces and I wondered how the hell I was going to pick up the bits.

And when I woke up next morning after a broken night I knew there was only one thing to do; to obey Slade, carry out his orders and deliver the damned package to Akureyri and hope to God I could get clear without further entanglement.

III

My mouth was dry with talking and smoking. I pitched the cigarette butt from the window and it lay on a stone sending a lonely smoke signal to the North Pole. 'That's it,' I said. 'I was blackmailed into it.'

Elin shifted in her seat. 'I'm glad you've told me. I was wondering why you had to fly to Akureyri so suddenly.' She leaned forward and stretched. 'But now you've delivered this mysterious package you have nothing more to worry about.'

'That's it,' I said. 'I didn't deliver it.' I told her about the four men at Akureyri Airport and she went pale. 'Slade flew here from London. He was annoyed.'

'He was *here*—in Iceland?'

I nodded. 'He said that I'm out of it, anyway; but I'm not, you know. Elin, I want you to stay clear of me—you might get hurt.'

She regarded me intently. 'I don't think you've told me everything.'

'I haven't,' I said. 'And I'm not going to. You're better out of this mess.'

'I think you'd better complete your story,' she said.

I bit my lip. 'Have you anywhere to stay—out of sight, I mean?'

She shrugged. 'There's the apartment in Reykjavik.'

'That's compromised,' I said. 'Slade knows about it and one of his men has it tagged.'

'I could visit my father,' she said.

'Yes, you could.' I had met Ragnar Thorsson once only; he was a tough old farmer who lived in the wilds of Strandasysla. Elin would be safe enough there. I said, 'If I tell you the full story will you go and stay with him until I send for you?'

'I give no guarantees,' she said uncompromisingly.

'Christ!' I said. 'If I get out of this you're going to make me one hell of a wife. I don't know if I'll be able to stand it.'

She jerked her head. 'What did you say?'

'In a left-handed way I was asking you to marry me.'

Things immediately got confused and it was a few minutes before we got ourselves untangled. Elin, pink-faced and tousle-haired, grinned at me impishly. 'Now tell!'

I sighed and opened the door. 'I'll not only tell you, but I'll show you.'

I went to the back of the Land-Rover and took the flat metal box from the girder to which I had taped it. I held it out to Elin on the palm of my hand. 'That's what the trouble is all about,' I said. 'You brought it up from Reykjavik yourself.'

She poked at it tentatively with her forefinger. 'So those men didn't take it.'

I said, 'What they got was a metal box which originally contained genuine Scottish fudge from Oban—full of cotton wadding and sand and sewn up in the original hessian.'

'What about some beer?' asked Elin.

I grimaced. The Icelandic brew is a prohibition beer, tasteless stuff bearing the same relationship to alcohol as candyfloss bears to sugar. Elin laughed. 'It's all right; Bjarni brought back a case of Carlsberg on his last flight from Greenland.'

That was better; the Danes really know about beer. I watched Elin open the cans and pour out the Carlsberg. 'I want you to go to stay with your father,' I said.

'I'll think about it.' She handed me a glass. 'I want to know why you still have the package.'

'It was a phoney deal,' I said. 'The whole operation stank to high heaven. Slade said Graham had been tagged by the opposition so he brought me in at the last minute. But Graham wasn't attacked—I was.' I didn't tell Elin about Lindholm; I didn't know how much strain I could put upon her. 'Doesn't that seem odd?'

She considered it. 'Yes, it is strange.'

'And Graham was watching our apartment which is funny behaviour for a man who knows he may be under observation by the enemy. I don't think Graham had been tagged at all; I think Slade has been telling a pack of lies.'

Elin seemed intent on the bubbles glistening on the side of her glass. 'Talking of the enemy—who is the enemy?'

'I think it's my old pals of the KGB,' I said. 'Russian Intelligence. I could be wrong, but I don't think so.'

I could see by her set face that she didn't like the sound of that, so I switched back to Slade and Graham. 'Another thing—Graham saw me being tackled at Akureyri Airport and he didn't do a bloody thing to help me. He could at least have followed the man who ran off with the camera case, but he didn't do a damned thing. What do you make of that?'

'I don't know.'

'Neither do I,' I admitted. 'That's why the whole thing smells rotten. Consider Slade—he is told by Graham that I've fallen down on the job so he flies from London. And what does he do? He gives me a slap on the wrist and tells me I've been a naughty boy. And that's too bloody uncharacteristic coming from Slade.'

Elin said, 'You don't trust Slade.' It was a statement.

I pointed over the sea towards Grimsey. 'I trust Slade as far as I can throw that island. He's cooked up a complicated deal and I'd like to find out where I fit in before the chopper falls because it might be designed to fall right on my neck.'

'And what about the package?'

'That's the ace.' I lifted the metal box. 'Slade thinks the opposition have it, but as long as they haven't there's no great harm done. The opposition think they have it, assuming they haven't opened it yet.'

'Is that a fair assumption?'

'I think so. Agents are not encouraged to pry too much. The quartet who took the package from me will have orders to take it to the boss unopened, I think.'

Elin looked at the box. 'I wonder what's in it?'

I looked at it myself, and it looked right back at me and said nothing. 'Maybe I'd better get out the can-opener,' I said. 'But not just yet. Perhaps it might be better not to know.'

Elin made a sound of exasperation. 'Why must you men make everything complicated? So what are you going to do?'

'I'm going to lie low,' I said mendaciously. 'While I do some heavy thinking. Maybe I'll post the damned thing to *post restante*, Akureyri, and telegraph Slade telling him where to pick it up.'

I hoped Elin would swallow that because I was going to do something quite different and infinitely more dangerous. Somebody was soon going to find out he'd been sold a pup; he was going to scream loudly and I wanted to be around to find out who was screaming. But I didn't want to have Elin around when that happened.

'Lie low,' repeated Elin thoughtfully. She turned to me. 'What about Asbyrgi for tonight?'

'Asbyrgi!' I laughed and drained my glass. 'Why not?'

V

In that dim and faraway time when the gods were young and Odin rode the arctic wastelands, he was out one day when his horse, Sleipnir, stumbled and planted a hoof

39

in Northern Iceland. The place where the hoof hit the ground is now known as Asbyrgi. So runs the legend but my geologist friends tell it a little differently.

Asbyrgi is a hoof-shaped rock formation about two miles across. Within it the trees, sheltered from the killing wind, grow quite strongly for Iceland, some of them attaining a height of nearly twenty feet. It is a green and fertile place nestling between the towering rock walls which surround it. There is nothing to draw one there but the legend and the unaccustomed sight of growing trees, but although it is a tourist attraction they don't stay the night. More to the point, it is quite off the main road.

We pushed through the narrow entrance to Asbyrgi and along the track made by the wheels of visiting cars until we were well inside at a place where the rock walls drew together and the trees were thick, and there we made camp. It was our custom to sleep on the ground when the climate allowed so I erected the awning which fitted on to the side of the Land-Rover, and brought out the air mattresses and sleeping bags while Elin began to prepare supper.

Perhaps we were sybaritic about our camping because we certainly didn't rough it. I took out the folding chairs and the table and set them up and Elin put down a bottle of Scotch and two glasses and joined me in a drink before she broiled the steak. Beef is a luxury I insist upon in Iceland; one can get awfully tired of mutton.

It was quiet and peaceful and we sat and enjoyed the evening, savouring the peaty taste of the whisky and talking desultorily of the things farthest from our minds. I think we both needed a respite from the nagging problem of Slade and his damned package, and the act of setting out our camp was a return to happier days which we both eagerly grasped.

Elin got up to cook supper and I poured another drink and wondered how I was to get rid of her. If she wouldn't go voluntarily then perhaps the best way would be to decamp early in the morning leaving her a couple of cans of food and a water bottle. With those and the sleeping bag she would be all right for a day or two until someone came into Asbyrgi and gave her a lift into civilization. She would be mad as a hornet but she would still be alive.

Because lying low wasn't good enough. I had to become

visible—set myself up like a tin duck at a shooting gallery so that someone would have a crack at me. I didn't want Elin around when the action started.

Elin brought the supper and we started to eat. She said, 'Alan, why did you leave the . . . the Department?'

I hesitated with my fork in the air. 'I had a difference of opinion,' I said shortly.

'With Slade?'

I laid down the fork gently. 'It was about Slade—yes. I don't want to talk about it, Elin.'

She brooded for a while, then said, 'It might be better if you talked about it. You don't want to keep things locked up.'

I laughed silently. 'That's funny,' I said. 'Telling that to an agent of the Department. Haven't you heard of the Official Secrets Act?'

'What's that?'

'If the Department found I'd talked out of turn I'd be slung into jail for the rest of my life.'

'Oh, that!' she said disparagingly. 'That doesn't count —not with me.'

'Try telling that to Sir David Taggart,' I said. 'I've told you more than enough already.'

'Then why not get it all out? You know I won't tell anyone.'

I looked down at my plate. 'Not of your own free will. I wouldn't want anyone to hurt you, Elin.'

'Who would hurt me?' she asked.

'Slade would, for one. Then there's a character called Kennikin who may be around, but I hope not.'

Elin said slowly, 'If I ever marry anyone it will be a man who has no secrets. This is not good, Alan.'

'So you think that a trouble shared is a trouble halved. I don't think the Department would go along with you on that. The powers that be don't think confession is good for the soul, and Catholic priests and psychiatrists are looked upon with deep suspicion. But since you're so persistent I'll tell you some of it—not enough to be dangerous.'

I cut into the steak again. 'It was on an operation in Sweden. I was in a counter-espionage group trying to penetrate the KGB *apparat* in Scandinavia. Slade was masterminding the operation. I'll tell you one thing about Slade;

he's very clever—devious and tricky, and he likes a ploy that wins coming and going.'

I found I had lost my appetite and pushed the plate away. 'A man called V. V. Kennikin was bossing the opposition, and I got pretty close to him. As far as he was concerned I was a Swedish Finn called Stewartsen, a fellow traveller who was willing to be used. Did you know I was born in Finland?'

Elin shook her head. 'You didn't tell me.'

I shrugged. 'I suppose I've tried to close off that part of my life. Anyway, after a lot of work and a lot of fright I was inside and accepted by Kennikin; not that he trusted me, but he used me on minor jobs and I was able to gather a lot of information which was duly passed on to Slade. But it was all trivial stuff. I was close to Kennikin, but not close enough.'

Elin said, 'It sounds awful. I'm not surprised you were frightened.'

'I was scared to death most of the time; double agents usually are.' I paused, trying to think of the simplest way to explain a complicated situation. I said deliberately, 'The time came when I had to kill a man. Slade warned me that my cover was in danger of being blown. He said the man responsible had not reported to Kennikin and the best thing to do was to eliminate him. So I did it with a bomb.' I swallowed. 'I never even saw the man I killed—I just put a bomb in a car.'

There was horror in Elin's eyes. I said harshly, 'We weren't playing patty-cake out there.'

'But someone you didn't know—that you had never seen!'

'It's better that way,' I said. 'Ask any bomber pilot. But that's not the point. The point is that I had trusted Slade and it turned out that the man I killed was a British agent—one of my own side.'

Elin was looking at me as though I had just crawled out from under a stone. I said, 'I contacted Slade and asked what the hell was going on. He said the man was a free-lance agent whom neither side trusted—the trade is lousy with them. He recommended that I tell Kennikin what I'd done, so I did and my stock went up with Kennikin. Apparently he had been aware of a leak in his organization and there was enough evidence around to point to the man I had killed. So I became one of his blue-eyed boys—we got really chummy—and that was his mistake because we managed to wreck his network completely.'

Elin let out her breath. 'Is that all?'

'By Christ, it's not all!' I said violently. I reached for the whisky bottle and found my hand was trembling. 'When it was all over I went back to England. I was congratulated on doing a good job. The Scandinavian branch of the Department was in a state of euphoria and I was a minor hero, for God's sake! Then I discovered that the man I had killed was no more a freelance agent than I was. His name—if it matters—was Birkby, and he had been a member of the Department, just as I was.'

I slopped whisky into the glass. 'Slade had been playing chess with us. Neither Birkby nor I were deep enough in Kennikin's outfit to suit him so he sacrificed a pawn to put another in a better position. But he had broken the rules as far as I was concerned—it was as though a chess player had knocked off one of his own pieces to checkmate the king, and that's not in the rules.'

Elin said in a shaking voice, 'Are there any rules in your dirty world?'

'Quite right,' I said. 'There aren't any rules. But I thought there were. I tried to raise a stink.' I knocked back the undiluted whisky and felt it burn my throat. 'Nobody would listen, of course—the job had been successful and was now being forgotten and the time had come to go on to bigger and better things. Slade had pulled it off and no one wanted to delve too deeply into how he'd done it.' I laughed humourlessly. 'In fact, he'd gone up a notch in the Department and any muck-raking would be tactless— a reflection on the superior who had promoted him. I was a nuisance and nuisances are unwanted and to be got rid of.'

'So they got rid of you,' she said flatly.

'If Slade had his way I'd have been got rid of the hard way—permanently. In fact, he told me so not long ago. But he wasn't too high in the organization in those days and he didn't carry enough weight.' I looked into the bottom of the glass. 'What happened was that I had a nervous breakdown.'

I raised my eyes to Elin. 'Some of it was genuine— I'd say about fifty-fifty. I'd been living on my nerve for a long time and this was the last straw. Anyway, the Department runs a hospital with tame psychiatrists for cases like mine. Right now there's a file stashed away somewhere full of stuff that would make Freud blush. If I step out of line there'll be a psychiatrist ready to give evidence that I suffer everything from enuresis to paranoic delusions of grandeur. Who would disbelieve evidence coming from an eminent medical man?'

Elin was outraged. 'But that's unethical! You're as sane as I am.'

'There are no rules—remember?' I poured out another drink, more gently this time. 'So I was allowed to retire. I was no use to the Department anyway; I had become that anomaly, the well-known secret service agent. I crept away to a Scottish glen to lick my wounds. I thought I was safe until Slade showed up.'

'And blackmailed you with Kennikin. Would he tell Kennikin where you are?'

'I wouldn't put it past him, on his past record. And it's quite true that Kennikin has a score to settle. The word is that he's no good to the girls any more, and he blames me for it. I'd just as soon he doesn't know where to find me.'

I thought of the last encounter in the dimness of the Swedish forest. I knew I hadn't killed him; I knew it as soon as I had squeezed the trigger. There is a curious prescience in the gunman which tells him if he has hit the mark at which he aims, and I knew the bullet had gone low and that I had only wounded him. The nature of the wound was something else, and I could expect no mercy from Kennikin if he caught up with me.

Elin looked away from me and across the little glade which was quiet and still in the fading light apart from the sleepy chirrup of birds bedding down for the night. She shivered and put her arms about her body, 'You come from another world—a world I don't know.'

'It's a world I'm trying to protect you from.'

'Was Birkby married?'

'I don't know,' I said. 'One thing did occur to me. If Slade had thought that Birkby had a better chance of getting next to Kennikin, then he'd have told him to kill me, and for the same reason. Sometimes I think it would have been better that way.'

'No, Alan!' Elin leaned forward and took my hand in hers. 'Never think that.'

'Don't worry; I'm not suicidally minded,' I said. 'Anyway, you now know why I don't like Slade and why I distrust him—and why I'm suspicious of this particular operation.'

Elin looked at me closely, still holding my hand. 'Alan, apart from Birkby, have you killed anyone else?'

'I have,' I said deliberately.

Her face seemed to close tight and her hand slipped from mine. She nodded slowly. 'I have a lot to think about, Alan. I'd like to take a walk.' She rose. 'Alone—if you don't mind.'

I watched her walk into the trees and then picked up the bottle hefting it in my hand and wondering if I wanted another drink. I looked at the level of liquid and discovered that four of my unmeasured slugs had nearly half-emptied the bottle. I put it down again—I have never believed in drowning my problems and this was no time to start.

I knew what was wrong with Elin. It's a shock for a woman to realize that the man accepted into her bed is a certified killer, no matter in how laudable a cause. And I had no illusions that the cause for which I had worked was particularly commendable—not to Elin. What would a peaceful Icelander know about the murkier depths of the unceasing undercover war between the nations?

I collected the dirty dishes and began to wash them, wondering what she would do. All I had going for me were the summers we had spent together and the hope that those days and nights of happiness would weigh in the balance of her mind. I hoped that what she knew of me as a man, a lover and a human being would count for more than my past.

I finished cleaning up and lit a cigarette. Light was slowly ebbing from the sky towards the long twilight of summer in northern lands. It would never really get dark —it was too close to Midsummer Day—and the sun would not be absent for long.

I saw Elin coming back, her white shirt glimmering among the trees. As she approached the Land-Rover she looked up at the sky. 'It's getting late.'

'Yes.'

She stooped, unzipped the sleeping bags, and then zipped them together to make one large bag. As she

turned her head towards me her lips curved in a half-smile.
'Come to bed, Alan,' she said, and I knew that nothing
was lost and everything was going to be all right.

Later that night I had an idea. I unzipped my side of the
bag and rolled out, trying not to disturb Elin. She said
sleepily, 'What are you doing?'

'I don't like Slade's mysterious box being in the open.
I'm going to hide it.'

'Where?'

'Somewhere under the chassis.'

'Can't it wait until morning?'

I pulled on a sweater. 'I might as well do it now. I can't
sleep—I've been thinking too much.'

Elin yawned. 'Can I help—hold a torch or something?'

'Go back to sleep.' I took the metal box, a roll of in-
sulating tape and a torch, and went over to the Land-
Rover. On the theory that I might want to get at the box
quickly I taped it inside the rear bumper. I had just
finished when a random sweep of my hand inside the
bumper gave me pause, because my fingers encountered
something that shifted stickily.

I nearly twisted my head off in an attempt to see what
it was. Squinting in the light of the torch I saw another
metal box, but much smaller and painted green, the same
colour as the Land-Rover but definitely not standard equipment as provided by the Rover Company. Gently I grasped
it and pulled it away. One side of the small cube was
magnetized so it would hold on a metal surface and, as
I held it in my hand, I knew that someone was being very
clever.

It was a radio bug of the type known as a 'bumper-
bleeper' and, at that moment, it would be sending out a
steady scream, shouting, *Here I am! Here I am!* Anyone
with a radio direction finder turned to the correct frequency would know exactly where to find the Land-Rover
any time he cared to switch on.

I rolled away and got to my feet, still holding the bug,
and for a moment was tempted to smash it. How long it
had been on the Land-Rover I didn't know—probably ever
since Reykjavik. And who else could have bugged it but
Slade or his man, Graham. Not content with warning
me to keep Elin out of it, he had coppered his bet by

making it easy to check on her. Or was it me he wanted to find?

I was about to drop it and grind it under my heel when I paused. That wouldn't be too clever—there were other, and better, ways of using it. Slade knew I was bugged, I knew I was bugged, but Slade didn't know that I knew, and that fact might yet be turned to account. I bent down and leaned under the Land-Rover to replace the bug. It attached itself to the bumper with a slight click.

And at that moment something happened. I didn't know what it was because it was so imperceptible—just a fractional alteration of the quality of the night silence—and if the finding of the bug had not made me preternaturally alert I might have missed it. I held my breath and listened intently and heard it again—the faraway metallic grunt of a gear change. Then there was nothing more, but that was enough.

CHAPTER THREE

I

I leaned over Elin and shook her. 'Wake up!' I said quietly.
'What's the matter?' she asked, still half-asleep.
'Keep quiet! Get dressed quickly.'
'But what . . .?'
'Don't argue—just get dressed.' I turned and stared into the trees, dimly visible in the half light. Nothing moved, nor could I hear anything—the quiet of the night was unbroken. The narrow entrance to Asbyrgi lay just under a mile away and I thought it likely that the vehicle would stop there. That would be a natural precaution—the stopper in the neck of the bottle.

It was likely that further investigation of Asbyrgi would be made on foot in a known direction given by radio direction finder and a known distance as given by a signal strength meter. Having a radio bug on a vehicle is as good as illuminating it with a searchlight.

Elin said quietly, 'I'm ready.'

I turned to her. 'We're about to have visitors,' I said in a low voice. 'In fifteen minutes—maybe less. I want you to hide.' I pointed. 'Over there would be best; find the closest cover you can among the trees and lie down—and don't come out until you hear me calling you.'

'But . . .'

'Don't argue—just do it,' I said harshly. I had never spoken to her before in that tone of voice and she blinked at me in surprise, but she turned quickly and ran into the trees.

I dived under the Land-Rover and groped for Lindholm's pistol which I had taped there in Reykjavik, but it had gone and all that was left was a sticky strand of insulation tape to show where it had been. The roads in Iceland are rough enough to shake anything loose and I was bloody lucky not to have lost the most important thing—the metal box.

So all I had was the knife—the *sgian dubh*. I stooped and picked it up from where it was lying next to the sleeping bag and tucked it into the waistband of my trousers. Then I withdrew into the trees by the side of the glade and settled down to wait.

It was a long time, nearer to half an hour, before anything happened. He came like a ghost, a dark shape moving quietly up the track and not making a sound. It was too dark to see his face but there was just enough light to let me see what he carried. The shape and the way he held it was unmistakable—there are ways of holding tools, and a man carries a rifle in a different way from he carries a stick. This was no stick.

I froze as he paused on the edge of the glade. He was quite still and, if I hadn't known he was there, it would have been easy for the eye to pass over that dark patch by the trees without recognizing it for what it was—a man with a gun. I was worried about the gun; it was either a rifle or a shotgun, and that was the sign of a professional. Pistols are too inaccurate for the serious business of killing —ask any soldier—and are liable to jam at the wrong moment. The professional prefers something more deadly.

If I was going to jump him I'd have to get behind him, which meant letting him pass me, but that would mean laying myself wide open for his friend—if he had a friend behind him. So I waited to see if the friend would turn up or if he was alone. I wondered briefly if he knew what would happen if he fired that gun in Asbyrgi; if he didn't then he'd be a very surprised gunman when he pulled the trigger.

There was a flicker of movement and he was suddenly gone, and I cursed silently. Then a twig cracked and I knew he was in the trees on the other side of the glade. This was a professional all right—a really careful boy. Never come from the direction in which you are expected, even if you don't think you'll be expected. Play it safe. He was in the trees and circling the glade to come in from the other side.

I also began to circle, but in the opposite direction. This was tricky because sooner or later we'd come face to face. I plucked the *sgian dubh* from my waist and held it loosely —puny protection against a rifle but it was all I had. Every step I took I tested carefully to make sure there was no twig underfoot, and it was slow and sweaty work.

I paused beneath a scrawny birch tree and peered into the semi-darkness. Nothing moved but I heard the faint click as of one stone knocking against another. I remained motionless, holding my breath, and then I saw him coming towards me, a dark moving shadow not ten yards away. I tightened my hold on the knife and waited for him.

Suddenly the silence was broken by the rustle of bushes and something white arose at his feet. It could only be one thing—he had walked right on to Elin where she had crouched in hiding. He was startled, retreated a step, and raised the rifle, I yelled, 'Get down, Elin!' as he pulled the trigger and a flash of light split the darkness.

It sounded as though a war had broken out, as though an infantry company had let off a rather ragged volley of rifle fire. The noise of the shot bounced from the cliffs of Asbyrgi, repeating from rock face to rock face in a diminishing series of multiple echoes which died away slowly in the far distance. That unexpected result of pulling the trigger unnerved him momentarily and he checked in surprise.

I threw the knife and there was the soft thud as it hit him. He gave a bubbling cry and dropped the rifle to claw at his chest. Then his knees buckled and he fell to the ground, thrashing and writhing among the bushes.

I ignored him and ran to where I had seen Elin, pulling the flashlight from my pocket as I went. She was sitting on the ground, her hand to her shoulder and her eyes wide with shock. 'Are you all right?'

She withdrew her hand and her fingers were covered in blood. 'He shot me,' she said dully.

I knelt beside her and looked at her shoulder. The bullet had grazed her, tearing the pad of muscle on top of the shoulder. It would be painful later, but it was not serious. 'We'd better put a dressing on that,' I said.

'He shot me!' Her voice was stronger and there was something like wonder in her tone.

'I doubt if he'll shoot anyone again,' I said, and turned the light on him. He was lying quite still with his head turned away.

'Is he dead?' asked Elin, her eyes on the haft of the knife which protruded from his chest.

'I don't know. Hold the light.' I took his wrist and felt the quick beat of the pulse. 'He's alive,' I said. 'He might even survive.' I pulled his head around so that I could see his face. It was Graham—and that was something of a.

surprise. I mentally apologized for accusing him of having been wet behind the ears; the way he had approached our camp had been all professional.

Elin said, 'There's a first-aid box in the Land-Rover.'

'Carry on,' I said. 'I'll bring him over.' I stooped and picked up Graham in my arms and followed Elin. She spread out the sleeping bag and I laid him down. Then she brought out the first-aid box and sank to her knees.

'No,' I said. 'You first. Take off your shirt.' I cleaned the wound on her shoulder, dusted it with penicillin powder, and bound a pad over it. 'You'll have trouble in raising your arm above your shoulder for the next week,' I said. 'Otherwise it's not too bad.'

She seemed mesmerized by the amber light reflected from the jewelled pommel of the knife in Graham's chest. 'That knife—do you always carry it?'

'Always,' I said. 'We have to get it out of there.' It had hit Graham in the centre of the chest just below the sternum and it had an upwards inclination. The whole of the blade was buried in him and God knows what it had sliced through.

I cut away his shirt, and said, 'Get an absorbent pad ready,' and then I put my hand on the hilt and pulled. The serrated back edge admitted air into the wound and made extraction easy and the knife came away cleanly. I half expected a gush of arterial blood which would have been the end of Graham, but there was just a steady trickle which ran down his stomach and collected in his navel.

Elin put the pad on the wound and strapped it down with tape while I took his pulse again. It was a little weaker than it had been.

'Do you know who he is?' asked Elin, sitting back on her heels.

'Yes,' I said matter-of-factly. 'He said his name is Graham. He's a member of the Department working with Slade.' I picked up the *sgian dubh* and began to clean it. 'Right now I'd like to know if he came alone or if he has any pals around here. We're sitting ducks.'

I got up and walked back into the trees and hunted about for Graham's rifle. I found it and took it back to the Land-Rover; it was a Remington pump action carbine chambered for .30/06 ammunition—a good gun for a murderer. The barrel not too long to get in the way, the fire rapid

51

—five aimed shots in five seconds—and a weight and velocity of slug enough to stop a man dead in his tracks. I operated the action and caught the round that jumped out. It was the ordinary soft-nosed hunting type, designed to spread on impact. Elin had been lucky.

She was bending over Graham wiping his brow. 'He's coming round.'

Graham's eyes flickered and opened and he saw me standing over him with the carbine in my hands. He tried to get up but a spasm of pain hit him and the sweat started out on his brow. 'You're not in a position to do much,' I said. 'You have a hole in your gut.'

He sagged back and moistened his lips. 'Slade said . . .' He fought for breath. '. . . said you weren't dangerous.'

'Did he, now? He was wrong, wasn't he?' I held up the carbine. 'If you'd come empty-handed without this you wouldn't be lying where you are now. What was supposed to be the idea?'

'Slade wanted the package,' he whispered.

'So? But the opposition have it. The Russians—I suppose they *are* Russians?'

Graham nodded weakly. 'But they didn't get it. That's why Slade sent me in here. He said you were playing a double game. He said you weren't straight.'

I frowned. 'Now, that's interesting,' I said, and sat on my heels next to him with the carbine across my knees. 'Tell me this, Graham—who told Slade the Russians hadn't got it? I didn't tell them, that's for sure. I suppose the Russkies obligingly told him they'd been fooled.'

A look of puzzlement came over his face. 'I don't know how he knew. He just told me to come and get it.'

I lifted the carbine. 'And he gave you this. I suppose I was to be liquidated.' I glanced at Elin, and then back at Graham. 'And what about Elin here? What was to happen to her?'

Graham closed his eyes. 'I didn't know she was here.'

'Maybe not,' I said. 'But Slade did. How the hell do you think that Land-Rover got here?' Graham's eyelids flickered. 'You know damned well you'd have to kill any witnesses.'

A trickle of blood crept from the corner of his mouth. 'You lousy bastard!' I said. 'If I thought you knew what you were doing I'd kill you now. So Slade told you I'd reneged and you took his word for it—you took the gun he gave you and followed his orders. Ever hear of a man called Birkby?'

Graham opened his eyes. 'No.'

'Before your time,' I said. 'It just happens that Slade has played that trick before. But never mind that now. Did you come alone?'

Graham closed his mouth tightly and a stubborn look came over his face. 'Don't be a hero,' I advised. 'I can get it out of you easily enough. How would you like me to stomp on your belly right now?' I heard Elin gasp, but ignored her. 'You have a bad gut wound, and you're liable to die unless we can get you to a hospital. And I can't do that if someone is going to take a crack at us as we leave Asbyrgi. I'm not going to put Elin into risk just for the sake of your hide.'

He looked beyond me to Elin, and then nodded. 'Slade,' he said. 'He's here . . . about a mile . . .'

'At the entrance to Asbyrgi?'

'Yes,' he said, and closed his eyes again. I took his pulse and found it very much fainter. I turned to Elin. 'Start to load; leave enough room for Graham to lie in the back on top of the sleeping bags.' I stood up and checked the load in the carbine.

'What are you going to do?'

'Maybe I can get close enough to Slade to talk to him,' I said. 'To tell him his boy is badly hurt. Maybe I won't—in that case I'll talk to him with this.' I held up the carbine.

She whitened. 'You'll kill him?'

'Christ, I don't know!' I said exasperatedly. 'All I know is that apparently he doesn't mind if I'm killed—and you, too. He's sitting at the entrance to Asbyrgi like a bloody cork in a bottle and this is the only corkscrew I've got.'

Graham moaned a little and opened his eyes. I bent down. 'How are you feeling?'

'Bad.' The trickle of blood at the corner of his mouth had increased to a rivulet which ran down his neck. 'It's funny,' he whispered. 'How *did* Slade know?'

I said, 'What's in the package?'

'Don't . . . know.'

'Who is bossing the Department these days?'

His breath wheezed. 'Ta . . . Taggart.'

If anyone could pull Slade off my back it would be Taggart. I said, 'All right; I'll go and see Slade. We'll have you out of here in no time.'

'Slade said . . .' Graham paused and began again. He seemed to have difficulty in swallowing and he coughed a little, bringing bright red bubbles foaming to his lips. 'Slade said . . .'

The coughing increased and there was sudden gush of red arterial blood from his mouth and his head fell sideways. I put my hand to his wrist and knew that Graham would never tell me what more Slade had said because he was dead. I closed his staring eyes, and stood up. 'I'd better talk to Slade.'

'He's dead!' said Elin in a shocked whisper.

Graham was dead—a pawn suddenly swept from the board. He had died because he followed orders blindly, just as I had done in Sweden; he had died because he didn't really understand what he was doing. Slade had told him to do something and he had tried and failed and come to his death. I didn't really understand what I was doing, either, so I'd better not fail in anything I attempted.

Elin was crying. The big tears welled from her eyes and trickled down her cheeks. She didn't sob but just stood there crying silently and looking down at the body of Graham. I said harshly, 'Don't cry for him—he was going to kill you. You heard him.'

When she spoke it was without a tremor, but still the tears came. 'I'm not crying for Graham,' she said desolately. 'I'm crying for you. Someone must.'

II

We struck camp quickly and loaded everything into the Land-Rover, and everything included the body of Graham. 'We can't leave him here,' I said. 'Someone will be sure to stumble across him soon—certainly within the week. To quote the Bard, we lug the guts into the neighbour room.'

A wan smile crossed Elin's face as she caught the allusion. 'Where?'

'Dettifoss,' I said. 'Or maybe Selfoss.' To go over a couple of waterfalls, one the most powerful in Europe, would batter the body beyond recognition and, with luck, disguise the fact that Graham had been stabbed. He would be a lone tourist who had had an accident.

So we put the body in the back of the Land-Rover.

I picked up the Remington carbine, and said, 'Give me half an hour, then come along as fast as you can.'

'I can't move fast if I have to be quiet,' she objected.

'Quietness won't matter—just belt towards the entrance as fast as you can, and use the headlights. Then slow down a bit so I can hop aboard.'

'And then?'

'Then we head for Dettifoss—but not by the main road. We keep on the track to the west of the river.'

'What are you going to do about Slade? You're going to kill him, aren't you?'

'He might kill me first,' I said. 'Let's have no illusions about Slade.'

'No more killing, Alan,' she said. 'Please—no more killing.'

'It might not be up to me. If he shoots at me then I'll shoot back.'

'All right,' she said quietly.

So I left her and headed towards the entrance to Asbyrgi, padding softly along the track and hoping that Slade wouldn't come looking for Graham. I didn't think it likely. Although he must have heard the shot he would have been expecting it, and then it would have taken Graham a half-hour to return after searching for the package. My guess was that Slade wouldn't be expecting Graham for another hour.

I made good time but slowed as I approached the entrance. Slade had not bothered to hide his car; it was parked in full sight and was clearly visible because the short northern night was nearly over and the sky was light. He knew what he was doing because it was impossible to get close to the car without being seen, so I settled behind a rock and waited for Elin. I had no relish for walking across that open ground only to stop a bullet.

Presently I heard her coming. The noise was quite loud as she changed gear and I saw a hint of movement from inside the parked car. I nestled my cheek against the stock of the carbine and aimed. Graham had been professional enough to put a spot of luminous paint on the foresight but it was not necessary in the pre-dawn light.

I settled the sight on the driving side and, as the noise behind me built up to a crescendo, I slapped three bullets in as many seconds through the windscreen which must have been made of laminated glass because it went totally opaque. Slade took off in a wide sweep and I saw that the only thing that had saved him was that the car had right-hand drive, English style, and I had shot holes in the wrong side of the windscreen.

But he wasn't waiting for me to correct the error and bucked away down the track as fast as he could go. The Land-Rover came up behind me and I jumped for it. 'Get going!' I yelled. 'Make it fast.'

Ahead, Slade's car skidded around a corner in a four-wheel drift, kicking up a cloud of dust. He was heading for the main road, but when we arrived at the corner Elin turned the other way as I had instructed her. It would have been useless chasing Slade—a Land-Rover isn't built for that and he had the advantage.

We turned south on to the track which parallels the *Jökulsá á Fjöllum*, the big river that takes the melt water north from Vatnajökull, and the roughness of the ground dictated a reduction in speed. Elin said, 'Did you talk to Slade?'

'I couldn't get near him.'

'I'm glad you didn't kill him.'

'It wasn't for want of trying,' I said. 'If he had a left-hand drive car he'd be dead by now.'

'And would that make you feel any better?' she asked cuttingly.

I looked at her. 'Elin,' I said. 'The man's dangerous. Either he's gone off his nut—which I think is unlikely—or . . .'

'Or what?'

'I don't know,' I said despondently. 'It's too damned complicated and I don't know enough. But I do know that Slade wants me dead. There's something I know—or something he thinks I know—that's dangerous for him; dangerous enough for him to want to kill me. Under the circumstances I don't want you around—you could get in the line of fire. You *did* get in the line of fire this morning.'

She slowed because of a deep rut. 'You can't survive alone,' she said. 'You need help.'

I needed more than help; I needed a new set of brains to work out this convoluted problem. But this wasn't the time to do it because Elin's shoulder was giving her hell. 'Pull up,' I said. 'I'll do the driving.'

We travelled south for an hour and a half and Ellin said,

'There's Dettifoss.'

I looked out over the rocky landscape towards the cloud of spray in the distance which hung over the deep gorge which the *Jökulsá á Fjöllum* has cut deep into the rock. 'We'll carry on to Selfoss,' I decided. 'Two waterfalls are better than one. Besides, there are usually campers at Dettifoss.'

We went past Dettifoss and, three kilometres farther on, I pulled off the road. 'This is as close to Selfoss as we can get.'

I got out. 'I'll go towards the river and see if anyone's around,' I said. 'It's bad form to be seen humping bodies about. Wait here and don't talk to any strange men.'

I checked to see if the body was still decently shrouded by the blanket with which we had covered it, and then headed towards the river. It was still very early in the morning and there was no one about so I went back and opened the rear door of the vehicle and climbed inside.

I stripped the blanket away from Graham's body and searched his clothing. His wallet contained some Icelandic currency and a sheaf of Deutschmarks, together with a German motoring club card identifying him as Dieter Buchner, as also did his German passport. There was a photograph of him with his arm around a pretty girl and a fascia board of a shop behind them was in German. The Department was always thorough about that kind of thing.

The only other item of interest was a packet of rifle ammunition which had been broken open. I put that on one side, pulled out the body and replaced the wallet in the pocket, and then carried him in a fireman's lift towards the river with Elin close on my heels.

I got to the lip of the gorge and put down the body while I studied the situation. The gorge at this point was curved and the river had undercut the rock face so that it was a straight drop right into the water. I pushed the body over the edge and watched it fall in a tumble of arms and legs until it splashed into the grey, swirling water. Buoyed by air trapped in the jacket it floated out until it was caught in the quick midstream current. We watched it go downstream until it disappeared over the edge of Selfoss to drop into the roaring cauldron below.

Elin looked at me sadly. 'And what now?'

'Now I go south,' I said, and walked away quickly

towards the Land-Rover. When Elin caught up with me I was bashing hell out of the radio-bug with a big stone.

'Why south?' she asked breathlessly.

'I want to get to Keflavik and back to London. There's a man I want to talk to—Sir David Taggart.'

'We go by way of Myvatn?'

I shook my head, and gave the radio-bug one last clout, sure now that it would tell no more tales. 'I'm keeping off the main roads—they're too dangerous. I go by way of the *Odádahraun* and by Askja—into the desert. But you're not coming.'

'We'll see,' she said, and tossed the car key in her hand.

III

God has not yet finished making Iceland.

In the last 500 years one-third of all the lava extruded from the guts of the earth to the face of the planet has surfaced in Iceland and, of 200 known volcanoes, thirty are still very much active. Iceland suffers from a bad case of geological acne.

For the last thousand years a major eruption has been recorded, on average, every five years. Askja—the ash volcano—last blew its top in 1961. Measurable quantities of volcanic ash settled on the roofs of Leningrad, 1,500 miles away. That didn't trouble the Russians overmuch but the effect was more serious nearer home. The country to north and east of Askja was scorched and poisoned by deep deposits of ash and, nearer to Askja, the lava flows overran the land, overlaying desolation with desolation. Askja dominates north-east Iceland and has created the most awesome landscape in the world.

It was into this wilderness, the *Odádahraun*, as remote and blasted as the surface of the moon, that we went. The name, loosely translated, means 'Murderers' Country', and was the last foothold of the outlaws of olden times, the shunned of men against whom all hands were raised.

There are tracks in the *Odádahraun*—sometimes. The tracks are made by those who venture into the interior; most of them scientists—geologists and hydrographers— few travel for pleasure in that part of the *Óbyggdir*. Each vehicle defines the track a little more, but when the winter snows come the tracks are obliterated—by water, by snow avalanche, by rock slip. Those going into the interior in the early summer, as we were, are in a very real sense trail blazers, sometimes finding the track anew and deepening it a fraction, very often not finding it and making another.

It was not bad during the first morning. The track was reasonable and not too bone-jolting and paralleled the *Jökulsá á Fjöllum* which ran grey-green with melt water to the Arctic Ocean. By midday we were opposite Möðrudalur which lay on the other side of the river, and Elin broke into that mournfully plaintive song which describes the plight of the Icelander in winter: 'Short are the mornings in the mountains of Möðrudal. There it is mid-morning at daybreak.' I suppose it fitted her mood; I know mine wasn't very much better.

I had dropped all thoughts of giving Elin the slip. Slade knew that she had been in Asbyrgi—the bug planted on the Land-Rover would have told him that—and it would be very dangerous for her to appear unprotected in any of the coastal towns. Slade had been a party to attempted murder and she was a witness, and I knew he would take extreme measures to silence her. As dangerous as my position was she was as safe with me as anywhere, so I was stuck with her.

At three in the afternoon we stopped at the rescue hut under the rising bulk of the great shield volcano called Herdubreid or 'Broad Shoulders'. We were both tired and hungry, and Elin said, 'Can't we stop here for the day?'

I looked across at the hut. 'No,' I said. 'Someone might be expecting us to do just that. We'll push on a little farther towards Askja. But there's no reason why we can't eat here.'

Elin prepared a meal and we ate in the open, sitting outside the hut. Halfway through the meal I was in mid-bite of a herring sandwich when an idea struck me like a bolt of lightning. I looked up at the radio mast next to the hut and then at the whip antenna on the Land-Rover. 'Elin, we can raise Reykjavik from here, can't we? I mean we can talk to anyone in Reykjavik who has a telephone.'

Elin looked up. 'Of course. We contact Gufunes Radio and they connect us into the telephone system.'

I said dreamily, 'Isn't it fortunate that the transatlantic

cables run through Iceland? If we can be plugged into the telephone system there's nothing to prevent a further patching so as to put a call through to London.' I stabbed my finger at the Land-Rover with its radio antenna waving gently in the breeze. 'Right from there.'

'I've never heard of it being done,' said Elin doubtfully.

I finished the sandwich. 'I see no reason why it can't be done. After all, President Nixon spoke to Neil Armstrong when he was on the moon. The ingredients are there —all we have to do is put them together. Do you know anyone in the telephone department?'

'I know Svein Haraldsson,' she said thoughtfully.

I would have taken a bet that she would know someone in the telephone department; everybody in Iceland knows somebody. I scribbled a number on a scrap of paper and gave it to her. 'That's the London number. I want Sir David Taggart in person.'

'What if this . . . Taggart . . . won't accept the call?'

I grinned. 'I have a feeling that Sir David will accept any call coming from Iceland right now.'

Elin looked up at the radio mast. 'The big set in the hut will give us more power.'

I shook my head. 'Don't use it—Slade might be monitoring the telephone bands. He can listen to what I have to say to Taggart but he mustn't know where it's coming from. A call from the Land-Rover could be coming from anywhere.'

Elin walked over to the Land-Rover, switched on that set and tried to raise Gufunes. The only result was a crackle of static through which a few lonely souls wailed like damned spirits, too drowned by noise to be understandable. 'There must be storms in the western mountains,' she said. 'Should I try Akureyri?' That was the nearest of the four radio-telephone stations.

'No,' I said. 'If Slade is monitoring at all he'll be concentrating on Akureyri. Try Seydisfjördur.'

Contacting Seydisfjördur in eastern Iceland was much easier and Elin was soon patched into the landline network to Reykjavik and spoke to her telephone friend, Svein. There was a fair amount of incredulous argument but she got her way. 'There's a delay of an hour,' she said.

'Good enough. Ask Seydisfjördur to contact us when the call comes through.' I looked at my watch. In an hour it would be 3:45 p.m. British Standard Time—a good hour to catch Taggart.

We packed up and on we pushed south towards the distant ice blink of Vatnajökull. I left the receiver switched on but turned it low and there was a subdued babble from the speaker.

Elin said, 'What good will it do to speak to this man, Taggart?'

'He's Slade's boss,' I said. 'He can get Slade off my back.'

'But will he?' she asked. 'You were supposed to hand over the package and you didn't. You disobeyed orders. Will Taggart like that?'

'I don't think Taggart knows what's going on here. I don't think he knows that Slade tried to kill me—and you. I think Slade is working on his own, and he's out on a limb. I could be wrong, of course, but that's one of the things I want to get from Taggart.'

'And if you *are* wrong? If Taggart instructs you to give the package to Slade? Will you do it?'

I hesitated. 'I don't know.'

Elin said, 'Perhaps Graham was right. Perhaps Slade really thought you'd defected—you must admit he would have every right to think so. Would he then . . .?'

'Send a man with a gun? He would.'

'Then I think you've been stupid, Alan; very, very stupid. I think you've allowed your hatred of Slade to cloud your judgment, and I think you're in very great trouble.'

I was beginning to think so myself. I said, 'I'll find that out when I talk to Taggart. If he backs Slade . . .' If Taggart backed Slade then I was Johnny-in-the-middle in danger of being squeezed between the Department and the opposition. The Department doesn't like its plans being messed around, and the wrath of Taggart would be mighty.

And yet there were things that didn't fit—the pointlessness of the whole exercise in the first place, Slade's lack of any real animosity when I apparently boobed, the ambivalence of Graham's role. And there was something else which prickled at the back of my mind but which I could not bring to the surface. Something which Slade had done or had not done, or had said or had not said—something which had rung a warning bell deep in my unconscious.

I braked and brought the Land-Rover to a halt, and Elin looked at me in surprise. I said, 'I'd better know what cards I hold before I talk to Taggart. Dig out the can-opener—I'm going to open the package.'

'Is that wise? You said yourself that it might be better not to know.'

'You may be right. But if you play stud poker without looking at your hole card you'll probably lose. I think I'd better know what it is that everyone wants so much.'

I got out and went to the rear bumper where I stripped the tape from the metal box and pulled it loose. When I got back behind the wheel Elin already had the can-opener—I think she was really as curious as I was.

The box was made of ordinary shiny metal of the type used for cans, but it was now flecked with a few rust spots due to its exposure. A soldered seam ran along four edges so I presumed that face to be the top. I tapped and pressed experimentally and found that the top flexed a little more under pressure than any of the other five sides, so it was probably safe to stab the blade of the can-opener into it.

I took a deep breath and jabbed the blade into one corner and heard the hiss of air as the metal was penetrated. That indicated that the contents had been vacuum-packed and I hoped I wasn't going to end up with a couple of pounds of pipe tobacco. The belated thought came to me that it could have been booby-trapped; there are detonators that operate on air pressure and that sudden equalization could have made the bloody thing blow up in my face.

But it hadn't, so I took another deep breath and began to lever the can-opener. Luckily it was one of the old-fashioned type that didn't need a rim to operate against; it made a jagged, sharp-edged cut—a really messy job—but it opened up the box inside two minutes.

I took off the top and looked inside and saw a piece of brown, shiny plastic with a somewhat electrical look about it—you can see bits of it in any radio repair shop. I tipped the contents of the box into the palm of my hand and looked at the gadget speculatively and somewhat hopelessly.

The piece of brown plastic was the base plate for an electronic circuit, a very complex one. I recognized resistors and transistors but most of it was incomprehensible. It had been a long time since I had studied radio and the technological avalanche of advances had long since passed me by. In my day a component was a component, but the micro-circuitry boys are now putting an entire and complicated circuit with dozens of components on to a chip of silicon you'd need a microscope to see.

'What is it?' asked Elin with sublime faith that I would know the answer.

'I'm damned if I know,' I admitted. I looked closer and tried to trace some of the circuits but it was impossible. Part of it was of modular construction with plates of printed circuits set on edge, each plate bristled with dozens of components; elsewhere it was of more conventional design, and set in the middle was a curious metal shape for which there was no accounting—not by me, anyway.

The only thing that made sense were the two ordinary screw terminals at the end of the base plate with a small engraved brass plate screwed over them. One terminal was marked '+' and the other '—', and above was engraved, '110 v. 60~'. I said, 'That's an American voltage and frequency. In England we use 240 volts and 50 cycles. Let's assume that's the input end.'

'So whatever it is, it's American.'

'Possibly American,' I said cautiously. There was no power pack and the two terminals were not connected so ably it would do what it was supposed to do when a 110 volt, 60 cycle current was applied across those terminals. But what it would do I had no idea at all.

Whatever kind of a whatsit it was, it was an advanced whatsit. The electronic whiz-kids have gone so far and fast that this dohickey, small enough to fit in the palm of my hand, could very well be an advanced computer capable of proving that $e=mc^2$ or, alternatively, disproving it.

It could also have been something that a whiz-kid might have jack-legged together to cool his coffee, but I didn't think so. It didn't have the jack-leg look about it; it was coolly professional, highly sophisticated and had the air of coming off a very long production line—a production line in a building without windows and guarded by hard-faced men with guns.

I said thoughtfully, 'Is Lee Nordlinger still at the base at Keflavik?'

'Yes,' said Elin. 'I saw him two weeks ago.'

I poked at the gadget. 'He's the only man in Iceland who might have the faintest idea of what this is.'

'Are you going to show it to him?'

'I don't know,' I said slowly. 'He might recognize it as a piece of missing US government property and, since he's a commander in the US Navy, he might think he has to take action. After all, I'm not supposed to have it, and there'd be a lot of questions.'

I put the gadget back into its box, laid the lid on top and taped it into place. 'I don't think this had better go underneath again now that I've opened it.'

'Listen!' said Elin. 'That's our number.'

I reached up and twisted the volume control and the voice became louder. 'Seydisfjördur calling seven, zero, that the gadget was not working at that moment. Presumfive; Seydisfjördur calling seven, zero, five.'

I unhooked the handset. 'Seven, zero, five answering Seydisfjördur.'

'Seydisfjördur calling seven, zero, five; your call to London has come through. I am connecting.'

'Thank you, Seydisfjördur.'

The characteristics of the noise coming through the speaker changed suddenly and a very faraway voice said, 'David Taggart here. Is that you, Slade?'

I said, 'I'm speaking on an open line—a very open line. Be careful.'

There was a pause, then Taggart said, 'I understand. Who is speaking? This is a very bad line.'

He was right, it was a bad line. His voice advanced and receded in volume and was mauled by an occasional burst of static. I said, 'This is Stewart here.'

An indescribable noise erupted from the speaker. It could have been static but more likely it was Taggart having an apoplexy. 'What the hell do you think you're doing?' he roared.

I looked at Elin and winced. From the sound of that it appeared that Taggart was not on my side, but it remained to be found if he backed Slade. He was going full blast. 'I talked to Slade this morning. He said you . . . er . . . tried to terminate his contract.' Another useful euphemism. 'And what's happened to Philips?'

'Who the hell is Philips?' I interjected.

'Oh! You might know him better as Buchner—or Graham.'

'His contract I did terminate,' I said.

'For Christ's sake!' yelled Taggart. 'Have you gone out of your mind?'

'I got in first just before he tried to terminate my contract,' I said. 'The competition is awful fierce here in Iceland. Slade sent him.'

'Slade tells it differently.'

'I'll bet he does,' I said. 'Either he's gone off his rocker or he's joined a competing firm. I came across some of their representatives over here, too.'

'Impossible!' said Taggart flatly.

'The competing representatives?'

'No—Slade. It's unthinkable.'

'How can it be unthinkable when I'm thinking it?' I said reasonably.

'He's been with us so long. You know the good work he's done.'

'Maclean,' I said. 'Burgess, Kim Philby, Blake, the Krogers, Lonsdale—all good men and true. What's wrong with adding Slade?'

Taggart's voice got an edge to it. 'This is an open line —watch your language. Stewart, you don't know the score. Slade says you still have the merchandise—is that true?'

'Yes,' I admitted.

Taggart breathed hard. 'Then you must go back to Akureyri. I'll fix it so that Slade finds you there. Let him have it.'

'The only thing I'll let Slade have is a final dismissal notice,' I said. 'The same thing I gave Graham—or whatever his name was.'

'You mean you're not going to obey orders,' said Taggart dangerously.

'Not so far as Slade is concerned,' I said. 'When Slade sent Graham my fiancée happened to be in the way.'

There was a long pause before Taggart said in a more conciliatory tone, 'Did anything . . .? Is she . . .?'

'She's got a hole in her,' I said baldly, and not giving a damn if it was an open line. 'Keep Slade away from me, Taggart.'

He had been called Sir David for so long that he didn't relish the unadorned sound of his own name, and it took some time for him to swallow it. At last he said, in a subdued voice, 'So you won't accept Slade.'

'I wouldn't accept Slade with a packet of Little Noddy's Rice Crispies. I don't trust him.'

'Who would you accept?'

That I had to think about. It had been a long time since I had been with the Department and I didn't know what the turnover had been. Taggart said, 'Would you accept Case?'

Case was a good man; I knew him and trusted him as far as I'd trust anyone in the Department. 'I'll accept Jack Case.'

'Where will you meet him? And when?'

I figured out the logic of time and distance. 'At Geysir —five p.m. the day after tomorrow.'

Taggart was silent and all I heard were the waves of static beating against my eardrum. Then he said, 'Can't be done—I still have to get him back here. Make it twenty-four hours later.' He slipped in a fast one. 'Where are you now?'

I grinned at Elin. 'Iceland.'

Even the distortion could not disguise the rasp in Taggart's voice; he sounded like a concrete-mixer. 'Stewart, I hope you know that you're well on your way to ruining a most important operation. When you meet Case you take your orders from him and you'll do precisely as he says. Understand?'

'He'd better not have Slade with him,' I said. 'Or all bets are off. Are you putting your dog on a leash, Taggart?'

'All right,' said Taggart reluctantly. 'I'll pull him back to London. But you're wrong about him, Stewart. Look what he did to Kennikin in Sweden.'

It happened so suddenly that I gasped. The irritant that had been festering at the back of my mind came to the surface and it was like a bomb going off. 'I want some information,' I said quickly. 'I might need it if I'm to do this job properly.'

'All right; what is it?' said Taggart impatiently.

'What have you got on file about Kennikin's drinking habits?'

'What the hell!' he roared. 'Are you trying to be funny?'

'I need the information,' I repeated patiently. I had Taggart by the short hairs and he knew it. I had the electronic gadget and he didn't know where I was. I was bargaining from strength and I didn't think he'd hold back apparently irrelevant information just to antagonize me. But he tried.

'It'll take time,' he said. 'Ring me back.'

'Now *you're* being funny,' I said. 'You have so many computers around you that electrons shoot out of your ears. All you have to do is to push a button and you'll have the answer in two minutes. Push it!'

'All right,' he said in an annoyed voice. 'Hold on.' He had every right to be annoyed—the boss isn't usually spoken to in that way.

I could imagine what was going on. The fast, computer-controlled retrieval of microfilm combined with the wonders of closed circuit television would put the answer on to the screen on his desk in much less than two minutes providing the right coding was dialled. Every known member of the opposition was listed in that microfilm file together with every known fact about him, so that his life was spread out like a butterfly pinned in a glass case. Apparent irrelevancies about a man could come in awfully useful if known at the right time or in the right place.

Presently Taggart said in a dim voice, 'I've got it.' The static was much worse and he was very far away. 'What do you want to know?'

'Speak up—I can hardly hear you. I want to know about his drinking habits.'

Taggart's voice came through stronger, but not much. 'Kennikin seems to be a bit of a puritan. He doesn't drink and, since his last encounter with you, he doesn't go out with women.' His voice was sardonic. 'Apparently you ruined him for the only pleasure in his life. You'd better watch . . .' The rest of the sentence was washed out in noise.

'What was that?' I shouted.

Taggart's voice came through the crashing static like a thin ghost. '. . . best of . . . knowledge . . . Kenni . . . Iceland . . . he's . . .'

And that was all I got, but it was enough. I tried unavailingly to restore the connection but nothing could be done. Elin pointed to the sky in the west which was black with cloud. 'The storm is moving east; you won't get anything more until it's over.'

I put the handset back into its clip. 'That bastard, Slade!' I said. 'I was right.'

'What do you mean?' asked Elin.

I looked at the clouds which were beginning to boil over Dyngjufjöll. 'I'd like to get off this track,' I said. 'We have twenty-four hours to waste and I'd rather not do it right here. Let's get up into Askja before that storm really breaks.'

CHAPTER FOUR

I

The great caldera of Askja is beautiful—but not in a storm. The wind lashed the waters of the crater lake far below and someone, possibly old Odin, pulled the plug out of the sky so that the rain fell in sheets and wind-driven curtains. It was impossible to get down to the lake until the water-slippery ash had dried out so I pulled off the track and we stayed right there, just inside the crater wall.

Some people I know get jumpy even at the thought of being inside the crater of what is, after all, a live volcano; but Askja had said his piece very loudly in 1961 and would probably be quiet for a while apart from a few minor exuberancies. Statistically speaking, we were fairly safe. I put up the top of the Land-Rover so as to get headroom, and presently there were lamb chops under the grill and eggs spluttering in the pan, and we were dry, warm and comfortable.

While Elin fried the eggs I checked the fuel situation. The tank held sixteen gallons and we carried another eighteen gallons in four jerrycans, enough for over 600 miles on good roads. But we weren't on good roads and, in the *Óbyggdir*, we'd be lucky to get even ten miles from a gallon. The gradients and the general roughness meant a lot of low gear work and that swallows fuel greedily, and the nearest filling station was a long way south. Still, I reckoned we'd have enough to get to Geysir.

Miraculously, Elin produced two bottles of Carlsberg from the refrigerator, and I filled a glass gratefully. I watched her as she spooned melted fat over the eggs and thought she looked pale and withdrawn. 'How's the shoulder?'

'Stiff and tender,' she said.

It would be. I said, 'I'll put another dressing on it after supper.' I drank from the glass and felt the sharp tingle of cold beer. 'I wish I could have kept you out of this, Elin.'

She turned her head and offered me a brief smile. 'But

you haven't.' With a dextrous twist of a spatula she lifted an egg on to a plate. 'I can't say I'm enjoying it much, though.'

'Entertainment isn't the object,' I said.

She put the plate down before me. 'Why did you ask about Kennikin's drinking habits? It seems pointless.'

'That goes back a long way,' I said. 'As a very young man Kennikin fought in Spain on the Republican side, and when that war was lost he lived in France for a while, stirring things up for Leon Blum's Popular Front, but I think even then he was an undercover man. Anyway, it was there he picked up a taste for Calvados—the Normandy applejack. Got any salt?'

Elin passed the salt cellar. 'I think maybe he had a drinking problem at one time and decided to cut it out because, as far as the Department is aware, he's a non-drinker. You heard Taggart on that.'

Elin began to cut into a loaf of bread. 'I don't see the point of all this,' she complained.

'I'm coming to it. Like a lot of men with an alcohol problem he can keep off the stuff for months at a time, but when the going becomes tough and the pressures build up then he goes on a toot. And, by God, there are enough tensions in our line of work. But the point is that he's a secret drinker; I only found out when I got next to him in Sweden. I visited him unexpectedly and found him cut to the eyeballs on Calvados—it's the only stuff he inhales. He was drunk enough to talk about it, too. Anyway, I poured him into bed and tactfully made my exit, and he never referred to the incident again when I was with him.'

I accepted a piece of bread and dabbed at the yolk of an egg. 'When an agent goes back to the Department after a job he is debriefed thoroughly and by experts. That happened to me when I got back from Sweden, but because I was raising a stink about what had happened to Jimmy Birkby maybe the de-briefing wasn't as thorough as it should have been, and the fact that Kennikin drinks never got put on record. It still isn't on record, as I've just found out.'

'I still don't see the point,' said Elin helplessly.

'I'm just about to make it,' I said. 'When Slade came to see me in Scotland he told me of the way I had wounded Kennikin, and made the crack that Kennikin would rather operate on me with a sharp knife than offer to split a bottle of Calvados. How in hell would Slade know about the Calvados? He's never been within a hundred miles of Kennikin and the fact isn't on file in the Department. It's been niggling at me for a long time, but the penny only dropped this afternoon.'

Elin sighed. 'It's a very small point.'

'Have you ever witnessed a murder trial? The point which can hang a man can be very small. But add this to it—the Russians took a package which they presumably discovered to be a fake. You'd expect them to come after the real thing, wouldn't you? But who did come after it, and with blood in his eye? None other than friend Slade.'

'You're trying to make out a case that Slade is a Russian agent,' said Elin. 'But it won't work. Who was really responsible for the destruction of Kennikin's network in Sweden?'

'Slade master-minded it,' I said. 'He pointed me in the right direction and pulled the trigger.'

Elin shrugged. 'Well, then? Would a Russian agent do that to his own side?'

'Slade's a big boy now,' I said. 'Right next to Taggart in a very important area of British Intelligence. He even lunches with the Prime Minister—he told me so. How important would it be to the Russians to get a man into that position?'

Elin looked at me as though I'd gone crazy. I said quietly, 'Whoever planned this has a mind like a pretzel, but it's all of a piece. Slade is in a top slot in British Intelligence—but how did he get there? Answer—by wrecking the Russian organization in Sweden. Which is more important to the Russians? To retain their Swedish network—which could be replaced if necessary? Or to put Slade where he is now?'

I tapped the table with the handle of my knife. 'You can see the same twisted thinking throughout. Slade put me next to Kennikin by sacrificing Birkby; the Russkies put Slade next to Taggart by sacrificing Kennikin and his outfit.'

'But this is silly!' burst out Elin. 'Why would Slade have to go to all that trouble with Birkby and you when the Russians would be co-operating with him, anyway?'

'Because it had to look good,' I said. 'The operation would be examined by men with very hard eyes and there had to be real blood, not tomato ketchup—no fakery at all. The blood was provided by poor Birkby—and Kennikin added some to it.' A sudden thought struck me. 'I wonder if Kennikin knew what was going on? I'll bet his organization was blasted from under him—the poor bastard wouldn't know his masters were selling him out just to bring Slade up a notch.' I rubbed my chin. 'I wonder if he's still ignorant of that?'

'This is all theory,' said Elin. 'Things don't happen that way.'

'Don't they? My God, you only have to read the *published* accounts of some of the spy trials to realize that bloody funny things happen. Do you know why Blake got a sentence of forty-two years in jail?'

She shook her head. 'I didn't read about it.'

'You won't find it in print, but the rumour around the Department was that forty-two was the number of our agents who came to a sticky end because he'd betrayed them. I wouldn't know the truth of it because he was in a different outfit—but think of what Slade could do!'

'So you can't trust anyone,' said Elin. 'What a life to lead!'

'It's not as bad as that. I trust Taggart to a point— and I trust Jack Case, the man I'm meeting at Geysir. But Slade is different; he's become careless and made two mistakes—one about the Calvados, and the other in coming after the package himself.'

Elin laughed derisively. 'And the only reason you trust Taggart and Case is because they've made no mistakes, as you call them?'

'Let me put it this way,' I said. 'I've killed Graham, a British intelligence agent, and so I'm in a hot spot. The only way I can get out of it is to prove that Slade is a Russian agent. If I can do that I'll be a bloody hero and the record will be wiped clean. And it helps a lot that I hate Slade's guts.'

'But what if you're wrong?'

I put as much finality into my voice as I could. 'I'm not wrong,' I said, and hoped it was true. 'We've had a long hard day, Elin; but we can rest tomorrow. Let me put a dressing on your shoulder.'

As I smoothed down the last piece of surgical tape, she said, 'What did you make of what Taggart said just before the storm came?'

I didn't like to think of that. 'I think,' I said carefully, 'that he was telling me that Kennikin is in Iceland.'

II

Tired though I was after a hard day's driving I slept badly. The wind howled from the west across the crater of Askja, buffeting the Land-Rover until it rocked on its springs, and the heavy rain drummed against the side. Once I heard a clatter as though something metallic had moved and I got up to investigate only to find nothing of consequence and got drenched to the skin for my pains. At last I fell into a heavy sleep, shot through with bad dreams.

Still, I felt better in the morning when I got up and looked out. The sun was shining and the lake was a deep blue reflecting the cloudless sky, and in the clear, rain-washed air the far side of the crater seemed a mere kilometre away instead of the ten kilometres it really was. I put water to boil for coffee and when it was ready I leaned over and dug Elin gently in the ribs.

'Umph!' she said indistinctly, and snuggled deeper into the sleeping bag. I prodded her again and one blue eye opened and looked at me malignantly through tumbled blonde hair. 'Stop it!'

'Coffee,' I said, and waved the cup under her nose.

She came to life and clutched the cup with both hands. I took my coffee and a jug of hot water and went outside where I laid my shaving kit on the bonnet and began to whisk up a lather. After shaving, I thought, it would be nice to go down to the lake and clean up. I was beginning to feel grubby—the Odàdahraun is a dusty place—and the thought of clean water was good.

I finished scraping my face and, as I rinsed the lather away, I ran through in my mind the things I had to do, the most important of which was to contact Taggart as soon as it was a reasonable hour to find him in his office. I wanted to give him the detailed case against Slade.

Elin came up with the coffee pot. 'More?'

'Thanks,' I said, holding out my cup. 'We'll have a lazy day.' I nodded towards the lake at the bottom of the crater. 'Fancy a swim?'

She pulled a face and moved her wounded shoulder.

'I can't do the crawl, but perhaps I can paddle with one arm.' She looked up at the sky, and said, 'It's a lovely day.'

I watched her face change. 'What's the matter?'

'The radio antenna,' she said. 'It's not there.'

I whirled around. 'Damn!' That was very bad. I climbed up and looked at the damage. It was easy to see what had happened. The rough ground in Central Iceland is enough to shake anything loose that isn't welded down; nuts you couldn't shift with a wrench somehow loosen themselves and wind off the bolts; split-pins jump out, even rivets pop. A whip antenna with its swaying motion is particularly vulnerable; I know one geologist who lost three in a month. The question here was when did we lose it?

It was certainly after I had spoken to Taggart, so it might have gone during the mad dash for Askja when we raced the storm. But I remembered the metallic clatter I had heard during the night; the antenna might have been loosened enough by the bumping to have been swept away by the strong wind. I said, 'It may be around here—quite close. Let's look.'

But we didn't get that far because I heard a familiar sound—the drone of a small aircraft. 'Get down!' I said quickly. 'Keep still and don't look up.'

We dropped flat next to the Land-Rover as the light plane came over the edge of the crater wall flying low. As it cleared the edge it dipped down into the crater to our left. I said, 'Whatever you do, don't lift your head. Nothing stands out so much as a white face.'

The plane flew low over the lake and then turned, spiralling out into a search pattern to survey the interior of the crater. It looked to me like a four-seater Cessna from the brief glimpse I got of it. The Land-Rover was parked in a jumble of big rocks, split into blocks by ice and water, and maybe it wouldn't show up too well from the air providing there was no movement around it.

Elin said quietly, 'Do you think it's someone looking for us?'

'We'll have to assume so,' I said. 'It could be a charter plane full of tourists looking at the *Óbyggdir* from the air, but it's a bit early in the day for that—tourists aren't awake much before nine o'clock.'

This was a development I hadn't thought of. Damn it, Slade was right; I *was* out of practice. Tracks in the

Óbyggdir are few and it would be no great effort to keep them under surveillance from the air and to direct ground transport by radio. The fact that my Land-Rover was the long wheelbase type would make identification easier—there weren't many of those about.

The plane finished quartering the crater and climbed again, heading north-west. I watched it go but made no move. Elin said, 'Do you think we were seen?'

'I don't know that, either. Stop asking unanswerable questions—and don't move because it may come back for another sweep.'

I gave it five minutes and used the time to figure out what to do next. There would be no refreshing swim in the lake, that was certain. Askja was as secluded a place as anywhere in Iceland but it had one fatal flaw—the track into the crater was a spur from the main track—a dead end—and if anyone blocked the way out of the crater there'd be no getting past, not with the Land-Rover. And I didn't have any illusions about the practicability of going anywhere on foot—you can get very dead that way in the *Óbyggdir*.

'We're getting out of here fast,' I said. 'I want to be on the main track where we have some choice of action. Let's move!'

'Breakfast?'

'Breakfast can wait.'

'And the radio antenna?'

I paused, indecisive and exasperated. We *needed* that antenna—I had to talk to Taggart—but if we had been spotted from the air then a car full of guns could be speeding towards Askja, and I didn't know how much time we had in hand. The antenna could be close by but, on the other hand, it might have dropped off somewhere up the track and miles away.

I made the decision. 'The hell with it! Let's go.'

There was no packing to do beyond collecting the coffee cups and my shaving kit and within two minutes we were climbing the narrow track on the way out of Askja. It was ten kilometres to the main track and when we got there I was sweating for fear of what I might find, but nothing was stirring. I turned right and we headed south.

An hour later I pulled up where the track forked. On the left ran the *Jökulsá á Fjöllum*, now near its source and no longer the mighty force it displayed at Dettifoss. I said, 'We'll have breakfast here.'

'Why here particularly?'

I pointed to the fork ahead. 'We have a three-way choice —we can go back or take either of those tracks. If that plane is going to come back and spot us I'd just as soon he did it here. He can't stay up there forever so we wait him out before we move on and leave him to figure which way we went.'

While Elin was fixing breakfast I took the rifle I had liberated from Graham and examined it. I unloaded it and looked down the bore. This was no way to treat a good gun; not to clean it after shooting. Fortunately, modern powder is no longer so violently corrosive and a day's wait before cleaning no longer such a heinous offence. Besides, I had neither gun oil nor solvent and engine oil would have to do.

I checked the ammunition after cleaning the rifle. Graham had loaded from a packet of twenty-five; he had shot one and I had popped off three at Slade—twenty-one rounds left. I set the sights of the rifle at a hundred yards. I didn't think that if things came to the crunch I'd be shooting at much over that range. Only film heroes can take a strange gun and unknown ammunition and drop the baddy at 500 yards.

I put the rifle where I could get at it easily and caught a disapproving glance from Elin. 'Well, what do you expect me to do?' I said defensively. 'Start throwing rocks?'

'I didn't say anything,' she said.

'No, you didn't,' I agreed. 'I'm going down to the river to clean up. Give me a shout when you're ready.'

But first I climbed a small knoll from where I could get a good view of the surrounding country. Nothing moved for as far as I could see, and in Iceland you can usually see a hell of a long way. Satisfied, I went down to the river which was the milky grey-green colour of melt water and shockingly cold, but after the first painful gasp it wasn't too bad. Refreshed, I went back to tuck into breakfast.

Elin was looking at the map. 'Which way are you going?'

'I want to get between Hofsjökull and Vatnajökull,' I said. 'So we take the left fork.'

'It's a one-way track,' said Elin and passed me the map.

True enough. Printed in ominous red alongside the dashed line which denoted the track was the stern injunction: *Adeins faert til austurs*—eastward travel only. We wanted to go to the west.

I frowned. Most people think that because Greenland is covered with ice and is wrongly named then so is Iceland, and there's not much ice about the place. They're dead wrong. Thirty-six icefields glaciate one-eighth of the country and one of them alone—Vatnajökull—is as big as all the glaciated areas in Scandinavia and the Alps put together.

The cold wastes of Vatnajökull lay just to the south of us and the track to the west was squeezed right up against it by the rearing bulk of Trölladyngja—the Dome of Trolls —a vast shield volcano. I had never been that way before but I had a good idea why the track was one way only. It would cling to the sides of cliffs and be full of hair-pin blind bends—quite hairy enough to negotiate without the unnerving possibility of running into someone head on.

I sighed and examined other possibilities. The track to the right would take us north, the opposite direction to which I wanted to go. More damaging, to get back again would triple the mileage. The geography of Iceland has its own ruthless logic about what is and what is not permitted and the choice of routes is restricted.

I said, 'We'll take our chances going the short way and hope to God we don't meet anyone. It's still early in the season and the chances are good.' I grinned at Elin. 'I don't think there'll be any police around to issue a traffic ticket.'

'And there'll be no ambulance to pick us up from the bottom of a cliff,' she said.

'I'm a careful driver; it may never happen.'

Elin went down to the river and I walked to the top of the knoll again. Everything was quiet. The track stretched back towards Askja and there was no tell-tale cloud of dust to indicate a pursuing vehicle, nor any mysterious aircraft buzzing about the sky. I wondered if I was letting my imagination get the better of me. Perhaps I was running away from nothing.

The guilty flee where no man pursueth. I was as guilty as hell! I had withheld the package from Slade on nothing more than intuition—a hunch Taggart found difficult to believe. And I had killed Graham! As far as the Department was concerned I would already have been judged, found guilty and sentenced, and I wondered what would be the attitude of Jack Case when I saw him at Geysir.

I saw Elin returning to the Land-Rover so I took one last look around and went down to her. Her hair was damp and her cheeks glowed pink as she scrubbed her face with a towel. I waited until she emerged, then said, 'You're in this as much as I am now, so you've got a vote. What do you think I should do?'

She lowered the towel and looked at me thoughtfully. 'I should do exactly what you are doing. You've made the plan. Meet this man at Geysir and give him that . . . that whatever-it-is.'

I nodded. 'And what if someone should try to stop us?'

She hesitated. 'If it is Slade, then give him the gadget. If it is Kennikin . . .' She stopped and shook her head slowly.

I saw her reasoning. I might be able to hand over to Slade and get away unscathed; but Kennikin would not be satisfied with that—he'd want my blood. I said, 'Supposing it is Kennikin—what would you expect me to do?'

She drooped. 'I think you would want to fight him— to use that rifle. You would want to kill him.' Her voice was desolate.

I took her by the arm. 'Elin, I don't kill people indiscriminately. I'm not a psychopath. I promise there will be no killing unless it is in self defence; unless my life is in danger—or yours.'

'I'm sorry, Alan,' she said. 'But a situation like this is so alien to me. I've never had to face anything like it.'

I waved towards the knoll. 'I was doing a bit of thinking up there. It occurred to me that perhaps my assessment of everything has been wrong—that I've misjudged people and events.'

'No!' she said definitely. 'You've made a strong case against Slade.'

'And yet you would want me to give him the gadget?'

'What is it to me?' she cried. 'Or to you? Let him have it when the time comes—let us go back to living our own lives.'

'I'd like to do that very much,' I said. 'If people would let me.' I looked up at the sun which was already high. 'Come on; let's be on our way.'

As we drove towards the fork I glanced at Elin's set face and sighed. I could quite understand her attitude, which was that of any other Icelander. Long gone are the days when the Vikings were the scourge of Europe, and the Icelanders have lived in isolation for so many years that the affairs of the rest of the world must seem remote and alien.

Their only battle has been to regain their political independence from Denmark and that was achieved by peaceful negotiation. True, they are not so isolated that their economy is separated from world trade—far from it—but trade is trade and war, whether open or covert, is something for other crazy people and not for sober, sensible Icelanders.

They are so confident that no one can envy their country enough to seize it that they have no armed forces. After all, if the Icelanders with their thousand years of experience behind them still find it most difficult to scratch a living out of the country then who else in his right mind would want it?

A peaceful people with no first-hand knowledge of war. It was hardly surprising that Elin found the shenanigans in which I was involved distasteful and dirty. I didn't feel too clean myself.

III

The track was bad.

It was bad right from where we had stopped and it got steadily worse after we had left the river and began to climb under Vatnajökull. I crunched down into low gear and went into four-wheel drive as the track snaked its way up the cliffs, doubling back on itself so often that I had a zany idea I might drive into my own rear. It was wide enough only for one vehicle and I crept around each corner hoping to God that no one was coming the other way.

Once there was a slide of rubble sideways and I felt the Land-Rover slip with rear wheels spinning towards the edge of a sheer drop. I poured on the juice and hoped for the best. The front wheels held their grip and hauled us to safety. Soon after that I stopped on a reasonably straight bit, and when I took my hands from the wheel they were wet with sweat.

I wiped them dry. 'This is bloody tricky.'

'Shall I drive for a while?' asked Elin.

I shook my head. 'Not with your bad shoulder. Besides, it's not the driving—it's the expectation of meeting someone around every corner.' I looked over the edge of the cliff. 'One of us would have to reverse out and that's a flat impossibility.' That was the best that could happen; the worst didn't bear thinking about. No wonder this track was one way only.

'I could walk ahead,' Elin said. 'I can check around the corners and guide you.'

'That would take all day,' I objected. 'And we've a long way to go.'

She jerked her thumb downwards. 'Better than going down there. Besides, we're not moving at much more than a walking pace as it is. I can stand on the front bumper while we go on the straight runs and jump off at the corners.'

It was an idea that had its points but I didn't like it much. 'It won't do your shoulder much good.'

'I can use the other arm,' she said impatiently, and opened the door to get out.

At one time in England there was a law to the effect that every mechanically propelled vehicle on the public highway must be preceded by a man on foot bearing a red flag to warn the unwary citizenry of the juggernaut bearing down upon them. I had never expected to be put in the same position, but that's progress.

Elin would ride the bumper until we approached a corner and jump off as I slowed down. Slowing down was no trick at all, even going down hill; all I had to do was to take my foot off the accelerator. I had dropped into the lowest gear possible which, on a Land-Rover is something wondrous. That final drive ratio of about 40:1 gives a lot of traction and a lot of engine braking. Driven flat out when cranked as low as that the old girl would make all of nine miles an hour when delivering ninety-five horsepower—and a hell of a lot of traction was just what I needed on that Icelandic roller-coaster. But it was hell on fuel consumption.

So Elin would guide me around a corner and then ride the bumper to the next one. It sounds as though it might have been a slow job but curiously enough we seemed to make better time. We went on in this dot-and-carry-one manner for quite a long way and then Elin held up her hand and pointed, not down the track but away in the air to the right. As she started to hurry back I twisted my neck to see what she had seen.

A helicopter was coming over Trölladyngja like a grasshopper, the sun making a spinning disc of its rotor and striking reflections from the greenhouse which designers put on choppers for their own weird reasons. I've flown by helicopter on many occasions and on a sunny day you feel like a ripening tomato under glass.

But I wasn't thinking about that right then because Elin had come up on the wrong side of the Land-Rover. 'Get to the other side,' I shouted. 'Get under cover.' I dived out of the door on the other side where the cliff face was.

She joined me. 'Trouble?'

'Could be.' I held open the door and grabbed the carbine. 'We've seen no vehicles so far, but two aircraft have been interested in us. That seems unnatural.'

I peered around the rear end of the Land-Rover, keeping the gun out of sight. The helicopter was still heading towards us and losing height. When it was quite close the nose came up and it bobbed and curtsied in the air as it came to a hovering stop about a hundred yards away. Then it came down like a lift until it was level with us.

I sweated and gripped the carbine. Sitting on the ledge we were like ducks in a shooting gallery, and all that was between us and any bullets was the Land-Rover. It's a stoutly built vehicle but at that moment I wished it was an armoured car. The chopper ducked and swayed and regarded us interestedly, but I could see no human movement beyond the reflections echoed from the glass of the cockpit.

Then the fuselage began to rotate slowly until it was turned broadside on, and I let out my breath in a long sigh. Painted in large letters along the side was the single word—NAVY—and I relaxed, put down the carbine and went into the open. If there was one place where Kennikin would not be it was inside a US Navy Sikorsky LH-34 chopper.

I waved, and said to Elin, 'It's all right; you can come out.'

She joined me and we looked at the helicopter. A door in the side slid open and a crewman appeared wearing a white bone-dome helmet. He leaned out, holding on with one hand, and made a whirling motion with the other and then put his fist to the side of his face. He did this two or three times before I tumbled to what he was doing.

'He wants us to use the telephone,' I said. 'A pity we can't.' I climbed on top of the Land-Rover and pointed as eloquently as I could to where the whip antenna had been. The crewman caught on fast; he waved and drew himself back inside and the door closed. Within a few seconds the helicopter reared up and gained height, the fuselage turning until it was pointing south-west, and then away it went until it disappeared into the distance with a fading roar.

I looked at Elin. 'What do you suppose that was about?'

'It seemed they want to talk to you. Perhaps the helicopter will land farther down the track.'

'It certainly couldn't land here,' I said. 'Maybe you're right. I could do with a trip back to Keflavik in comfort.' I looked into the thin air into which the chopper had vanished. 'But nobody told me the Americans were in on this.'

Elin gave me a sidelong look. 'In on what?'

'I don't know, damn it! I wish to hell I did.' I retrieved the carbine. 'Let's get on with it.'

So on we went along that bastard of a track, round and round, up and down, but mostly up, until we had climbed right to the edge of Vatnajökull, next to the ice. The track could only go one way from there and that was away, so it turned at right-angles to the ice field and from then on the direction was mostly down. There was one more particularly nasty bit where we had to climb an outlying ridge of Trölladyngja but from then on the track improved and I called Elin aboard again.

I looked back the way we had come and was thankful for one thing; it had been a bright, sunny day. If there had been mist or much rain it would have been impossible. I checked the map and found we were through the one-way section for which I was heartily thankful.

Elin looked tired. She had done a lot of walking over rough ground and a lot of jumping up and down, and her face was drawn. I checked the time, and said, 'We'll feel better after we've eaten, and hot coffee would go down well. We'll stop here a while.'

And that was a mistake.

I discovered it was a mistake two and a half hours later. We had rested for an hour and eaten, and then continued for an hour and a half until we came to a river which was brimming full. I pulled up at the water's edge where the track disappeared into the river, and got out to look at the problem.

I estimated the depth and looked at the dry stones in the banks. 'It's still rising, damn it! If we hadn't stopped we could have crossed an hour ago. Now, I'm not so sure.'

Vatnajökull is well named the 'Water Glacier'. It dominates the river system of Eastern and Southern Iceland —a great reservoir of frozen water which, in slowly melting, covers the land with a network of rivers. I had been thankful it had been a sunny day, but now I was not so sure because sunny days mean full rivers. The best time to cross a glacier is at dawn when it is low. During the day, especially on a clear, sunny day, the melt water increases and the flow grows to a peak in the late afternoon. This particular river had not yet reached its peak but it was still too damned deep to cross.

Elin consulted the map. 'Where are you making for? Today, I mean.'

'I wanted to get to the main Sprengisandur route. That's more or less a permanent track; once we're on it getting to Geysir should be easy.'

She measured the distance. 'Sixty kilometres,' she said, and paused.

I saw her lips moving. 'What's the matter?'

She looked up, 'I was counting,' she said. 'Sixteen rivers to cross in that sixty kilometres before we hit the Sprengisandur track.'

'For Christ's sake!' I said. Normally in my travels in Iceland I had never been in a particular hurry to get anywhere. I had never counted the rivers and if an unfordable one had barred my path it was no great hardship to camp for a few hours until the level dropped. But the times were a-changing.

Elin said, 'We'll have to camp here.'

I looked at the river and knew I had to make up my mind quickly. 'I think we'll try to get over,' I said.

Elin looked at me blankly. 'But why? You won't be able to cross the others until tomorrow.'

I tossed a pebble into the water. If it made any ripples I didn't see them because they were obliterated by the swift flowing current. I said, ' "By the pricking of my thumbs, something evil this way comes." ' I swung around and pointed back along the track. 'And I think it will come from that direction. If we have to stop I'd rather it was on the other side of this river.'

Elin looked doubtfully at the fast rip in the middle. 'It will be dangerous.'

'It might be more dangerous to stay here.' I had an uneasy feeling which, maybe, was no more than the automatic revulsion against being caught in a position from which it was impossible to run. It was the reason I had left Askja, and it was the reason I wanted to cross this river. Perhaps it was just my tactical sense sharpening up after lying dormant for so long. I said, 'And it'll be more dangerous to cross in fifteen minutes, so let's move it.'

I checked whether, in fact, the place where the track crossed the river was the most practicable. This turned out to be a waste of time but it had to be done. Anywhere upstream or downstream was impossible for various reasons, either deep water or high banks—so I concentrated on the ford and hoped the footing was sound.

Dropping again into the lowest gear possible I drove slowly into the river. The quick water swirled against the wheels and built up into waves which slapped against the side of the cab. Right in midstream the water was deep and any moment I expected to find it flowing under the door. More ominously the force of the water was so great that for one hair-raising second I felt the vehicle shift sideways and there was a curiously lifting lurch preparatory to being swept downstream.

I rammed my foot down and headed for shallower water and the opposite bank. The front wheels bit into the bed of the river but the back of the Land-Rover actually lifted and floated so that we got to the other side broadside on and climbed out awkwardly over a moss-crusted hummock of lava, streaming water like a shaggy dog just come from a swim.

I headed for the track and we bucked and lurched over the lava, and when we were finally on reasonably level ground I switched off the engine and looked at Elin. 'I don't think we'll cross any more rivers today. That one was enough. Thank God for four-wheel drive.'

She was pale. 'That was an unjustifiable risk,' she said. 'We could have been swept downstream.'

'But we weren't,' I said, and switched on the engine again. 'How far to the next river? We'll camp there and cross at dawn.'

She consulted the map. 'About two kilometres.'

So we pushed on and presently came to river number two which was also swollen with sun-melted water from Vatnajökull. I turned the vehicle and headed towards a jumble of rocks behind which I parked, out of sight of both the river and the track—again on good tactical principles.

I was annoyed. It was still not very late and there were several hours of daylight left which we could have used for mileage if it hadn't been for those damned rivers. But there was nothing for it but to wait until the next day when the flow would drop. I said, 'You look tired; you've had a hard day.'

Elin nodded dispiritedly and got out of the cab. I noticed her favouring her right arm, and said, 'How is the shoulder?'

She grimaced. 'Stiff.'

'I'd better take a look at it.'

I put up the collapsible top of the Land-Rover and set water to boil, and Elin sat on a bunk and tried to take off her sweater. She couldn't do it because she couldn't raise her right arm. I helped her take it off but, gentle though I was, she gasped in pain. Reasonably enough, she wasn't wearing a brassière under the sweater because the shoulder strap would have cut right into the wound.

I took off the pad and looked at her shoulder. The wound was angry and inflamed but there was no sign of any pus which would indicate infection. I said, 'I told you that you'd begin to feel it. A graze like this can hurt like the devil, so don't be too stiff-upper-lipped about it—I know how it feels.'

She crossed her arms across her breasts. 'Has it ever happened to you?'

'I was grazed across the ribs once,' I said, as I poured warm water into a cup.

'So that's how you got that scar.'

'Yours is worse because it's across the trapezius muscle and you keep pulling it. You really should have your arm

85

in a sling—I'll see what I can find.' I washed the wound and put on a new medicated dressing from the first-aid box, then helped her put on the sweater. 'Where's your scarf—the new woollen one?'

She pointed. 'In that drawer.'

'Then that's your sling.' I took out the scarf and fitted it to her arm so as to immobilize the shoulder as much as possible. 'Now, you just sit there and watch me cook supper.'

I thought this was an appropriate time to open the goody box—the small collection of luxuries we kept for special occasions. We both needed cheering up and there's nothing like a first-class meal under the belt to lift the spirits. I don't know if Mr Fortnum and Mr Mason are aware of the joy they bring to sojourners in far-flung lands, but after the oyster soup, the whole roast quails and the pears pickled in cognac I felt almost impelled to write them a letter of appreciation.

The colour came back into Elin's cheeks as she ate. I insisted that she didn't use her right hand and she didn't have to—the dark, tender flesh fell away from the quail at the touch of a fork and she managed all right. I made coffee and we accompanied it with brandy which I carried for medicinal purposes.

As she sipped her coffee she sighed. 'Just like old times, Alan.'

'Yes,' I said lazily. I was feeling much better myself. 'But you'd better sleep. We make an early start tomorrow.' I calculated it would be light enough to move at three a.m. when the rivers would also be at their lowest. I leaned over and took the binoculars.

'Where are you going?' she asked.

'Just to have a look around. You go to bed.'

Her eyes flickered sleepily. 'I *am* tired,' she admitted.

That wasn't surprising. We'd been on the run for a long time, and bouncing about in the *Óbyggdir* wasn't helping—we'd managed to fall into every damned pothole on the track. I said, 'Get your head down—I won't be long.'

I hung the lanyard of the binoculars around my neck, opened the back door and dropped to the ground. I was about to walk away when I turned back on impulse, reached into the cab and picked up the carbine. I don't think Elin saw me do that.

First I inspected the river we had to cross. It was flowing

well but exposed wet stones showed that the level was already dropping. By dawn the crossing would be easy, and we should be able to get across all the other rivers that lay between us and Sprengisandur before the increased flow made it impossible.

I slung the carbine over my shoulder and walked back along the track towards the river we had crossed which lay a little over a mile away. I approached cautiously but everything was peaceful. The river flowed and chuckled and there was nothing in sight to cause alarm. I checked the distant view with the binoculars, then sat down with my back against a mossy boulder, lit a cigarette and started to think.

I was worried about Elin's shoulder; not that there was anything particularly alarming about its condition, but a doctor would do a better job than I could, and this bouncing about the wilderness wasn't helping. It might be difficult explaining to a doctor how Elin had come by an unmistakable gunshot wound, but accidents do happen and I thought I could get away with it by talking fast.

I stayed there for a couple of hours, smoking and thinking and looking at the river, and at the end of that time I had come up with nothing new despite my brain beating. The added factor of the American helicopter was a piece of the jigsaw that wouldn't fit anywhere. I looked at my watch and found it was after nine o'clock, so I buried all the cigarette stubs, picked up the carbine and prepared to go back.

As I stood up I saw something that made me tense— a plume of dust in the far distance across the river. I laid down the carbine and lifted the glasses and saw the little dot of a vehicle at the head of that feather of dust like a high-flying jet at the head of a contrail. I looked around —there was no cover near the river but about two hundred yards back a spasm of long gone energy had heaved up the lava into a ridge which I could hide behind. I ran for it.

The vehicle proved to be a Willys jeep—as good for this country in its way as my Land-Rover. It slowed as it came to the river, nosed forward and came to a stop at the water's edge. The night was quiet and I heard the click of the door handle as a man got out and walked forward to look at the water. He turned and said something to the driver and, although I could not hear the words, I knew he was speaking neither Icelandic nor English.

He spoke Russian.

The driver got out, looked at the water and shook his head. Presently there were four of them standing there, and they seemed to be having an argument. Another jeep came up behind and more men got out to study the problem until there were eight in all—two jeeps full. One of them, the one who made the decisive gestures and who seemed to be the boss, I thought I recognized.

I lifted the glasses and his face sprang into full view in the dimming light. Elin had been wrong; crossing the river had *not* been an unjustifiable risk, and the justification lay in the face I now saw. The scar was still there, running from the end of the right eyebrow to the corner of the mouth, and the eyes were still grey and hard as stones. The only change in him was that his close-cropped hair was no longer black but a grizzled grey and his face was puffier with incipient wattles forming on his neck.

Kennikin and I were both four years older but I think I may have worn better than he had.

CHAPTER FIVE

I

I put my hand out to the carbine and then paused. The light was bad and getting worse, the gun was strange and it hadn't the barrel to reach out and knock a man down at a distance. I estimated the range at a shade under three hundred yards and I knew that if I hit anyone at that range and in that light it would be by chance and not by intention.

If I had my own gun I could have dropped Kennikin as easily as dropping a deer. I have put a soft-nosed bullet into a deer and it has run for half a mile before dropping dead, and that with an exit wound big enough to put your fist in. A man can't do that—his nervous system is too delicate and can't stand the shock.

But I hadn't my own rifle, and there was no percentage in opening fire at random. That would only tell Kennikin I was close, and it might be better if he didn't know. So I let my fingers relax from the carbine and concentrated on watching what was going to happen next.

The arguing had stopped with Kennikin's arrival, and I knew why, having worked with him. He had no time for futile blathering; he would accept your facts—and God help you if they were wrong—and then he would make the decisions. He was busily engaged in making one now.

I smiled as I saw someone point out the tracks of the Land-Rover entering the water and then indicate the other bank of the river. There were no tracks where we had left the water because we had been swept sideways a little, and that must have been puzzling to anyone who hadn't seen it happen.

The man waved downstream eloquently but Kennikin shook his head. He wasn't buying that one. Instead he said something, snapping his fingers impatiently, and someone else rushed up with a map. He studied it and then pointed off to the right and four of the men got into a jeep, reversed up the track, and then took off across country in a bumpy ride.

That made me wrinkle my brows until I remembered there was a small group of lakes over in that direction called Gaesavötn. If Kennikin expected me to be camping at Gaesavötn he'd draw a blank, but it showed how thorough and careful he was.

The crew from the other jeep got busy erecting a camp just off the track, putting up tents rather inexpertly. One of them went to Kennikin with a vacuum flask and poured out a cup of steaming hot coffee which he offered obsequiously. Kennikin took it and sipped it while still standing at the water's edge looking across the impassable river. He seemed to be staring right into my eyes.

I lowered the glasses and withdrew slowly and cautiously, being careful to make no sound. I climbed down from the lava ridge and then slung the carbine and headed back to the Land-Rover at a fast clip, and checked to make sure there were no tyre marks to show where we had left the track. I didn't think Kennikin would have a man swim the river—he could lose a lot of men that way—but it was best to make sure we weren't stumbled over too easily.

Elin was asleep. She lay on her left side, buried in her sleeping bag, and I was thankful that she always slept quietly and with no blowing or snoring. I let her sleep; there was no reason to disturb her and ruin her night. We weren't going anywhere, and neither was Kennikin. I switched on my pocket torch shading it with my hand to avoid waking her, and rummaged in a drawer until I found the housewife, from which I took a reel of black thread.

I went back to the track and stretched a line of thread right across it about a foot from the ground, anchoring each end by lumps of loose lava. If Kennikin came through during the night I wanted to know it, no matter how stealthily he went about it. I didn't want to cross the river in the morning only to run into him on the other side.

Then I went down to the river and looked at it. The water level was still dropping and it might have been been barely feasible to cross there and then had the light been better. But I wouldn't risk it without using the headlights and I couldn't do that because they'd certainly show in the sky. Kennikin's mob wasn't all that far away.

I dropped into my berth fully clothed. I didn't expect to sleep under the circumstances but nevertheless I set the alarm on my wrist watch for two a.m. And that was the last thing I remember until it buzzed like a demented mosquito and woke me up.

I I

We were ready to move at two-fifteen. As soon as the alarm buzzed I woke Elin, ruthlessly disregarding her sleepy protests. As soon as she knew how close Kennikin was she moved fast. I said, 'Get dressed quickly. I'm going to have a look around.'

The black thread was still in place which meant that no vehicle had gone through. Any jeep moving at night would *have* to stick to the track; it was flatly impossible to cross the lava beds in the darkness. True, someone on foot might have gone through, but I discounted that.

The water in the river was nice and low and it would be easy to cross. As I went back I looked in the sky towards the east; already the short northern night was nearly over and I was determined to cross the river at the earliest opportunity and get as far ahead of Kennikin as I could.

Elin had different ideas. 'Why not stay here and let him get ahead? Just let him go past. He'd have to go a long way before he discovered he's chasing nothing.'

'No,' I said. 'We know he has two jeeps, but we don't know if he has more. It could happen that, if we let him get ahead, we could be the meat in a sandwich and that might be uncomfortable. We cross now.'

Starting an engine quietly is not easy. I stuffed blankets around the generator in an attempt to muffle that unmistakable rasp, the engine caught and purred sweetly, and I took the blankets away. And I was very light-footed on the accelerator as we drove towards the river. We got across easily, although making more noise than I cared for, and away we went towards the next river.

I told Elin to keep a sharp eye to the rear while I concentrated on moving as fast as possible compatible with quietness. In the next four kilometres we crossed two more rivers and then there was a long stretch where the track swung north temporarily, and I opened up. We were now far enough away from Kennikin to make speed more important than silence.

Sixteen rivers in sixty kilometres, Elin had said. Not

counting the time spent in crossing rivers we were now averaging a bone-jarring twenty-five kilometres an hour —too fast for comfort in this country—and I estimated we would get to the main Sprengisandur track in about four hours. It actually took six hours because some of the rivers were bastards.

In reaching the Sprengisandur track we had crossed the watershed and all the rivers from now on would be flowing south and west instead of north and east. We hit the track at eight-thirty, and I said, 'Breakfast. Climb in the back and get something ready.'

'You're not stopping?'

'Christ, no! Kennikin will have been on the move for hours. There's no way of knowing how close he is and I've no urgent inclination to find out the hard way. Bread and cheese and beer will do fine.'

So we ate on the move and stopped only once, at ten o'clock, to fill up the tank from the last full jerrycan. While we were doing that up popped our friend of the previous day, the US Navy helicopter. It came from the north this time, not very low, and floated over us without appearing to pay us much attention.

I watched it fly south, and Elin said, 'I'm puzzled about that.'

'So am I,' I said.

'Not in the same way that I am,' she said. 'American military aircraft don't usually overfly the country.' She was frowning.

'Now you come to mention it, that *is* odd.' There's a certain amount of tension in Iceland about the continuing American military presence at Keflavik. A lot of Icelanders take the view that it's an imposition and who can blame them? The American authorities are quite aware of this tension and try to minimize it, and the American Navy in Iceland tries to remain as inconspicuous as possible. Flaunting military aircraft in Icelandic skies was certainly out of character.

I shrugged and dismissed the problem, concentrating on getting the last drop out of the jerrycan, and then we carried on with not a sign of anything on our tail. We were now on the last lap, running down the straight, if rough, track between the River Thjórsá and the ridge of Búdarháls with the main roads only seventy kilometres ahead, inasmuch as any roads in Iceland can be so described.

But even a lousy Icelandic road would be perfection when compared with the tracks of the *Óbyggdir*, especially when we ran into trouble with mud. This is one of the problems of June when the frozen earth of winter melts into a gelatinous car trap. Because we were in a Land-Rover it didn't stop us but it slowed us down considerably, and the only consolation I had was that Kennikin would be equally hampered when he hit the stuff.

At eleven o'clock the worst happened—a tyre blew. It was a front tyre and I fought the wheel as we jolted to a stop. 'Let's make this fast,' I said, and grabbed the wheel brace.

If we had to have a puncture it wasn't a bad place to have it. The footing was level enough to take the jack without slipping and there was no mud at that point. I jacked up the front of the Land-Rover and got busy on the wheel with the brace. Because of Elin's shoulder she wasn't of much use in this kind of job, so I said, 'What about making coffee—we could do with something hot.'

I took the wheel off, rolled it away and replaced it with the spare. The whole operation took a little under ten minutes, time we couldn't afford—not there and then. Once we were farther south we could lose ourselves on a more-or-less complex road network, but these wilderness tracks were too restricted for my liking.

I tightened the last wheel nut and then looked to see what had caused a blowout and to put the wheel back into its rack. What I saw made my blood run cold. I fingered the jagged hole in the thick tyre and looked up at the Búdarháls ridge which dominated the track.

There was only one thing that could make a hole like that—a bullet. And somewhere up on the ridge, hidden in some crevice, was a sniper—and even then I was probably in his sights.

III

How in hell did Kennikin get ahead of me? That was my first bitter thought. But idle thoughts were no use and action was necessary.

I heaved up the wheel with its ruined tyre on to the bonnet and screwed it down securely. While I rotated the wheel brace I glanced covertly at the ridge. There was a lot of open ground before the ridge heaved itself into the air—at least two hundred yards—and the closest a sniper could have been was possibly four hundred yards and probably more.

Any man who could put a bullet into a tyre at over four hundred yards—a quarter mile—was a hell of a good shot. So good that he could put a bullet into me any time he liked—so why the devil hadn't he? I was in plain view, a perfect target, and yet no bullets had come my way. I tightened down the last nut and turned my back to the ridge, and felt a prickling feeling between my shoulder blades—that was where the bullet would hit me if it came.

I jumped to the ground and put away the brace and jack, concentrating on doing the natural thing. The palms of my hands were slippery with sweat. I went to the back of the Land-Rover and looked in at the open door. 'How's the coffee coming?'

'Just ready,' said Elin.

I climbed in and sat down. Sitting in that confined space gave a comforting illusion of protection, but that's all it was—an illusion. For the second time I wished the Land-Rover had been an armoured car. From where I was sitting I could inspect the slopes of the ridge without being too obvious about it and I made the most of the opportunity.

Nothing moved among those red and grey rocks. Nobody stood up and waved or cheered. If anyone was still up there he was keeping as quiet as a mouse which, of course, was the correct thing to do. If you pump a bullet at someone you'd better scrunch yourself up small in case he starts shooting back.

But was anybody still up there? I rather thought there was. Who in his right mind would shoot a hole in the tyre of a car and then just walk away? So he was still up there, waiting and watching. But if he was still there why hadn't he nailed me? It didn't make much sense—unless he was just supposed to immobilize me.

I stared unseeingly at Elin who was topping up a jar with sugar. If that was so, then Kennikin had men coming in from both sides. It wouldn't be too hard to arrange if he knew where I was—radio communication is a wonderful thing. That character up on the ridge would have been instructed to stop me so that Kennikin could catch up; and that meant he wanted me alive.

I wondered what would happen if I got into the driving seat and took off again. The odds were that another bullet would rip open another tyre. It would be easier this time on a sitting target. I didn't take the trouble to find out—there was a limit to the number of spare tyres I carried, and the limit had already been reached.

Hoping that my chain of reasoning was not too shaky I began to make arrangements to get out from under that gun. I took Lindholm's cosh from under the mattress where I had concealed it and put it into my pocket, then I said, 'Let's go and . . .' My voice came out as a hoarse croak and I cleared my throat. 'Let's have coffee outside.'

Elin looked up in surprise. 'I thought we were in a hurry.'

'We've been making good time,' I said. 'I reckon we're far enough ahead to earn a break. I'll take the coffee pot and the sugar; you bring the cups.' I would have dearly loved to have taken the carbine but that would have been too obvious; an unsuspecting man doesn't drink his coffee fully armed.

I jumped out of the rear door and Elin handed out the coffee pot and the sugar jar which I set on the rear bumper before helping her down. Her right arm was still in the sling but she could carry the cups and spoons in her left hand. I picked up the coffee pot and waved it in the general direction of the ridge. 'Let's go over there at the foot of the rocks.' I made off in that direction without giving her time to argue.

We trudged over the open ground towards the ridge. I had the coffee pot in one hand and the sugar jar in the other, the picture of innocence. I also had the *sgian dubh* tucked into my left stocking and a cosh in my pocket, but those didn't show. As we got nearer the ridge a miniature cliff reared up and I thought our friend up on top might be getting worried. Any moment from now he would be losing sight of us, and he might just lean forward a little to keep us in view.

I turned as though to speak to Elin and then turned back quickly, glancing upwards as I did so. There was no one to be seen but I was rewarded by the glint of something—a reflection that flickered into nothing. It might have been the sun reflecting off a surface of glassy lava, but I didn't think so. Lava doesn't jump around when left to its own devices—not after it has cooled off, that is.

I marked the spot and went on, not looking up again, and we came to the base of the cliff which was about twenty feet high. There was a straggly growth of birch; gnarled trees all of a foot high. In Iceland bonsai grow naturally and I'm surprised the Icelanders don't work up an export trade to Japan. I found a clear space, set down the coffee pot and the sugar jar, then sat down and pulled up my trouser leg to extract the knife.

Elin came up. 'What are you doing?'

I said, 'Now don't jump out of your pants, but there's a character on the ridge behind us who just shot a hole in that tyre.'

Elin stared at me wordlessly. I said, 'He can't see us here, but I don't think he's worried very much about that. All he wants to do is to stop us until Kennikin arrives—and he's doing it very well. As long as he can see the Land-Rover he knows we aren't far away.' I tucked the knife into the waistband of my trousers—it's designed for a fast draw only when wearing a kilt.

Elin sank to her knees. 'You're sure?'

'I'm positive. You don't get a natural puncture like that in the side wall of a new tyre.' I stood up and looked along the ridge. 'I'm going to winkle out that bastard; I think I know where he is.' I pointed to a crevice at the end of the cliff, a four-foot high crack in the rock. 'I want you to get in there and wait. Don't move until you hear me call—and make bloody sure it is me.'

'And what if you don't come back?' she said bleakly.

She was a realist. I looked at her set face and said deliberately, 'In that case, if nothing else happens, you stay where you are until dark, then make a break for the Land-Rover and get the hell out of here. On the other hand, if Kennikin pitches up, try to keep out of his way—and do that by keeping out of sight.' I shrugged. 'But I'll try to get back.'

'Do you have to go at all?'

I sighed. 'We're stuck here, Elin. As long as that joker can keep the Land-Rover covered we're stuck. What do you want me to do? Wait here until Kennikin arrives and then just give myself up?'

'But you're not armed?'

I patted the hilt of the knife. 'I'll make out. Now, just do as I say.' I escorted her to the cleft and saw her inside. It can't have been very comfortable; it was a foot and a half wide by four feet high and so she had to crouch. But there are worse things than being uncomfortable.

Then I contemplated what I had to do. The ridge was seamed by gullies cut by water into the soft rock and they offered a feasible way of climbing without being seen. What I wanted to do was to get above the place where I had seen the sudden glint. In warfare—and this was war—he who holds the high ground has the advantage.

I set out, moving to the left and sticking close in to the rocks. There was a gully twenty yards along which I rejected because I knew it petered out not far up the ridge. The next one was better because it went nearly to the top, so I went into it and began to climb.

Back in the days when I was being trained I went to mountain school and my instructor said something very wise. 'Never follow a watercourse or a stream, either uphill or downhill,' he said. The reasoning was good. Water will take the quickest way down any hill and the quickest way is usually the steepest. Normally one sticks to the bare hillside and steers clear of ravines. Abnormally, on the other hand, one scrambles up a damned steep, slippery, waterworn crack in the rock or one gets one's head blown off.

The sides of the ravine at the bottom of the ridge were about ten feet high, so there was no danger of being seen. But higher up the ravine was shallower and towards the end it was only about two feet deep and I was snaking upwards on my belly. When I had gone as far as I could I reckoned I was higher than the sniper, so I cautiously pushed my head around a pitted chunk of lava and assessed the situation.

Far below me on the track, and looking conspicuously isolated, was the Land-Rover. About two hundred feet to the right and a hundred feet below was the place where I thought the sniper was hiding. I couldn't see him because of the boulders which jutted through the sandy skin of the ridge. That suited me; if I couldn't see him then he couldn't see me, and that screen of boulders was just what I needed to get up close.

But I didn't rush at it. It was in my mind that there might be more than one man. Hell, there could be a dozen scattered along the top of the ridge for all I knew!

I just stayed very still and got back my breath, and did a careful survey of every damned rock within sight.

Nothing moved, so I wormed my way out of cover of the ravine and headed towards the boulders, still on my belly. I got there and rested again, listening carefully. All I heard was the faraway murmur of the river in the distance. I moved again, going upwards and around the clump of boulders, and now I was holding the cosh.

I pushed my head around a rock and saw them, fifty feet below in a hollow in the hillside. One was lying down with a rifle pushed before him, the barrel resting on a folded jacket; the other sat farther back tinkering with a walkie-talkie. He had an unlighted cigarette in his mouth.

I withdrew my head and considered. One man I might have tackled—two together were going to be tricky, especially without a gun. I moved carefully and found a better place from which to observe and where I would be less conspicuous—two rocks came almost together but not quite, and I had a peephole an inch across.

The man with the rifle was very still and very patient. I could imagine that he was an experienced hunter and had spent many hours on hillsides like this waiting for his quarry to move within range. The other man was more fidgety; he eased his buttocks on the rock on which he was sitting, he scratched, he slapped at an insect which settled on his leg, and he fiddled with the walkie-talkie.

At the bottom of the ridge I saw something moving and held my breath. The man with the rifle saw it, too, and I could see the slight tautening of his muscles as he tensed. It was Elin. She came out of cover from under the cliff and walked towards the Land-Rover.

I cursed to myself and wondered what the hell she thought she was doing. The man with the rifle settled the butt firmly into his shoulder and took aim, following her all the way with his eye glued to the telescopic sight. If he pulled that trigger I would take my chances and jump the bastard there and then.

Elin got to the Land-Rover and climbed inside. Within a minute she came out again and began to walk back towards the cliff. Half-way there she called out and tossed something into the air. I was too far away to see what it was but I thought it was a packet of cigarettes. The joker with the rifle would be sure of what it was because he was equipped with one of the biggest telescopic sights

I had ever seen.

Elin vanished from sight below and I let out my breath. She had deliberately play-acted to convince these gunmen that I was still there below, even if out of sight. And it worked, too. The rifleman visibly relaxed and turned over and said something to the other man. I couldn't hear what was said because he spoke in low tones, but the fidget laughed loudly.

He was having trouble with the walkie-talkie. He extended the antenna, clicked switches and turned knobs, and then tossed it aside on to the moss. He spoke to the rifleman and pointed upwards, and the rifleman nodded. Then he stood up and turned to climb towards me.

I noted the direction he was taking, then turned my head to find a place to ambush him. There was a boulder just behind me about three feet high, so I pulled away from my peephole and dropped behind it in a crouch and took a firm hold of the cosh. I could hear him coming because he wasn't making much attempt to move quietly. His boots crunched on the ground and once there was a flow of gravel as he slipped and I heard a muttered curse. Then there was a change in the light as his shadow fell across me, and I rose up behind him and hit him.

There's quite a bit of nonsense talked about hitting men on the head. From some accounts—film and TV script writers—it's practically as safe as an anaesthetic used in an operating theatre; all that happens is a brief spell of unconsciousness followed by a headache not worse than a good hangover. A pity it isn't so because if it were the hospital anaesthetists would be able to dispense with the elaborate equipment with which they are now lumbered in favour of the time-honoured blunt instrument.

Unconsciousness is achieved by imparting a sharp acceleration to the skull bone so that it collides with the contents—the brain. This results in varying degrees of brain damage ranging from slight concussion to death, and there is always lasting damage, however slight. The blow must be quite heavy and, since men vary, a blow that will make one man merely dizzy will kill another. The trouble is that until you've administered the blow you don't know what you've done.

I wasn't in any mood for messing about so I hit this character hard. His knees buckled under him and he collapsed, and I caught him before he hit the ground. I eased him down and turned him so that he lay on his back. A mangled cigar sagged sideways from his mouth, half bitten through, and blood trickled from the cigar butt to show he had bitten his tongue. He was still breathing.

I patted his pockets and came upon the familiar hard shape, and drew forth an automatic pistol—a Smith & Wesson .38, the twin to the one I had taken from Lindholm. I checked the magazine to see if it was full and then worked the action to put a bullet into the breech.

The collapsed figure at my feet wasn't going to be much use to anybody even if he did wake up, so I didn't have to worry about him. All I had to do now was to take care of Daniel Boone—the man with the rifle. I returned to my peephole to see what he was doing.

He was doing precisely what he had been doing ever since I had seen him—contemplating the Land-Rover with inexhaustible patience. I stood up and walked into the hollow, gun first. I didn't worry overmuch about keeping quiet; speed was more important than quietness and I reckoned he might be more alarmed if I pussyfooted around than if I crunched up behind him.

He didn't even turn his head. All he did was to say in a flat Western drawl, 'You forgotten something, Joe?'

I caught my jaw before it sagged too far. A Russian I expected; an American I didn't. But this was no time to worry about nationalities—a man who throws bullets at you is automatically a bastard, and whether he's a Russian bastard or an American bastard makes little difference. I just said curtly, 'Turn around, but leave the rifle where it is or you'll have a hole in you.'

He went very still, but the only part of him that he turned was his head. He had china-blue eyes in a tanned, narrow face and he looked ideal for type-casting as Pop's eldest son in a TV horse opera. He also looked dangerous. 'I'll be goddamned!' he said softly.

'You certainly will be if you don't take your hands off that rifle,' I said. 'Spread your arms out as though you were being crucified.'

He looked at the pistol in my hand and reluctantly extended his arms. A man prone in that position finds it difficult to get up quickly. 'Where's Joe?' he asked.

'He's gone beddy-byes.' I walked over to him and put the muzzle of the pistol to the nape of his neck and I felt him shudder. That didn't mean much; it didn't mean he was afraid—I shudder involuntarily when Elin kisses me on the nape of the neck. 'Just keep quiet,' I advised, and picked up the rifle.

I didn't have time to examine it closely then, but I did afterwards, and it was certainly some weapon. It had a mixed ancestry and probably had started life as a Browning, but a good gunsmith had put in a lot of time in reworking it, giving it such refinements as a sculptured stock with a hole in it to put your thumb, and other fancy items. It was a bit like the man said, 'I have my grand-father's axe—my father replaced the blade and I gave it a new haft.'

What it had ended up as was the complete long-range assassin's kit. It was bolt action because it was a gun for a man who picks his target and who can shoot well enough not to want to send a second bullet after the first in too much of a hurry. It was chambered for a .375 magnum load, a heavy 300 grain bullet with a big charge behind it —high velocity, low trajectory. This rifle in good hands could reach out half a mile and snuff out a man's life if the light was good and the air still.

To help the aforesaid good hands was a fantastic tele-scopic sight—a variable-powered monster with a top mag-nification of 30. To use it when fully racked out would need a man with no nerves—and thus no tremble—or a solid bench rest. The scope was equipped with its own range-finding system, a multiple mounting of graduated dots on the vertical cross hair for various ranges, and was sighted in at five hundred yards.

It was a hell of a lot of gun.

I straightened and rested the muzzle of the rifle lightly against my friend's spine. 'That's your gun you can feel,' I said. 'You don't need me to tell you what would happen if I pulled the trigger.'

His head was turned sideways and I saw a light film of sweat coating the tan. He didn't need to let his imagination work because he was a good craftsman and knew his tools enough to *know* what would happen—over 5,000 foot-pounds of energy would blast him clean in two.

I said, 'Where's Kennikin?'

'Who?'

'Don't be childish,' I said. 'I'll ask you again—where's Kennikin?'

'I don't know any Kennikin,' he said in a muffled voice. He found difficulty in speaking because the side of his face was pressed against the ground.

'Think again.'

'I tell you I don't know him. All I was doing was following orders.'

'Yes,' I said. 'You took a shot at me.'

'No,' he said quickly. 'At your tyre. You're still alive, aren't you? I could have knocked you off any time.'

I looked down the slope at the Land-Rover. That was true; it would be like a Bisley champion shooting tin ducks at a fairground. 'So you were instructed to stop me. Then what?'

'Then nothing.'

I increased the pressure on his spine slightly. 'You can do better than that.'

'I was to wait until someone showed up and then quit and go home.'

'And who was the someone?'

'I don't know—I wasn't told.'

That sounded crazy; it was even improbable enough to be true. I said, 'What's your name?'

'John Smith.'

I smiled and said, 'All right, Johnny; start crawling—backwards and slowly. And if I see more than half an inch of daylight between your belly and the ground I'll let you have it.'

He wriggled back slowly and painfully away from the edge and down into the hollow, and then I stopped him. Much as I would have liked to carry on the interrogation I had to put an end to it because time was wasting. I said, 'Now, Johnny; I don't want you to make any sudden moves because I'm a very nervous man, so just keep quite still.'

I came up on his blind side, lifted the butt of the rifle and brought it down on the back of his head. It was no way to treat such a good gun but it was the only thing I had handy. The gun butt was considerably harder than the cosh and I regretfully decided I had fractured his skull. Anyway, he wouldn't be causing me any more trouble.

I walked over to pick up the jacket he had been using as a gun rest. It was heavy and I expected to find a pistol in the pocket, but the weight was caused by an unbroken box of rounds for the rifle. Next to the jacket was an open box. Both were unlabelled.

I checked the rifle. The magazine was designed to hold five rounds and contained four, there was one in the breech ready to pop off, and there were nineteen rounds in the opened box. Mr Smith was a professional; he had filled the magazine, jacked one into the breech, and then taken out the magazine and stuffed another round into it so he would have six rounds in hand instead of five. Not that he needed them—he had bust the tyre on a moving vehicle at over four hundred yards with just one shot.

He was a professional all right, but his name wasn't Smith because he carried an American passport in the name of Wendell George Fleet. He also carried a pass that would get him into the more remote corners of Keflavik Naval Base, the parts which the public are discouraged from visiting. He didn't carry a pistol; a rifleman as good as he usually despises handguns.

I put the boxes of ammunition into my pocket where they weighed heavy, and I stuck Joe's automatic pistol into the waistband of my trousers, unloading it first so I didn't do a Kennikin on myself. Safety catches are not all that reliable and a lot of men have ruined themselves for their wives by acting like a character in a TV drama.

I went to see how Joe was doing and found that he was still asleep and that his name wasn't even Joe according to his passport. It turned out he was Patrick Aloysius McCarthy. I regarded him speculatively; he looked more Italian than Irish to me. Probably all the names were phoney, just as Buchner who wasn't Graham turned out to be Philips.

McCarthy carried two spare magazines for the Smith & Wesson, both of them full, which I confiscated. I seemed to be building up quite an armoury on this expedition—from a little knife to a high-powered rifle in one week wasn't doing too bad. Next up the scale ought to be a burp gun or possibly a fully-fledged machine-gun. I wondered how long it would take me to graduate to something really lethal, such as an Atlas ICBM.

McCarthy had been going somewhere when I thumped him. He had been trying to contact someone by radio, but the walkie-talkie had been on the blink so he'd decided to walk, and that put whoever it was not very far away. I stared up towards the top of the ridge and decided to take a look over the next rise. It was a climb of perhaps two hundred yards and when I poked my head carefully over the top I caught my breath in surprise.

The yellow US Navy helicopter was parked about four hundred yards away and two crewmen and a civilian sat in front of it, talking casually. I lifted Fleet's rifle and looked at them through the big scope at maximum magnification. The crewmen were unimportant but I thought I might know the civilian. I didn't, but I memorized his face for future reference.

For a moment I was tempted to tickle them up with the rifle but I shelved the idea. It would be better to depart quietly and without fuss. I didn't want that chopper with me the rest of the way, so I withdrew and went back down the hill. I had been away quite a while and Elin would be becoming even more worried, if that were possible.

From where I was I had a good view along the track so I looked to see if Kennikin was yet in sight. He was! Through the scope I saw a minute black dot in the far distance crawling along the track, and I estimated that the jeep was about three miles away. There was a lot of mud along there and I didn't think he'd be making much more than ten miles an hour, so that put him about fifteen minutes behind.

I went down the hillside fast.

Elin was squashed into the crack in the rock but she came out when I called. She ran over and grabbed me as though she wanted to check whether I was all in one piece and she was laughing and crying at the same time. I disentangled myself from her arms. 'Kennikin's not far behind; let's move.'

I set out towards the Land-Rover at a dead run, holding Elin's arm, but she dragged free. 'The coffee pot!'

'The hell with it!' Women are funny creatures; this was not a time to be thinking of domestic economy. I grabbed her arm again and dragged her along.

Thirty seconds later I had the engine going and we were bouncing along the track too fast for either safety or comfort while I decided which potholes it would be safe to put the front wheels into. Decisions, decisions, nothing but bloody decisions—and if I decided wrongly we'd have a broken half-axle or be stuck in the mud and the jig would be up.

We bounced like hell all the way to the Tungnaá River and the traffic got thicker—one car passed us going the other way, the first we had seen since being in the *Óbyggdir*. That was bad because Kennikin was likely to stop it and ask the driver if he had seen a long wheelbase Land-Rover lately. It was one thing to chase me through the wilderness without knowing where I was, and quite another to know that I was actually within spitting distance. The psychological spur would stimulate his adrenal gland just that much more.

On the other hand, seeing the car cheered me because it meant that the car transporter over the Tungnaá would be on our side of the river and there would be no waiting. I have travelled a lot in places where water crossings are done by ferry—there are quite a few in Scotland—and it's a law of nature that the ferry is always on the other side when you arrive at the water's edge. But that wouldn't be so this time.

Not that this was a ferry. You cross the Tungnaá by means of a contraption—a platform slung on an overhead cable. You drive your car on to the platform and winch yourself across, averting your eyes from the white water streaming below. According to the *Ferdahandbokin*, which every traveller in the *Óbyggdir* ought to consult, extreme care is necessary for people not acquainted with the system. Personally, I don't recommend it for those with queasy stomachs who have to cross in a high wind.

We arrived at the Tungnaá and the contraption was, indeed, on our side. I checked that it was secured and safe, and then drove on carefully. 'Stay in the cab,' I said to Elin. 'You can't winch with that broken wing.'

I got out and began to operate the winch, keeping an eye open for Kennikin's imminent arrival. I felt very exposed and naked and I hoped I had kept my fifteen-minute lead because crossing the Tungnaá is a slow job. But we made it without incident and I drove off the platform with a great sense of relief.

'Now we can stop the bastard,' I said as we drove away.

Elin sat up straight. 'You're not going to break the cable!' There was a note of indignation in her voice. Being shot at was all right but the wanton destruction of public property was unethical.

I grinned at her. 'I'd do it if I could, but it would take a stronger man than me.' I pulled the car off the road and looked back; the river was out of sight. 'No, I'm going to chain up the platform so Kennikin can't pull it across. He'll be stuck on the other side until someone going the other way can release it, and God knows when that will be —there's not much traffic. Stay here.'

I got out, rummaged in the tool kit, and found the snow chains. It wasn't at all likely we'd need them in the summer and they could do a better job keeping Kennikin off my neck than lying where they were. I lifted them out and ran back down the track.

You can't really tie a chain into a knot but I tethered that platform with such a tangle of iron that would take anyone at least half an hour to free unless he happened to have an oxy-acetylene cutting torch handy. I had nearly completed the job when Kennikin arrived on the other side and the fun started.

The jeep came to a halt and four men got out, Kennikin in the lead. I was hidden behind the platform and no one saw me at first. Kennikin studied the cable and then read the instructions that are posted in Icelandic and English. He got the hang of it and ordered his men to haul the platform back across the river.

They duly hauled and nothing happened.

I was working like hell to finish the job and just got it done in time. The platform lurched away and then stopped, tethered by the chain. There was a shout from the other side and someone went running along the bank so as to get into a position to see what was stopping the platform. He saw it all right—he saw me. The next moment he had whipped out a gun and started to shoot.

The pistol is a much over-rated weapon. It has its place, which is about ten yards from its target or, better still, ten feet. The popgun that was shooting at me was a short-barrelled .38 revolver—a belly gun—with which I wouldn't trust to hit anything I couldn't reach out and touch. I was pretty safe as long as he aimed at me; if he started to shoot anywhere else I might get hit by accident, but that was a slim chance.

The others opened up as I snagged the last bit of chain into place. A bullet raised the dust two yards away and that was as close as they came. Yet it's no fun being shot at so I turned and belted away up the track at a dead run.

Elin was standing by the Land-Rover, her face full of concern, having heard the barrage of shots. 'It's all right,' I said. 'The war hasn't broken out.' I reached inside and took out Fleet's rifle. 'Let's see if we can discourage them.'

She looked at the rifle with abhorrence. 'Oh, God! Must you kill them? Haven't you done enough?'

I stared at her and then the penny dropped. She thought I'd got hold of that rifle by killing Fleet; she seemed to think that you couldn't take that much gun away from a man without killing him. I said, 'Elin; those men across the river were trying to kill me. The fact they didn't succeed doesn't alter their intention. Now, I'm not going to kill anyone—I said I'll discourage them.' I held up the rifle. 'And I didn't kill the man I took this from, either.'

I walked away down the track but veered away from it before I reached the river. I hunted around until I found suitable cover and then lay and watched Kennikin and his crew unsuccessfully trying to get at the platform. A 30-power scope was a bit too much optical glass for a range of a hundred yards but it had variable power so I dropped it to a magnification of six which was as low as it would go. A rock in front of me formed a convenient rest and I settled the butt against my shoulder and looked into the eyepiece.

I wasn't going to kill anyone. Not that I didn't want to, but bodies you can't get rid of are inconvenient and lead to the asking of awkward questions by the appropriate authorities. A wounded Russian, on the other hand, would be eliminated just as much as a dead one. He would be smuggled by his friends on to the trawler which was undoubtedly to hand, probably already in Reykjavik harbour. The Russians have more non-fishing trawlers than any other nation on earth.

No, I wasn't going to kill anyone, but someone would soon wish to God he were dead.

Kennikin had disappeared and the three other men were engaged in a heated discussion about how to solve their little problem. I broke it up by firing five spaced shots in thirty seconds. The first hit the man standing next to the jeep in the kneecap, and suddenly there wasn't anyone else around to shoot at. He lay on the ground, writhing and shouting, and he'd have one leg shorter than the other for the rest of his life—if he was got into a hospital quickly. If not, he'd be lucky to have a leg at all.

I re-sighted and squeezed the trigger again, this time shooting at the off-side front tyre of the jeep. The rifle was one of the best I've ever handled and, at a hundred yards, the trajectory was so flat that I could put a bullet exactly where I wanted it. The tyre wasn't just punctured; under the close-range hammer blow of that big .375 bullet it exploded into bits, as did the other front tyre when I let fly again.

Someone popped off with a pistol. I ignored that and fed another round into the breech. I centred the cross hairs on to the front of the radiator and fired again, and the jeep rocked on its springs under the impact. This rifle was chambered to shoot big game and anything that can crack open the frontal skull bone of a buffalo wouldn't do an engine block much good. I put the last bullet in the same place in the hope of putting the jeep permanently out of action and then withdrew, keeping my head down.

I walked up to the Land-Rover, and said to Elin, 'It's a good rifle.'

She looked at me nervously. 'I thought I heard someone scream.'

'I didn't kill anyone,' I said. 'But they won't be driving that jeep very far. Let's go on. You can drive for a bit.' I was suddenly very tired.

CHAPTER SIX

I

We drove out of the *Óbyggdir* and hit the main road system. Even if Kennikin was able to follow us we would have a good chance of losing him because this was one of the main areas of population and there was a network of roads harder to police than the simple choices of the *Óbyggdir*. Elin drove while I relaxed in the passenger seat, and once we were on the good roads were able to pick up speed.

'Where to?' she asked.

'I'd like to get this vehicle out of sight,' I said. 'It's too damned conspicuous. Any suggestions?'

'You have to be at Geysir tomorrow night,' she said. 'I have friends at Laugarvatn—you must remember Gunnar.'

'Weren't you running around with him before you met me?'

She smiled. 'It wasn't serious—and we're still friends. Besides, he's married now.'

Marriage, to a lot of men, doesn't mean an automatic cancellation of their hunting licence, but I let it lie; a more-or-less civilized butting match with Elin's old boyfriend was preferable to a more deadly encounter with Kennikin. 'All right,' I said. 'Head for Laugarvatn.'

We were silent for a while, then I said, 'Thank you for what you did back there when I was on Búdarháls. It was a damned silly thing to do, but it helped.'

'I thought it might distract their attention,' she said.

'It sure as hell distracted mine for a minute. Did you know you were in the sights of a rifle all the way—and there was a finger on the trigger?'

'I did feel uneasy,' she admitted, and shivered involuntarily. 'What happened up there?'

'I gave headaches to a couple of men. One of them will probably wind up in hospital at Keflavik.'

She looked at me sharply. 'Keflavik!'

'Yes,' I said. 'They were Americans.' I told her about

Fleet, McCarthy and the waiting helicopter. 'I've been trying to make sense out of it ever since—without much success.'

She thought about it too, and said. 'But it *doesn't* make sense. Why would the Americans co-operate with the Russians? Are you sure they were Americans?'

'They were as American as Mom's apple-pie—at least Fleet was. I didn't get to talk to McCarthy.'

'They could be sympathizers,' said Elin. 'Fellow-travellers.'

'Then they're travelling closer than a flea to a dog.' I took out Fleet's pass to the remoter recesses of Keflavik Air Base. 'If they're fellow-travellers then the Yanks had better watch it—their furniture is riddled with woodworm.' I examined the pass and thought about the helicopter. 'It's just about the most ridiculous thing I've heard of.'

'Then what other explanation is there?'

The idea of a nest of communist sympathizers being convenient to hand at Keflavik and able to lay their hands on a navy helicopter at a moment's notice was untenable. I said, 'I doubt if Kennikin rang up Keflavik and said, "Look, boys; I'm chasing a British spy and I need your help. Can you lay on a chopper and a sharpshooter and stop him for me?" But there's someone else who could do it.'

'Who?'

'There's a man called Helms in Washington who could pick up a telephone and say, "Admiral, there'll be a couple of guys dropping in at Keflavik pretty soon. Let them have a helicopter and a crew—and don't ask too many questions about what they want it for." And the Admiral would say, 'Yes, sir; yes, sir; three bags full, sir," because Helms is the boss of the CIA.'

'But why?'

'I'm damned if I know,' I said. 'But it's a bloody sight more likely than Keflavik being white-anted by Russian agents.' I thought of my brief and unsatisfactory conversation with Fleet. 'Fleet said that his orders were to pin us down until someone—presumably Kennikin—arrived. He said he'd never heard of Kennikin. He also said that when Kennikin arrived his job was over and he could go home. There's one more question I should have asked him.'

'What's that?'

'Whether his instructions called for him to show himself

to Kennikin or whether they specifically forbade it. I'd give a lot to know the answer to that one.'

'You're sure we were chased by Russians? I mean, you're sure it *was* Kennikin?'

'That's a face I'll never forget,' I said. 'And there was a lot of swearing in Russian back at the Tungnaá River.'

I could almost see the wheels whizzing round as Elin thought about it. 'Try this,' she said. 'Supposing Slade is also chasing us, and suppose he asked the Americans to co-operate—but what he didn't know was that Kennikin was closer to us. The Americans were supposed to hold us up until Slade arrived—not Kennikin.'

'It's barely possible,' I conceded. 'But it shows lousy liaison. And why go to all the trouble of a sniper hidden on a hill? Why not have the Americans just make a simple pinch?' I shook my head. 'Besides, the Department isn't all that chummy with the CIA—the special relationship has its limits.'

'My explanation is the more reasonable,' said Elin.

'I'm not sure there *is* any reason involved—it's turning into a thoroughly unreasonable situation. It reminds me of what a physicist once said about his job: "The universe is not only queerer than we imagine but, perhaps, queerer than we can imagine." I can see his point now.'

Elin laughed, and I said, 'What the hell's so funny? Slade has already taken a crack at us, and may do again if Taggart hasn't pulled him off. Kennikin is sweating blood trying to get at me—and now the Americans have put in their oar. Any minute from now I'm expecting the West Germans to pitch up, or maybe the Chilean Secret Service. I wouldn't be surprised at anything. But there's one thing that really worries me.'

'What?'

I said, 'Suppose I give this gadget to Case tomorrow night. Kennikin won't know that, will he? I can't see Jack Case writing him a letter—"Dear Vaslav, Stewart doesn't have the football any more; I've got it—come and chase *me*." I'll be just as much up the creek as before. Farther, in fact, because if Kennikin catches me and I *haven't* got the damned thing then he'll be even madder than he is now, if that's possible.'

I wasn't so sure I was going to give the gadget to Case, after all. If I was going to be up the creek, I'd better retain the paddle.

Laugarvatn is a district educational centre which takes in children from a wide rural area. The country is so big relative to the population, and the population so scattered, that the educational system is rather peculiar. Most of the rural schools are boarding schools and in some of them the pupils spend a fortnight at school and a fortnight at home, turn and turn about, during the winter teaching terms. The children from farther away spend all winter at school. In the summer the schools are turned into hotels for four months.

Because Laugarvatn is conveniently close to Thingvellir, Geysir, Gullfoss and other tourist attractions its two large schools come in very useful as summer hotels, and Laugarvatn had become a pony-trekking centre very popular with visitors. Personally, I've never cared much for horses, not even the multi-coloured Icelandic variety which is better-looking than most. I think the horse is a stupid animal—any animal which allows another to ride it must be stupid—and I prefer to be bounced by a Land-Rover rather than by a stubborn pony who would rather go home.

Gunnar Arnarsson was a schoolteacher in the winter and in summer ran a pony-trekking operation. Very versatile people, these Icelanders. He was away when we arrived, but his wife, Sigurlin Asgeirsdottir, made us welcome with much clucking at the sight of Elin's arm in an improvised sling.

One of the problems in Iceland is sorting out the single from the married people, because the woman does not change her name when she gets married. In fact, the whole problem of names is a trap into which foreigners usually fall with a loud thump. The surname just tells everyone who your father was; Sigurlin was the daughter of Asgeir, just as Gunnar was the son of Arnar. If Gunnar had a son and decided to name the boy after his grandfather he'd be called Arnar Gunnarsson. All very difficult and the reason why the Icelandic telephone directory is listed alphabetically under given names. Elin Ragnarsdottir was listed under 'E'.

Gunnar appeared to have done well for himself because

Sigurlin was one of those tall, leggy, svelte, Scandinavian types who go over big when they get to Hollywood, and what the hell has acting got to do with it, anyway? The widespread belief that the Nordic nations are populated exclusively on the distaff side by these tow-headed goddesses is, however, a regrettable illusion.

From the way she welcomed us Sigurlin knew about me, but not all, I hoped. At any rate she knew a lot—enough to hear the distant chime of wedding bells. It's funny, but as soon as a girl gets married she wants to get all her old girl-friends caught in the same trap. Because of Kennikin there weren't going to be any immediate wedding bells—the tolling of a single funeral note was more likely—but, disregarding Kennikin, I wasn't going to be pressured by any busty blonde with a match-making glint in her eye.

I put the Land-Rover into Gunnar's empty garage with some relief. Now it was safely off the road and under cover I felt much better. I saw that the collection of small arms was decently concealed and then went into the house to find Sigurlin just coming downstairs. She gave me a peculiar look and said abruptly, 'What did Elin do to her shoulder?'

I said cautiously, 'Didn't she tell you?'

'She said she was climbing and fell against a sharp rock.'

I made an indeterminate noise expressive of agreement, but I could see that Sigurlin was suspicious. A gunshot wound tends to look like nothing else but, even to someone who has never seen one before. I said hastily, 'It's very good of you to offer us a bed for the night.'

'It's nothing,' she said. 'Would you like some coffee?'

'Thank you, I would.' I followed her into the kitchen. 'Have you known Elin long?'

'Since we were children.' Sigurlin dumped a handful of beans into a coffee grinder. 'And you?'

'Three years.'

She filled an electric kettle and plugged it in, then swung around to face me. 'Elin looks very tired.'

'We pushed it a bit in the *Óbyggdir*.'

That can't have sounded convincing because Sigurlin said, 'I wouldn't want her to come to any harm. That wound . . .'

'Well?'

'She didn't fall against a rock, did she?'

There was a brain behind those beautiful eyes. 'No,' I said. 'She didn't.'

'I thought not,' she said. 'I've seen wounds like that. Before I married I was a nurse at Keflavik. An American sailor was brought into hospital once—he'd been cleaning his gun and shot himself accidentally. Whose gun was Elin cleaning?'

I sat down at the kitchen table. 'There's a certain amount of trouble,' I said carefully. 'And it's best you're not involved, so I'm not going to tell you anything about it—for your own good. I tried to keep Elin out of it from the beginning, but she's headstrong.'

Sigurlin nodded. 'Her family always was stubborn.'

I said, 'I'm going to Geysir tomorrow evening and I'd like Elin to stay here. I'll want your co-operation on that.'

Sigurlin regarded me seriously. 'I don't like trouble with guns.'

'Neither do I. I'm not exactly shouting for joy. That's why I want Elin out of it. Can she stay here for a while?'

'A gunshot wound should be reported to the police.'

'I know,' I said wearily. 'But I don't think your police are equipped to cope with this particular situation. It has international ramifications and there is more than one gun involved. Innocent people could get killed if it's not carefully handled, and with no disrespect to your police, I think they'd be likely to blunder.'

'This trouble, as you call it—is it criminal?'

'Not in the normal sense. You might call it an extreme form of political action.'

Sigurlin turned down the corners of her mouth. 'The only good thing I've heard about this is that you want to keep Elin out of it,' she said waspishly. 'Tell me, Alan Stewart; are you in love with her?'

'Yes.'

'Are you going to marry her?'

'If she'll have me after all this.'

She offered me a superior smile. 'Oh, she'll have you. You're hooked like a salmon and you won't get away now.'

'I'm not so sure of that,' I said. 'There are certain things that have come up lately that don't add to my charms in Elin's eyes.'

'Such as guns?' Sigurlin poured coffee. 'You don't need

to answer that. I won't probe.' She put the cup before me. 'All right; I'll keep Elin here.'

'I don't know how you're going to do it,' I said. 'I've never been able to make her do anything she didn't want to do.'

'I'll put her to bed,' said Sigurlin. 'Strict medical supervision. She'll argue, but she'll do it. You do what you have to do and Elin will stay here. But I won't be able to keep her long. What happens if you don't come back from Geysir?'

'I don't know,' I said. 'But don't let her go back to Reykjavik. To go to the apartment would be extremely unwise.'

Sigurlin took a deep breath. 'I'll see what I can do.' She poured herself a cup of coffee and sat down. 'If it weren't for the concern you show for Elin I'd be inclined to . . .' She shook her head irritably. 'I don't like any of this, Alan. For God's sake get it cleared up as quickly as you can.'

'I'll do my best.'

III

The next day seemed very long.

At breakfast Sigurlin read the paper and suddenly said, 'Well, well! Someone tied up the cable transport on the Tungnaá just the other side of Hald. A party of tourists was stranded on the farther side for several hours. I wonder who could have done that?'

'It was all right when we came across,' I said blandly. 'What does it say about the tourists? Anyone hurt?'

She looked at me speculatively across the breakfast table. 'Why should anyone be hurt? No, it says nothing about that.'

I changed the subject quickly. 'I'm surprised that Elin is still asleep.'

Sigurlin smiled. 'I'm not. She didn't know it, but she had a sleeping draught last night. She'll be drowsy when she wakes and she won't want to jump out of bed.'

That was one way of making sure of Elin. I said, 'I noticed your garage was empty—don't you have a car?'

'Yes. Gunnar left it at the stables.'

'When will he be back?'

'In two days—providing the party doesn't get saddle-sore.'

'When I go to Geysir I'd just as soon not use the Land-Rover,' I said.

'You want the car? All right—but I want it back in one piece.' She told me where to find it. 'You'll find the key in the glove locker.'

After breakfast I regarded the telephone seriously and wondered whether to ring Taggart. I had a lot to tell him but I thought it would be better to let it go until I heard what Jack Case had to say. Instead I went out to the Land-Rover and cleaned Fleet's rifle.

It really was a good tool. With its fancy hand-grip and free-style stock it had obviously been tailor-made to suit Fleet, whom I suspected of being an enthusiast. In every field of human endeavour there are those who push perfection to its ultimate and absurd end. In hi-fi, for example, there is the maniac who has seventeen loud-speakers and one test record. In shooting there is the gun nut.

The gun nut believes that there is no standard, off-the-shelf weapon that could be possibly good enough for him and so he adapts and chisels until he finally achieves something that looks like one of the more far-out works of modern sculpture. He also believes that the ammunition manufacturers know damn-all about their job and so he loads his own cases, carefully weighing each bullet and matching it with an amount of powder calculated to one-tenth of a grain. Sometimes he shoots very well.

I checked the ammunition from the opened box and, sure enough, found the telltale scratches from a crimping tool. Fleet was in the habit of rolling his own, something I have never found necessary, but then my own shooting has not been of the type necessary to get a perfect grouping at x-hundred yards. It also explained why the box was unlabelled.

I wondered why Fleet should have carried as many as fifty rounds; after all, he was a good shot and had brought us to a standstill with one squeeze of the trigger. He had loaded the rifle with ordinary hunting ammunition, soft-nosed and designed to spread on impact. The closed box contained twenty-five rounds of jacketed ammunition—the military load.

It's always seemed odd to me that the bullet one shoots at an animal is designed to kill as quickly and as mercilessly as possible, whereas the same bullet shot at a man is illegal under the Geneva Convention. Shoot a hunting load at a man and you're accused of using dum-dum bullets and that's against the rules. You can roast him to death with napalm, disembowel him with a jump mine, but you can't shoot him with the same bullet you would use to kill a deer cleanly.

I looked at the cartridge in the palm of my hand and wished I had known about it earlier. One of those going into the engine of Kennikin's jeep was likely to do a hell of a lot more damage than the soft-nosed bullet I had used. While a .375 jacketed bullet with a magnum charge behind it probably wouldn't drill through a jeep from end to end at a range of a hundred yards, I wouldn't like to bet on it by standing behind the jeep.

I filled the magazine of the rifle with a mixed load, three soft-nosed and two jacketed, laid alternately. Then I examined McCarthy's Smith & Wesson automatic pistol, a more prosaic piece of iron than Fleet's jazzed-up rifle. After checking that it was in order I put it into my pocket, together with the spare clips. The electronic gadget I left where it was under the front seat. I wasn't taking it with me when I went to see Jack Case, but I wasn't going empty-handed either.

When I got back to the house Elin was awake. She looked at me drowsily, and said, 'I don't know why I'm so tired.'

'Well,' I said judiciously. 'You've been shot and you've been racketing around the *Óbyggdir* for two days with not much sleep. I'm not surprised you're tired. I haven't been too wide awake myself.'

Elin opened her eyes wide in alarm and glanced at Sigurlin who was arranging flowers in a vase. I said, 'Sigurlin knows you didn't fall on any rock. She knows you were shot, but not how or why—and I don't want you to tell her. I don't want you to discuss it with Sigurlin or anyone else.' I turned to Sigurlin. 'You'll get the full story at the right time, but at the moment the knowledge would be dangerous.'

Sigurlin nodded in acceptance. Elin said, 'I think I'll sleep all day. I'm tired now, but I'll be ready by the time we have to leave for Geysir.'

Sigurlin crossed the room and began to plump up the pillows behind Elin's head. The heartless professionalism

117

spoke of the trained nurse. 'You're not leaving for anywhere,' she said sharply. 'Not for the next two days at least.'

'But I must,' protested Elin.

'But you must not. Your shoulder is bad enough.' Her lips compressed tightly as she looked down at Elin. 'You should really see a doctor.'

'Oh, no!' said Elin.

'Well, then, you'll do as I say.'

Elin looked at me appealingly. I said, 'I'm only going to see a man. As a matter of fact, Jack Case wouldn't say a word in your presence, anyway—you're not a member of the club. I'm just going to Geysir, have a chat with the man, and then come back here—and you might as well keep your turned-up nose out of it for once.'

Elin looked flinty, and Sigurlin said, 'I'll leave you to whisper sweet nothings into each other's ear.' She smiled. 'You two are going to lead interesting lives.'

She left the room, and I said gloomily, 'That sounds like the Chinese curse—"May you live in interesting times."'

'All right,' said Elin in a tired voice. 'I won't give you any trouble. You can go to Geysir alone.'

I sat on the edge of the bed. 'It's not a matter of you giving trouble; I just want you out of this. You disturb my concentration, and if I run into difficulties I don't want to have to watch out for you as well as myself.'

'Have I been a drag?'

I shook my head. 'No, Elin; you haven't. But the nature of the game may change. I've been chased across Iceland and I'm pretty damn tired of it. If the opportunity offers I'll turn around and do a bit of chasing myself.'

'And I'd get in the way,' she said flatly.

'You're a civilized person,' I said. 'Very law-abiding and full of scruples. I doubt if you've had as much as a parking ticket in your life. I might manage to retain a few scruples while I'm being hunted; not many, but some. But when I'm the hunter I can't afford them. I think you might be horrified at what I'd do.'

'You'd kill,' she said. It was a statement.

'I might do worse,' I said grimly, and she shivered. 'It's not that I want to—I'm no casual murderer; I didn't want to have any part of this but I've been conscripted against my will.'

118

'You dress it in fine words,' she said. 'You don't have to kill.'

'No fine words,' I said. 'Just one—survival. A drafted American college boy may be a pacifist, but when the Viet Cong shoot at him with those Russian 7.62 milli-metre rifles he'll shoot right back, you may depend on it. And when Kennikin comes after me he'll deserve all he runs into. I didn't ask him to shoot at me on the Tungnaá River—he didn't need my permission—but he can't have been very surprised when I shot back. Hell, he would expect it!'

'I can see the logic,' said Elin. 'But don't expect me to like it.'

'Christ!' I said. 'Do you think I like it?'

'I'm sorry, Alan,' she said, and smiled wanly.

'So am I.' I stood up. 'After that bit of deep philosophy you'd better have breakfast. I'll see what Sigurlin can offer.'

IV

I left Laugarvatn at eight that night. Punctuality may be a virtue but it has been my experience that the virtuous often die young while the ungodly live to a ripe age. I had arranged to meet Jack Case at five o'clock but it would do him no great harm to stew for a few hours, and I had it in mind that the arrangement to meet him had been made on an open radio circuit.

I arrived at Geysir in Gunnar's Volkswagen beetle and parked inconspicuously quite a long way from the sum-mer hotel. A few people, not many, were picking their way among the pools of boiling water, cameras at the ready. Geysir itself—the Gusher—which has given its name to all the other spouters in the world, was quiescent. It has been a long time since Geysir spouted. The habit of prodding it into action by tossing rocks into the pool finally proved too much as the pressure chamber was blocked. However, Strokkur—the Churn—was blasting off with commendable efficiency and sending up its feathery plume of boiling water at seven-minute intervals.

I stayed in the car for a long time and used the field-glasses assiduously. There were no familiar faces to be seen in the next hour, a fact that didn't impress me much, however. Finally I got out of the car and walked towards the Hotel Geysir, one hand in my pocket resting on the butt of the pistol.

Case was in the lounge, sitting in a corner and reading a paperback. I walked up to him and said, 'Hello, Jack; that's a nice tan—you must have been in the sun.'

He looked up. 'I was in Spain. What kept you?'

'This and that.'

I prepared to sit down, but he said, 'This is too public—let's go up to my room. Besides, I have a bottle.'

'That's nice.'

I followed him to his room. He locked the door and turned to survey me. 'That gun in your pocket spoils the set of your coat. Why don't you use a shoulder holster?'

I grinned at him. 'The man I took the gun from didn't have one. How are you, Jack? It's good to see you.'

He grunted sourly. 'You might change your mind about that.' With a flip of his hand he opened a suitcase lying on a chair and took out a bottle. He poured a heavy slug into a tooth glass and handed it to me. 'What the devil have you been doing? You've got Taggart really worked up.'

'He sounded pretty steamy when I spoke to him,' I said, and sipped the whisky. 'Most of the time I've been chased from hell-and-gone to here.'

'You weren't followed here?' he asked quickly.

'No.'

'Taggart tells me you killed Philips. Is that true?'

'If Philips was a man who called himself Buchner and Graham it's true.'

He stared at me. 'You admit it!'

I relaxed in the chair. 'Why not, since I did it? I didn't know it was Philips, though. He came at me in the dark with a gun.'

'That's not how Slade described it. He says you took a crack at him too.'

'I did—but that was after I'd disposed of Philips. He and Slade came together.'

'Slade says differently. He says that he was in a car with Philips when you ambushed it.'

I laughed. 'With what?' I drew the *sgian dubh* from my stocking and flipped it across the room, where it stuck in the top of the dressing-table, quivering. 'With that?'

'He says you had a rifle.'

'Where would I get a rifle?' I demanded. 'He's right, though; I took the rifle from Philips after I disposed of him with that little pig-sticker. I put three shots into Slade's car and missed the bastard.'

'Christ!' said Case. 'No wonder Taggart is doing his nut. Have you gone off your little rocker?'

I sighed. 'Jack, did Taggart say anything about a girl?'

'He said you'd referred to a girl. He didn't know whether to believe you.'

'He'd better believe me,' I said. 'That girl isn't far from here, and she has a bullet wound in her shoulder that was given to her by Philips. He was within an ace of killing her. Now, there's no two ways about that, and I can take you to her and show you the wound. Slade says I ambushed him. Is it likely I'd do it with my fiancée watching? And why in hell would I want to ambush him?' I slid in a trick question. 'What did he say he'd done with Philips's body?'

Case frowned. 'I don't think the question came up.'

'It wouldn't,' I said. 'The last I saw of Slade he was driving away like a maniac—and there was no body in his car. I disposed of it later.'

'This is all very well,' said Case. 'But it happened after Akureyri, and in Akureyri you were supposed to deliver a package to Philips. You didn't, and you didn't give it to Slade either. Why not?'

'The operation stank,' I said, and went into it in detail.

I talked for twenty minutes and by the time I had finished Case was pop-eyed. He swallowed and his Adam's apple jumped convulsively. 'Do you really believe that Slade is a Russian agent? How do you expect Taggart to swallow that? I've never heard such a cock-and-bull story in my life.'

I said patiently, 'I followed Slade's instructions at Keflavik and nearly got knocked off by Lindholm; Slade sent Philips after me into Asbyrgi—how *did* he know the Russians were holding a fake? There's the Calvados; there's . . .'

Case held up his hands. 'There's no need to go through it all again. Lindholm might have been lucky in catching you—there's nothing to say all the roads around Keflavik weren't staked out. Slade says he didn't go after you in Asbyrgi. As for the Calvados . . .' He threw up his hands.

'There's only your word for that.'

'What the hell are you, Jack? Prosecutor, judge and jury, too? Or have I already been judged and you're the executioner?'

'Don't fly off the handle,' he said wearily. 'I'm just trying to find out how complicated a cock-up you've made, that's all. What did you do after you left Asbyrgi?'

'We went south in the wilderness,' I said. 'And then Kennikin pitched up.'

'The one who drinks Calvados? The one you had the hassle with in Sweden?'

'The same. My old pal, Vaslav. Don't you think that was bloody coincidental, Jack? How would Kennikin know which track to chase along? But Slade knew, of course; he knew which way we went after we left Asbyrgi.'

Case regarded me thoughtfully. 'You know you're very convincing sometimes. I'm getting so I might believe this silly story if I'm not careful. But Kennikin didn't catch you.'

'It was nip and tuck,' I said. 'And the bloody Yanks didn't help.'

Case sat up. 'How do they come into this?'

I pulled out Fleet's pass and skimmed it across the room into Case's lap. 'That chap shot a hole in my tyre at very long range. I got out of there with Kennikin ten minutes behind.' I told Case all about it.

His mouth was grim. 'Now you really have gone overboard. I suppose you'll now claim Slade is a member of the CIA,' he said sarcastically. 'Why should the Americans hold you up just so Kennikin could grab you?'

'I don't know,' I said feelingly. 'I wish I did.'

Case examined the card. 'Fleet—I know that name; it came up when I was in Turkey last year. He's a CIA hatchetman and he's dangerous.'

'Not for the next month,' I said. 'I cracked his skull.'

'So what happened next?'

I shrugged. 'I went hell-for-leather with Kennikin and his boys trying to climb up my exhaust pipe—there was a bit of an affray at a river, and then I lost him. I suppose he's around here somewhere.'

'And you've still got the package?'

'Not on me, Jack,' I said softly. 'Not on me—but quite close.'

'I don't want it,' he said, and crossed the room to take my empty glass. 'The plan's changed. You're to take the package to Reykjavik.'

'Just like that,' I said. 'What if I don't want to?'

'Don't be a fool. Taggart wants it that way, and you'd better not annoy him any more. Not only have you loused up his operation but you've killed Philips, and for that he can have your hide. I have a message from him—take the package to Reykjavik and all is forgiven.'

'It must be really important,' I said, and checked my fingers. 'Let's see—I've killed two men, damn near shot the leg off another, and maybe fractured a couple of skulls —and Taggart says he can sweep all that under the carpet?'

'The Russkies and the Americans can take care of their own—they bury their own dead, if any,' said Case brutally. 'But Taggart—and only Taggart—can clear you on our side. By killing Philips you set yourself up as a legitimate target. Do as he says or he'll set the dogs on you.'

I remembered I had used a phrase like that when speaking to Taggart. I said, 'Where is Slade now?'

Case turned away from me and I heard the clink of glass against bottle. 'I don't know. When I left London Taggart was trying to contact him.'

'So he could still be in Iceland,' I said slowly. 'I don't know that I like that.'

Case whirled around. 'What you like has ceased to matter. For God's sake, what's got into you, Alan? Look, it's only a hundred kilometres to Reykjavik; you can be there in two hours. Take the bloody package and go.'

'I have a better idea,' I said. 'You take it.'

He shook his head. 'That's not on. Taggart wants me back in Spain.'

I laughed. 'Jack, the easiest way to get to the International Airport at Keflavik is through Reykjavik. You could drop off the package on the way. What's so important about me and the package together?'

He shrugged. 'My instructions are that you take it. Don't ask me why because I don't know.'

'What's in the package?'

'I don't know that either; and the way this operation is shaping I don't want to know.'

I said, 'Jack, at one time I'd have called you a friend.

But you've just tried to con me with this nonsense about being pulled back to Spain, and I don't believe a bloody word of it. But I do believe you when you say you don't know what's going on. I don't think anyone in this operation knows what's going on except, maybe, one man.'

Case nodded. 'Taggart has his hands on the strings,' he said. 'Neither you nor I need to know much in order to do the job.'

'I wasn't thinking of Taggart,' I said. 'I don't think he knows what's going on either. He might think he does, but he doesn't.' I looked up. 'I was thinking of Slade. This whole weird operation is warped to the pattern of his mind. I've worked with him before and I know how he thinks.'

'So we get back to Slade,' said Case grimly. 'You're obsessed, Alan.'

'Maybe,' I said. 'But you can make Taggart happy by telling him I'll take his damned package to Reykjavik. Where do I deliver it?'

'That's better.' Case looked down at my glass which had been held, forgotten, in his hand. He gave it to me. 'You know the Nordri Travel Agency?'

'I know it.' It was the firm for which Elin had once worked.

'I don't, but I'm told that as well as running the agency they have a big souvenir shop.'

'You were told correctly.'

'I have here a piece of wrapping paper from the souvenir shop; it's the standard stuff they gift-wrap with. You have the package neatly wrapped up. You walk in and go to the back of the shop where they sell the woollen goods. A man will be standing there carrying a copy of the *New York Times*, and under his arm will be an identical package. You make light conversation by saying, 'It's colder here than in the States,'' to which he will reply . . .'

' "It's even colder than Birmingham." I've been through the routine before.'

'All right; once there's a mutual identification you put your package on the counter, and so will he. From then on it's a simple exchange job.'

'And when is this simple exchange job to take place?'

'At midday tomorrow.'

'Supposing I'm not there at midday tomorrow? For all I know there may be a hundred Russians spaced out along that road at one kilometre intervals.'

'There'll be a man in the shop every midday until you turn up,' said Case.

'Taggart has a touching faith in me,' I said. 'According to Slade the Department is afflicted with a manpower shortage, and here is Taggart being spendthrift. What happens if I don't turn up for a year?'

Case didn't smile. 'Taggart brought up that problem. If you're not there within a week then someone will come looking for you, and I'd regret that because, in spite of that snide crack you made about friendship, I still love you, you silly bastard.'

'Smile when you say that, stranger.'

He grinned and sat down again. 'Now let's go through all this again, right from the beginning—right from the time Slade came to see you in Scotland.'

So I repeated my tale of woe again in great detail, with all the pros and cons, and we talked for a long time. At the end of it Case said seriously, 'If you're right and Slade has been got at then this is big trouble.'

'I don't think he's been got at,' I said. 'I think he's been a Russian agent all along. But there's something else worrying me just as much as Slade—where do the Americans fit in? It's not like them to be cosy with people like Kennikin.'

Case dismissed the Americans. 'They're just a problem of this particular operation. Slade is different. He's a big boy now and has a hand in planning and policy. If he's gone sour the whole department will have to be organized.'

He made a sudden sweeping motion with his hand. 'Jesus, you've got me going now! I'm actually beginning to believe you. This is nonsense, Alan.'

I held out my empty glass. 'I could do with a refill—this is thirsty work.' As Case picked up the depleted bottle, I said, 'Let me put it this way. The question has been asked and, once asked, it can't be unasked. If you put my case against Slade to Taggart, just as I've put it to you, then he'll be forced to take action. He can't afford not to. He'll have Slade under a microscope and I don't think Slade can stand close inspection.'

Case nodded. 'There's just one thing, Alan. Be sure—be very, very sure—that your prejudices aren't shouting too loud. I know why you left the Department and I know why you hate Slade's guts. You're biased. This is a serious accusation you're making, and if Slade comes out of it cleaner than the driven snow then you're in big trouble. He'll demand your head on a platter—and he'll get it.'

'He'll deserve it,' I said. 'But the problem won't arise. He's as guilty as hell.' I may have sounded confident but there was the nagging fear that perhaps I was wrong. Case's warning about bias and prejudice was sound, and I hastily re-examined the indictment against Slade. I found no flaw.

Case looked at his watch. 'Eleven-thirty.'

I put down the whisky untasted. 'It's late—I'd better be going.'

'I'll tell Taggart all about it,' said Case. 'And I'll also tell him about Fleet and McCarthy. Maybe he can get a line on that angle through Washington.'

I retrieved the *sgian dubh* from the dressing-table and slipped it into my stocking-top. 'Jack, you really haven't any idea of what this operation is all about?'

'Not the faintest clue,' he said. 'I didn't know anything about it until I was pulled out of Spain. Taggart was angry, and justifiably so, in my opinion. He said you refused to have anything to do with Slade, and you wouldn't even tell him where you were. He said you'd agree to meet me here. All I am is a messenger boy, Alan.'

'That's what Slade told me I was,' I said morosely. 'I'm getting tired of running blind; I'm getting tired of *running*. Maybe if I stood my ground for once in a while I'd be better off.'

'I wouldn't advise it,' said Case. 'Just follow orders and get the package to Reykjavik.' He put on his jacket. 'I'll walk with you to your car. Where is it?'

'Up the road.'

He was about to unlock the door when I said, 'Jack, I don't think you've been entirely frank with me. You've dodged a couple of issues in this conversation. Now there have been some bloody funny things going on lately, such as a member of the Department coming after me with a gun—so I just want to tell you one thing. It's likely that I'll be stopped on the way to Reykjavik, and if you have any part in that I'll go right through you, friendship or no friendship. I hope you understand that.'

He smiled and said, 'For God's sake, you're imagining things.'

But the smile was strained and there was something

about his expression I couldn't place, and it worried me. It was only a long time afterwards that I identified the emotion. It was pity but by then the identification had come too late.

CHAPTER SEVEN

I

We went outside to find it was as dark as it ever gets in the Icelandic summer. There was no moon but there was visibility of sorts in a kind of ghostly twilight. There was a soft explosion among the hot pools and the eerie spectre of Strokkur rose into the air, a fading apparition which dissipated into wind-blown shreds. There was a stink of sulphur in the air.

I shivered suddenly. It's no wonder that the map of Iceland is littered with place names which tell of the giant trolls who dwell in the roots of the mountains, or that the old men still hand down the legends of man in conflict with spirits. The young Icelanders, geared to the twentieth century with their transistor radios and casual use of aircraft, laugh and call it superstition. Maybe they're right, but I've noticed that they tend to force their laughter sometimes and it has a quality of unease about it. All I know is that if I had been one of the old Vikings and had come upon Strokkur unexpectedly one dark night I'd have been scared witless.

I think Case caught something of the atmosphere because he looked across at the thinning curtain of mist as Strokkur disappeared, and said softly, 'It's really something, isn't it?'

'Yes,' I said shortly. 'The car's over there. It's quite a way.'

We crunched on the crushed lava of the road and walked past the long row of white-painted pillars which separate the road from the pools. I could hear the bubbling of hot water and the stench of sulphur was stronger. If you looked at the pools in daylight you would find them all colours, some as white and clear as gin, others a limpid blue or green, and all close to boiling point. Even in the darkness I could see the white vapour rising in the air.

Case said, 'About Slade. What was the . . .?'

I never heard the end of that question because three heavier patches of darkness rose up about us suddenly.

Someone grabbed me and said, '*Stewartsen, stanna! Förstar Ni?*' Something hard jabbed into my side.

I stopped all right, but not in the way that was expected. I let myself go limp, just as McCarthy had done when I hit him with the cosh. My knees buckled and I went down to the ground. There was a muffled exclamation of surprise and momentarily the grip on my arm relaxed and the movement in a totally unexpected direction dislodged the gun from my ribs.

As soon as I was down I spun around fast with one leg bent and the other extended rigidly. The outstretched leg caught my Swedish-speaking friend behind the knees with a great deal of force and he fell to the ground. His pistol was ready for use because there was a bang as he fell and I heard the whine of a ricocheting bullet.

I rolled over until I was prone against one of the pillars. I would be too conspicuous against that painted whiteness so I wormed off the road and into the darkness, pulling the pistol from my pocket as I went. Behind me there was a shout of '*Spheshíte!*' and another voice in a lower tone said, '*Net! Slúshayte!*' I kept very still and heard the thudding of boots as someone ran towards the hotel.

Only Kennikin's mob would have addressed me as Stewartsen and in Swedish, and now they were bellowing in Russian. I kept my head close to the ground and looked back towards the road so I could see anyone there silhouetted against the paler sky. There was a flicker of movement quite close and a crunch of footsteps, so I put a bullet in that direction, picked myself up, and ran for it.

And that was damned dangerous because, in the darkness, I could very well run headlong into a bottomless pool of boiling water. I counted my paces and tried to visualize the hot pools area as I had often seen it in daylight under less unnerving conditions. The pools vary in size from a piddling little six inches in diameter to the fifty-foot giant economy size. Heated by the subterranean volcanic activity, the water continually wells out of the pools to form a network of hot streams which covers the whole area.

After I had covered a hundred yards I stopped and dropped on one knee. Ahead of me steam rose and lay in a level blanket and I thought that was Geysir itself. That means that Strokkur was somewhere to my left and a little behind. I wanted to keep clear of Strokkur—getting too close would be dicey in the extreme.

I looked back and saw nothing, but I heard footsteps following in the line I had come, and others away to the right and getting closer. I didn't know if my pursuers knew the lie of the ground or not but, intentionally or accidentally, I was being herded right into the pools. The man on the right switched on a flash lamp, a big thing like a miniature searchlight. He directed it at the ground which was lucky for me, but he was more troubled about turning himself into goulash.

I lifted my pistol and banged off three shots in that direction and the light went out suddenly. I don't think I hit him but he had come to the acute realization that his light made a good target. I wasn't worried about making a noise; the more noise the better as far as I was concerned. Five shots had been fired, five too many in the quiet Icelandic night, and already lights were popping on in the hotel and I heard someone call from that direction.

The man behind me let fly with two shots and I saw the muzzle flare of his pistol very close, not more than ten yards away. The bullets went wide; one I don't know where, but the other raised a fountain in the pool of Geysir. I didn't return the fire but ran to the left, skirting the pool. I stumbled through a stream of hot water, but it was barely two inches deep and I went through fast enough not to do any damage to myself and being more concerned that the splashing noise would give away my position.

There were more cries from the hotel and the slam of windows opening. Someone started up a car with a rasping noise and headlights were switched on. I paid little attention to that, but carried on, angling back towards the road. Whoever started that car had a bright idea—and no pun intended. He swung around and drove towards the pools, his headlamps illuminating the whole area.

It was fortunate for me that he did because it prevented me from running headlong into one of the pools. I saw the reflections strike from the water just in time to skid to a halt, and I teetered for a moment right on the edge. My balancing act wasn't improved much when someone took a shot at me from an unexpected direction—the other side of the pool—and something tugged briefly at the sleeve of my jacket.

130

Although I was illuminated by the lights of that damned car my attacker was in an even worse position because he was between me and the light and marvellously silhouetted. I slung a shot at him and he flinched with his whole body and retreated. Briefly the headlights of the car swung away and I hastily ran around the pool while he put a bullet in roughly the place I had been.

Then the lights came back and steadied and I saw him retreating backwards, his head moving from side to side nervously. He didn't see me because by this time I was flat on my belly. Slowly he went backwards until he put a foot into six inches of boiling water and jerked apprehensively. He moved fast but not fast enough, because the big gas bubble which heralds the blasting of Strokkur was already rising in the pool behind him like a monster coming to the surface.

Strokkur exploded violently. Steam, superheated by the molten magma far below, drove a column of boiling water up the shaft so that it fountained sixty feet above the pool and descended in a downpour of deadly rain. The man screamed horribly, but his shrill piping was lost in the roar of Strokkur. He flung his arms wide and toppled into the pool.

I moved fast, casting a wide circle away from the revealing lights and heading eventually towards the road. There was a confused babble of shouting and more cars were started up to add their lights to the scene, and I saw a crowd of people running towards Strokkur. I came to a pool and tossed the pistol into it, together with the spare clips of ammunition. Anyone found carrying a gun that night would be likely to spend the rest of his life in jail.

At last I got to the road and joined the crowd. Someone said, 'What happened?'

'I don't know,' I flung my hand towards the pool. 'I heard shooting.'

He dashed past me, avid for vicarious excitement—he would have run just as fast to see a bloody motor smash —and I discreetly melted into the darkness behind the line of parked cars drawn up with headlamps blazing.

After I had gone a hundred yards up the road in the direction of the Volkswagen I turned and looked back. There was a lot of excitement and waving of arms, and long shadows were cast on to the shifting vapour above the hot pools, and there was a small crowd about Strokkur, edging closer but not too close because Strokkur has a short, seven-minute cycle. I realized, with some astonishment, that from the time Case and I had seen Strokkur blow when we left the hotel until the man had fallen into the pool had been only seven minutes.

Then I saw Slade.

He was standing clearly visible in the lights of a car and looking out towards Strokkur. I regretted throwing away the pistol because I would have shot him there and then had I been able, regardless of the consequences. His companion raised his arm and pointed and Slade laughed. Then his friend turned around and I saw it was Jack Case.

I found myself trembling all over, and it was with an effort that I dragged myself away up the road and looked for the Volkswagen. It was where I had left it and I got behind the driving wheel, switched on the engine, and then sat there for a moment, letting the tension drain away. No one I know has ever been shot at from close range and retained his equanimity—his autonomic nervous system sees to that. The glands work overtime and the chemicals stir in the blood, the muscles tune up and the belly goes loose, and it's even worse when the danger has gone.

I found that my hands were trembling violently and rested them on the wheel, and presently they grew still and I felt better. I had just put the car into gear when I felt a ring of cold metal applied to the back of my neck, and a harsh, well-remembered voice said, '*God dag, Herr Stewartsen. Var forsiktig.*'

I sighed, and switched off the engine. 'Hello, Vaslav,' I said.

II

'I am surrounded by a pack of idiots of an incomparable stupidity,' said Kennikin. 'Their brains are in their trigger fingers. It was different in our day; eh, Stewartsen?'

'My name is Stewart now,' I said.

'So? Well, Herr Stewart; you may switch on your engine and proceed. I will direct you. We will let my incompetent assistants find their own way.'

The muzzle of the gun nudged me. I switched on, and said, 'Which way?'

'Head towards Laugarvatn.'

I drove out of Geysir slowly and carefully. The gun no longer pressed into the back of my neck but I knew it wasn't far away, and I knew Kennikin well enough not to go in for any damn-fool heroics. He was disposed to make light conversation. 'You've caused a lot of trouble, Alan —and you can solve a problem that's been puzzling me. Whatever happened to Tadeusz?'

'Who the hell is Tadeusz?'

'The day you landed at Keflavik he was supposed to stop you.'

'So that was Tadeusz—he called himself Lindholm. Tadeusz—that sounds Polish.'

'He's Russian; his mother is Polish, I believe.'

'She'll miss him,' I said.

'So!' He was silent for a while, then he said, 'Poor Yuri had his leg amputated this morning.'

'Poor Yuri ought to have known better than to wave a belly gun at a man armed with a rifle,' I said.

'But Yuri didn't know you had a rifle,' said Kennikin. 'Not that rifle, anyway. It came as quite a surprise.' He clicked his tongue. 'You really shouldn't have wrecked my jeep like that. It wasn't nice.'

Not *that* rifle! He expected a rifle, but not the block-buster I'd taken from Fleet. That was interesting because the only other rifle was the one I'd taken from Philips and how could he know about that? Only from Slade —another piece of evidence.

I said, 'Was the engine wrecked?'

'There was a hole shot through the battery,' he said. 'And the cooling system was wrecked. We lost all the water. That must be quite a gun.'

'It is,' I said. 'I hope to use it again.'

He chuckled. 'I doubt if you will. That little episode was most embarrassing; I had to talk fast to get out of it. A couple of inquisitive Icelanders asked a lot of questions which I didn't really feel like answering. Such as why the cable car was tied up, and what had happened to the jeep. And there was the problem of keeping Yuri quiet.'

'It must have been most uncomfortable,' I said.

'And now you've done it again,' said Kennikin. 'And in public this time. What really happened back there?'

'One of your boys got himself parboiled,' I said. 'He got too close to a spouter.'

'You see what I mean,' said Kennikin. 'Incompetents, the lot of them. You'd think three to one would be good odds, wouldn't you? But no; they bungled it.'

The odds had been three to two, but what had happened to Jack Case? He hadn't lifted a finger to help. The image of him standing and talking to Slade still burned brightly in my mind and I felt the rage boil up within me. Every time I had turned to those I thought I could trust I had been betrayed, and the knowledge burned like acid.

Buchner/Graham/Philips I could understand; he was a member of the Department fooled by Slade. But Case knew the score—he knew my suspicions of Slade—and he had not done one damned thing to help when I had been jumped by Kennikin's men. And ten minutes later he was hob-nobbing with Slade. It seemed as though the whole Department was infiltrated although, Taggart excepted, Case was the last man I would have thought to have gone over. I thought sourly that even Taggart might be on the Moscow pay-roll—that would wrap the whole bundle into one neat package.

Kennikin said, 'I'm glad I didn't underestimate you. I rather thought you'd get away from the morons I've had wished on me, so I staked out this car. A little forethought always pays, don't you think?'

I said, 'Where are we going?'

'You don't need to know in detail,' he said. 'Just concentrate on the driving. And you will go through Laugarvatn very carefully, observing all the speed limits and refraining from drawing attention. No sudden blasts on the horn, for example.' The cold steel momentarily touched my neck. 'Understand?'

'I understand.' I felt a sudden relief. I had thought that perhaps he knew where I had spent the last twenty-four hours and that we were driving to Gunnar's house. It wouldn't have surprised me overmuch; Kennikin seemed to know everything else. He had been lying in wait at Geysir, and that had been a neat trick. The thought of Elin being taken and what might have happened to Sigurlin had made my blood freeze.

We went through Laugarvatn and on to Thingvellir, and took the Reykjavik road, but eight kilometres out of Thingvellir Kennikin directed me to turn left on a secondary road. It was a road I knew well, and it led around the lake of Thingvallavatn. I wondered where the hell we were going.

I didn't have to wonder long because at a word from Kennikin I turned off the road again and we went down a bumpy track towards the lake and the lights of a small house. One of the status symbols in Reykjavik is to have a summer chalet on the shores of Thingvallavatn, even more prized because the building restrictions have forbidden new construction and so the price has shot up. Owning a chalet on Thingvallavatn is the Icelandic equivalent of having a Rembrandt on the wall.

I pulled up outside the house, and Kennikin said, 'Blow the horn.'

I tooted and someone came out. Kennikin put the pistol to my head. 'Careful, Alan,' he said. 'Be very careful.'

He also was very careful. I was taken inside without the faintest possibility of making a break. The room was decorated in that generalized style known as Swedish Modern; when done in England it looks bleak and a little phoney, but when done by the Scandinavians it looks natural and good. There was an open fire burning which was something of a surprise. Iceland has no coal and no trees to make log fires, and an open blaze is something of a rarity; a lot of the houses are heated by natural hot water, and those that aren't have oil-fired central heating. This fire was of peat which glowed redly with small flickering blue flames.

Kennikin jerked his gun. 'Sit by the fire, Alan; make yourself warm. But first Ilyich will search you.'

Ilyich was a squarely-built man with a broad, flat face. There was something Asiatic about his eyes which made me think that at least one of his parents hailed from the farther side of the Urals. He patted me thoroughly, then turned to Kennikin and shook his head.

'No gun?' said Kennikin. 'That was wise of you.' He smiled pleasantly at Ilyich, then turned to me and said, 'You see what I mean, Alan? I am surrounded by idiots. Draw up the left leg of your trousers and show Ilyich your pretty little knife.'

I obeyed, and Ilyich blinked at it in astonishment while Kennikin reamed him out. Russian is even richer than English in cutting invective. The *sgian dubh* was confiscated and Kennikin waved me to the seat while Ilyich, red-faced, moved behind me.

Kennikin put away his gun. 'Now, what will you have to drink, Alan Stewart?'

'Scotch—if you have it.'

'We have it.' He opened a cupboard near the fireplace and poured a drink. 'Will you have it neat or with water? I regret we have no soda.'

'Water will do,' I said. 'Make it a weak one.'

He smiled. 'Oh, yes; you have to keep a clear head,' he said sardonically. 'Section four, Rule thirty-five; when offered a drink by the opposition request a weak one.' He splashed water into the glass then brought it to me. 'I hope that is to your satisfaction.'

I sipped it cautiously, then nodded. If it had been any weaker it wouldn't have been able to crawl out of the glass and past my lips. He returned to the cupboard and poured himself a tumbler-full of Icelandic *brennivin* and knocked back half the contents with one gulp. I watched with some astonishment as he swallowed the raw spirit without twitching a hair. Kennikin was going downhill fast if he now did his drinking openly. I was surprised the Department hadn't caught on to it.

I said, 'Can't you get Calvados here in Iceland, Vaslav?'

He grinned and held up the glass. 'This is my first drink in four years, Alan. I'm celebrating.' He sat in the chair opposite me. 'I have reason to celebrate—it's not often that old friends meet in our profession. Is the Department treating you well?'

I sipped the watery scotch and set the glass on the low table next to my chair. 'I haven't been with the Department for four years.'

He raised his eyebrows. 'My information is different.'

'Maybe,' I said. 'But it's wrong. I quit when I left Sweden.'

'I also quit,' said Kennikin. 'This is my first assignment in four years. I have you to thank for that. I have you to thank for many things.' His voice was slow and even. 'I didn't quit of my own volition, Alan; I was sent to sort papers in Ashkhabad. Do you know where that is?'

'Turkmenistan.'

'Yes.' He thumped his chest. 'Me—Vaslav Viktorovich Kennikin—sent to comb the border for narcotics smugglers and to shuffle papers at a desk.'

'Thus are the mighty fallen,' I said. 'So they dug you up for this operation. That must have pleased you.'

He stretched out his legs. 'Oh, it did. I was very pleased when I discovered you were here. You see, at one time I thought you were my friend.' His voice rose slightly. 'You were as close to me as my own brother.'

'Don't be silly,' I said. 'Don't you know intelligence agents have no friends?' I remembered Jack Case and thought bitterly that I was learning the lesson the hard way, just as Kennikin had.

He went on as though I had not spoken. 'Closer to me than my brother. I would have put my life in your hands —I *did* put my life in your hands.' He stared into the colourless liquid in his glass. 'And you sold me out.' Abruptly he lifted the glass and drained it.

I said derisively, 'Come off it, Vaslav; you'd have done the same in my position.'

He stared at me. 'But I trusted you,' he said almost plaintively. 'That is what hurt most.' He stood up and walked to the cupboard. Over his shoulder he said, 'You know what my people are like. Mistakes aren't condoned. And so . . .' He shrugged '. . . the desk in Ashkhabad. They wasted me.' His voice was harsh.

'It could have been worse,' I said. 'It could have been Siberia. Khatanga, for instance.'

When he returned to his chair the tumbler was full again. 'It very nearly was,' he said in a low voice. 'But my friends helped—my true Russian friends.' With an effort he pulled himself back to the present. 'But we waste time. You have a certain piece of electronic equipment which is wrongfully in your possession. Where is it?'

'I don't know what you're talking about.'

He nodded. 'Of course, you would have to say that; I expected nothing else. But you must realize that you will give it to me eventually.' He took a cigarette case from his pocket. 'Well?'

'All right,' I said. 'I know I've got it, and you know I've got it; there's no point in beating around the bush. We know each other too well for that, Vaslav. But you're not going to get it.'

He took a long Russian cigarette from the case. 'I think I will, Alan; I *know* I will.' He put the case away and searched his pockets for a lighter. 'You see, this is not just an ordinary operation for me. I have many reasons for wanting to hurt you that are quite unconnected with this electronic gear. I am quite certain I shall get it. Quite certain.'

His voice was cold as ice and I felt an answering shudder run down my spine. *Kennikin will want to operate on you with a sharp knife.* Slade had said that, and Slade had delivered me into his hands.

He made a sound of annoyance as he discovered he had no means of lighting his cigarette, and Ilyich stepped from behind me, a cigarette lighter in his hand. Kennikin inclined his head to accept a light as the flint sparked. It sparked again but no flame appeared, and he said irritably, 'Oh, never mind!'

He leaned forward and picked up a spill of paper from the hearth, ignited it at the fire, and lit his cigarette. I was interested in what Ilyich was doing. He had not returned to his post behind my chair but had gone to the cupboard where the liquor was kept—behind Kennikin.

Kennikin drew on the cigarette and blew a plume of smoke, and then looked up. As soon as he saw that Ilyich was not in sight the pistol appeared in his hand. 'Ilyich, what are you doing?' The gun pointed steadily at me.

Ilyich turned with a refill cylinder of butane gas in his hand. 'Filling the lighter.'

Kennikin blew out his cheeks and rolled his eyes upwards. 'Never mind that,' he said curtly. 'Go outside and search the Volkswagen. You know what to look for.'

'It's not there, Vaslav,' I said.

'Ilyich will make sure of it,' said Kennikin.

Ilyich put the butane cylinder back into the liquor cupboard and left the room. Kennikin did not put away the pistol again but held it casually. 'Didn't I tell you? The team they have given me has been scraped from the bottom of the barrel. I'm surprised you didn't try to take advantage.'

I said, 'I might have done if you hadn't been around.'

'Ah, yes,' he said. 'We know each other very well. Perhaps too well.' He balanced the cigarette in an ashtray and picked up his glass. 'I don't really know if I will get any pleasure from working on you. Don't you English have a proverb—"It hurts me as much as it hurts you."' He waved his hand. 'But perhaps I've got it wrong.'

'I'm not English,' I said. 'I'm a Scot.'

'A difference that makes no difference is no difference. But I'll tell you something—you made a great difference to me and to my life.' He took a gulp of *brennivin*. 'Tell me —that girl you've been running around with—Elin Ragnarsdottir; are you in love with her?'

I felt myself tighten. 'She's got nothing to do with this.'

He laughed. 'Do not trouble yourself. I have no intention of harming her. Not a hair of her head shall be touched. I don't believe in the Bible, but I'm willing to swear on it.' His voice turned sardonic. 'I'll even swear it on the Works of Lenin, if that's an acceptable substitute. Do you believe me?'

'I believe you,' I said. I did, too. There was no comparison between Kennikin and Slade. I wouldn't have taken Slade's word had he sworn on a thousand bibles, but in this I would accept Kennikin's lightest word and trust him as he had once trusted me. I knew and understood Kennikin and I liked his style; he was a gentleman— savage, but still a gentleman.

'Well, then; answer my question. Are you in love with her?'

'We're going to be married.'

He laughed. 'That's not exactly a straight answer, but it will do.' He leaned forward. 'Do you sleep with her, Alan? When you come to Iceland do you lie under the stars together and clasp each other's bodies, and work at each other until your sweat mingles? Do you call each other by names that are sweet and soft and handle each other until that last gust of passion, that flare of ecstasy in each of you, mutually quenches the other and ebbs away into languor? Is that how it is, Alan?'

His voice was purring and cruel. 'Do you remember our last encounter in the pine woods when you tried to kill me? I wish you had been a better shot. I was in hospital in Moscow for a long time while they patched me up, but there was one patch they couldn't put back, Alan. And that is why, if you come out of this alive— and that is something I haven't yet decided—you will be no good to Elin Ragnarsdottir or to any other woman.'

I said, 'I'd like another drink.'

'I'll make it stronger this time,' he said. 'You look as though you need it.' He came across and took my glass, and backed towards the liquor cupboard. Still holding the pistol he poured whisky into the glass and added a little water. He brought it back. 'You need some colour in your cheeks,' he said.

I took the whisky from him. 'I understand your bitterness —but any soldier can expect to be wounded; it's an occupational hazard. What really hurts is that you were sold out. That's it, Vaslav; isn't it?'

'That among other things,' he agreed.

I sampled the whisky; it was strong this time. 'Where you go wrong is in your identification of who did it. Who was your boss at that time?'

'Bakayev—in Moscow.'

'And who was my boss?'

He smiled. 'That eminent British nobleman, Sir David Taggart.'

I shook my head. 'No. Taggart wasn't interested; there were bigger fish to occupy his attention at the time. You were sold out by Bakayev, your own boss, in collaboration with my boss, and I was just the instrument.'

Kennikin roared with laughter. 'My dear Alan; you've been reading too much Fleming.'

I said, 'You haven't asked who my boss was.'

He was still shaking with chuckles as he said, 'All right; who was he?'

'Slade,' I said.

The laughter suddenly stopped. I said, 'It was very carefully planned. You were sacrificed to give Slade a good reputation. It had to look good—it had to look very authentic. That's why you weren't told. All things considered, you put up a good fight, but all the time your foundations were being nibbled away by Bakayev who was passing information to Slade.'

'This is nonsense, Stewartsen,' he said; but his face had gone pale and the livid cicatrice stood out on his cheek.

'So you failed,' I said. 'And, naturally, you had to be punished, or it still wouldn't look right. Yes, we know how your people do things, and if you hadn't been sent to Ashkhabad or somewhere like it we'd have been suspicious. So you spent four years in exile to make it look right; four years of paper shuffling for doing your duty. You've been had, Vaslav.'

His eyes were stony. 'This Slade I don't know,' he said shortly.

'You ought to. He's the man you take orders from in

Iceland. You thought it natural, perhaps, that you shouldn't be in command on this operation. Your people wouldn't want to give sole responsibility to a man like yourself who failed once. A reasonable attitude, you would think; and maybe you could retrieve your reputation and your honour and aspire to your former dizzy heights by a successful completion of this mission.' I laughed. 'And who do they give you for a boss? None other than the man who torpedoed you in Sweden.'

Kennikin stood up. The pistol pointed unwaveringly at my chest. 'I know who ruined the Swedish operation,' he said. 'And I can touch him from here.'

'I just took orders,' I said. 'Slade did the brainwork. Do you remember Jimmy Birkby?'

'I've never heard of the man,' said Kennikin stonily.

'Of course not. You'd know him better as Sven Hornlund—the man I killed.'

'The British agent,' said Kennikin. 'I remember. It was that one act of yours that made me sure of you.'

'Slade's idea,' I said. 'I didn't know who I killed. That's why I left the Department—I had a flaming row.' I leaned forward. 'Vaslav, it fits the pattern, don't you see that? Slade sacrificed one good man to make you trust me. It meant nothing to him how many of our agents were killed. But he and Bakayev sacrificed you to make Taggart trust Slade the more.'

Kennikin's grey eyes were like stones. His face was quite still except for one corner of his mouth where the scar ran down which twitched with a slight tic.

I leaned back in the chair and picked up the glass. 'Slade's sitting pretty now. He's here in Iceland running both sides of an operation. My God, what a position to be in! But it went wrong when one of the puppets refused to jump when he pulled the strings. That must have worried the hell out of him.'

'I don't know this man Slade,' repeated Kennikin woodenly.

'No? Then why are you all worked up?' I grinned at him. 'I'll tell you what to do. Next time you speak to him why don't you ask him for the truth. Not that he'll tell you; Slade never told anyone the truth in his life. But he might give himself away to such a perceptive person as yourself.'

Lights flickered through the drawn curtains and there

was the sound of a car pulling up outside. I said, 'Think of the past, Vaslav; think of the wasted years in Ashkhabad. Put yourself in the position of Bakayev and ask yourself which is the more important—an operation in Sweden which can be reconstituted at any time, or the chance to put a man high in the hierarchy of British Intelligence —so high that he lunches with the British Prime Minister?'

Kennikin moved uneasily and I knew I had got to him. He was deep in thought and the pistol no longer pointed directly at me. I said, 'As a matter of interest, how long did it take to build up another Swedish outfit? Not long, I'll bet. I daresay Bakayev had an organization already working in parallel ready to go into action when you dropped out.'

It was a shot at random but it went home. It was like watching a one-armed bandit come up with the jackpot; the wheels went round and whirred and clicked and a mental bell rang loud and clear. Kennikin snorted and turned away. He looked down into the fire and the hand holding the pistol was down at his side.

I tensed myself, ready to jump him, and said softly, 'They didn't trust you, Vaslav. Bakayev didn't trust you to wreck your own organization and make it look good. I wasn't trusted either; but I was sold out by Slade who is one of your mob. You're different; you've been kicked in the teeth by your own people. How does it feel?'

Vaslav Kennikin was a good man—a good agent—and he gave nothing away. He turned his head and looked at me. 'I've listened to this fairy-story with great interest,' he said colourlessly. 'The man, Slade, I don't know. You tell a fine tale, Alan, but it won't get you out of trouble. You're not . . .'

The door opened and two men came in. Kennikin turned impatiently, and said, 'Well?'

The bigger of the men said in Russian, 'We've just got back.'

'So I see,' said Kennikin emotionlessly. He waved at me. 'Let me introduce Alan Stewartsen, the man you were supposed to bring here. What went wrong? Where's Igor?'

They looked at each other, and the big man said, 'He was taken to hospital. He was badly scalded when . . .'

'That's fine!' said Kennikin caustically. 'That's marvellous!' He turned and appealed to me. 'What do you think of this, Alan? We get Yuri safely and secretly to the

142

trawler but Igor must go to a hospital where questions are asked. What would you do with an idiot like this?'

I grinned, and said hopefully, 'Shoot him.'

'It's doubtful if a bullet would penetrate his thick skull,' said Kennikin acidly. He looked balefully at the big Russian. 'And why, in God's name, did you start shooting? It sounded like the outbreak of revolution.'

The man gestured towards me helplessly. 'He started it.'

'He should never have been given the opportunity. If three men can't take another one quietly, then . . .'

'There were two of them.'

'Oh!' Kennikin glanced at me. 'What happened to him?'

'I don't know—he ran away,' said the big man.

I said casually, 'It's hardly surprising. He was just a guest from the hotel.' I seethed internally. So Case had just run away and left me to it. I wouldn't sell him to Kennikin but there'd be an account to settle if I got out of this mess.

'He probably raised the alarm at the hotel,' said Kennikin. 'Can't you do anything right?'

The big man started to expostulate, but Kennikin cut him short. 'What's Ilyich doing?'

'Taking a car to pieces.' His voice was sullen.

'Go and help him.' They both turned, but Kennikin said sharply, 'Not you, Gregor. Stay here and watch Stewartsen.' He handed his pistol to the smaller man.

I said, 'Can I have another drink, Vaslav?'

'Why not?' said Kennikin. 'There's no danger of you turning into an alcoholic. You won't live that long. Watch him, Gregor.'

He left the room, closing the door behind him, and Gregor planted himself in front of it and looked at me expressionlessly. I drew up my legs very slowly and got to my feet. Gregor lifted the pistol and I grinned at him, holding up my empty glass. 'You heard what the boss said; I'm allowed a last drink.'

The muzzle of the pistol dropped. 'I'll be right behind you,' he said.

I walked across to the liquor cupboard, talking all the time. 'I'll bet you're from the Crimea, Gregor. That accent is unmistakable. Am I right?'

He was silent, but I persevered with my patter. 'There doesn't seem to be any vodka here, Gregor. The nearest to it is *brennivin*, but that comes a bad second—I don't go for it myself. Come to that, I don't like vodka very much either. Scotch is my tipple, and why not, since I'm a Scot?'

I clattered bottles and heard Gregor breathing down my neck. The scotch went into the glass to be followed by water, and I turned with it raised in my hand to find Gregor a yard away with the pistol trained on my navel. As I have said, there *is* a place for the pistol, and this was it. It's a dandy indoor weapon. If I had done anything so foolish as to throw the drink into his face he would have drilled me clear through the spine.

I held up the glass at mouth level. '*Skal*—as we say in Iceland.' I had to keep my hand up otherwise the cylinder of butane gas would have dropped out of my sleeve, so I walked across the room in a pansyfied manner and sat in my chair again. Gregor looked at me with something like contempt in his eyes.

I sipped from the glass and then transferred it from one hand to the other. When I had finished wriggling about the butane cylinder was tucked in between the cushion and the arm of the chair. I toasted Gregor again and then looked at the hot-burning peat fire with interest.

On each refill cylinder of butane there is a solemn warning: EXTREMELY INFLAMMABLE MIXTURE. DO NOT USE NEAR FIRE OR FLAME. KEEP OUT OF THE REACH OF CHILDREN. DO NOT PUNCTURE OR INCINERATE. Commercial firms do not like to put such horrendous notices on their products and usually do so only under pressure of legislation, so that in all cases the warnings are thoroughly justified.

The peat fire was glowing hot with a nice thick bed of red embers. I thought that if I put the cylinder into the fire one of two things were likely to happen—it would either explode like a bomb or take off like a rocket—and either of these would suit me. My only difficulty was that I didn't know how long it would take to blow up. Putting it into the fire might be easy, but anyone quick enough could pull it out—Gregor, for instance. Kennikin's boys couldn't possibly be as incompetent as he made them out to be.

Kennikin came back. 'You were telling the truth,' he said.

'I always do; the trouble is most people don't recognize it when they hear it. So you agree with me about Slade.'

He frowned. 'I don't mean that stupid story. What I am looking for is not in your car. Where is it?'

'I'm not telling you, Vaslav.'

'You will.'

A telephone bell rang somewhere. I said, 'Let's have a bet on it.'

'I don't want to get blood on the carpet in here,' he said. 'Stand up.' Someone took the telephone receiver off the hook.

'Can't I finish my drink first?'

Ilyich opened the door and beckoned to Kennikin, who said, 'You'd better have finished that drink by the time I get back.'

He left the room and Gregor moved over to stand in front of me. That wasn't very good because as long as he stood there I wouldn't have a chance of jamming the butane cylinder into the fire. I touched my forehead and found a thin film of sweat.

Presently Kennikin came back and regarded me thoughtfully. 'The man you were with at Geysir—a guest at the hotel, I think you said.'

'That's right.'

'Does the name—John Case—mean anything to you?' I looked at him blankly. 'Not a thing.'

He smiled sadly. 'And you are the man who said he always told the truth.' He sat down. 'It seems that what I am looking for has ceased to have any importance. More accurately, its importance has diminished relative to yourself. Do you know what that means?'

'You've lost me,' I said, and I really meant it. This was a new twist.

Kennikin said, 'I would have gone to any length necessary to get the information from you. However, my instructions have changed. You will not be tortured, Stewartsen, so put your mind at ease.'

I let out my breath. 'Thanks!' I said wholeheartedly.

He shook his head pityingly. 'I don't want your thanks. My instructions are to kill you immediately.'

The telephone bell rang again.

My voice came out in a croak. 'Why?'

He shrugged. 'You are getting in the way.'

I swallowed. 'Hadn't you better answer that telephone? It might be a change of instruction.'

He smiled crookedly. 'A last minute reprieve, Alan? I don't think so. Do you know why I told you of these instructions? It's not normally done, as you know.'

I knew all right, but I wouldn't give him the satisfaction of telling him. The telephone stopped ringing.

'There are some good things in the Bible,' he said. 'For instance—"An eye for an eye, and a tooth for a tooth." I had everything planned for you, and I regret my plans cannot now be implemented. But at least I can watch you sweat as you're sweating now.'

Ilyich stuck his head around the door. 'Reykjavik,' he said.

Kennikin made a gesture of annoyance. 'I'm coming.' He rose. 'Think about it—and sweat some more.'

I put out my hand. 'Have you a cigarette?'

He stopped in mid-stride and laughed aloud. 'Oh, very good, Alan. You British are strong on tradition. Certainly you may have the traditional last cigarette.' He tossed me his cigarette case. 'Is there anything else you would like?'

'Yes,' I said. 'I would like to be in Trafalgar Square on New Year's Eve in the year 2000.'

'My regrets,' he said, and left the room.

I opened the case, stuck a cigarette in my mouth, and patted my pockets helplessly; then I stooped very slowly to pick up one of the paper spills from the hearth. I said to Gregor, 'I'm just going to light my cigarette,' and bent forward to the fire, hoping to God he wouldn't move from the door.

I held the spill in my left hand and leaned forward so that my right hand was screened by my body, and thrust the cylinder into the embers at the same time as I lifted the flaming spill and returned to my seat. Waving it in a circle to attract Gregor's eyes from the fire, I applied it to the tip of the cigarette, drew in smoke and blew a plume in his direction. I deliberately allowed the flame to burn down so that it touched my fingers.

'Ouch!' I exclaimed, and shook my hand vigorously. Anything to keep him from looking directly at the fire. It took all the willpower I had to refrain from glancing at it myself.

The telephone was slammed down and Kennikin came stalking back. 'Diplomats!' he said in a scathing voice. 'As though I don't have enough troubles.' He jerked his thumb at me. 'All right; on your feet.'

I held up the cigarette. 'What about this?'

'You can finish it outside. There'll be just enough . . .'

The blast of the exploding cylinder was deafening in that enclosed area, and it blew the peat fire all over the room. Because I was expecting it I was quicker off the mark than anyone else. I ignored the red-hot ember which stung my neck, but Gregor found he couldn't do the same with the ember which alighted on the back of his hand. He gave a yell and dropped the gun.

I dived across the room, seized the pistol and shot him twice through the chest. Then I turned to nail Kennikin before he could recover. He had been beating red-hot bits of peat from his jacket but now he was turning at the sound of the shots. I lifted the pistol and he grabbed a table-lamp and threw it at me. I ducked, my shot went wild, and the table-lamp sailed over my head to hit Ilyich straight in the face as he opened the door to find out what the hell was going on.

That saved me the trouble of opening it. I shouldered him aside and stumbled into the hall to find that the front door was open. Kennikin had given me a bad time, and much as I would have liked to have fought it out with him this was not the time for it. I ran out of the house and past the Volkswagen which was minus all four wheels, and on the way took a snap shot at the big Russian to encourage him to keep his head down. Then I ran into the darkness which, by now, was not as dark as I would have liked, and took to the countryside fast.

The countryside thereabouts consisted of humpy lava covered by a thick layer of moss and occasional patches of dwarf birch. At full speed and in broad daylight a man might make one mile an hour without breaking an ankle. I sweated over it, knowing that if I broke my ankle, or as much as sprained it, I would be picked up easily and probably shot on the spot.

I went about four hundred yards, angling away from the lake shore and up towards the road, before I stopped. Looking back I saw the windows of the room in which I had been held; there was a curious flickering and I saw that the curtains were going up in flames. There were distant shouts and someone ran in front of the window, but it seemed that no one was coming after me. I don't think any of them knew which direction I'd taken.

The view ahead was blocked by the bulk of an old lava flow and I reckoned the road was on the other side of that.

I moved forward again and began to climb over it. It would be dawn soon and I wanted to get out of sight of the house.

I went over the top of the lava flow on my belly and once safely screened on the other side I got to my feet. Dimly, in the distance, I could see a straight dark line which could only be the road, and I was just about to make for it when someone put a stranglehold on my neck and a hand clamped on my wrist with bone-crushing pressure. 'Drop the gun!' came a hoarse whisper in Russian.

I dropped the pistol and was immediately flung away so that I stumbled and fell. I looked up into the glare of a flashlight which illumined a pistol held on me. 'Christ, it's you!' said Jack Case.

'Put that bloody light out,' I said, and massaged my neck. 'Where the hell were you when the whistle blew at Geysir?'

'I'm sorry about that,' said Case. 'He was at the hotel when I arrived.'

'But you said . . .'

There was a note of exasperation in Case's voice. 'Jesus, I couldn't tell you he was there. In the mood you were in you'd have slaughtered him.'

'A fine friend you turned out to be,' I said bitterly. 'But this is no time to go into it. Where's your car—we can talk later.'

'Just off the road down there.' He put away his gun.

I came to a snap decision; this was no time to trust Case or anyone else. I said, 'Jack, you can tell Taggart I'll deliver his package to Reykjavik.'

'All right, but let's get out of here.'

I moved close to him. 'I don't trust you, Jack,' I said, and sank three rigid fingers into his midriff. The air exploded violently from his lungs and he doubled up. I chopped at the back of his neck and he collapsed at my feet. Jack and I had always been level on the unarmed combat mat and I don't think I could have taken him so easily had he known what was coming.

In the distance a car started and its engine throbbed. I saw the glow of headlights to my right and dropped flat. I could hear the car coming up the spur track towards the road, but it turned away and moved in the opposite direction—the way I had driven in from Thingvellir.

When it was out of earshot I reached out and began

to search Case's pockets. I took his keys and stripped him of his shoulder holster and pistol. Gregor's pistol I wiped clean and threw away. Then I went to look for Case's car.

It was a Volvo and I found it parked just off the road. The engine turned over easily at the touch of a button and I moved away without lights. I would be going all the way around Thingvallavatn and it would be a long way to Laugarvatn, but I certainly didn't feel like going back.

CHAPTER EIGHT

I

I got into Laugarvatn just before five in the morning and parked the car in the drive. As I got out I saw the curtains twitch and Elin ran out and into my arms before I got to the front door. 'Alan!' she said. 'There's blood on your face.'

I touched my cheek and felt the caked blood which had oozed from a cut. It must have happened when the butane cylinder went up. I said, 'Let's get inside.'

In the hall we met Sigurlin. She looked me up and down, then said, 'Your jacket's burnt.'

I glanced at the holes in the fabric. 'Yes,' I said. 'I was careless, wasn't I?'

'What happened?' asked Elin urgently.

'I had . . . I had a talk with Kennikin,' I said shortly. The reaction was hitting me and I felt very weary. I had to do something about it because there was no time to rest. 'Do you have any coffee?' I asked Sigurlin.

Elin gripped my arm. 'What happened? What did Kenni . . .?'

'I'll tell you later.'

Sigurlin said, 'You look as though you haven't slept for a week. There's a bed upstairs.'

I shook my head. 'No. I . . . we . . . are moving out.'

She and Elin exchanged glances, and then Sigurlin said practically, 'You can have your coffee, anyway. It's all ready—we've been drinking the stuff all night. Come into the kitchen.'

I sat down at the kitchen table and spooned a lot of sugar into a steaming cup of black coffee. It was the most wonderful thing I've ever tasted. Sigurlin went to the window and looked at the Volvo in the drive. 'Where's the Volkswagen?'

I grimaced. 'It's a write-off.' The big Russian had said that Ilyich was taking it to pieces, and from the fleeting glimpse I had of it he had been right. I said, 'What's it worth, Sigurlin?' and put my hand in my pocket for my cheque-book.

She made an impatient gesture. 'That can wait.' There was an edge to her voice. 'Elin told me everything. About Slade—about Kennikin—everything.'

'You shouldn't have done that, Elin,' I said quietly.

'I had to talk about it to someone,' she burst out.

'You must go to the police,' said Sigurlin.

I shook my head. 'So far this has been a private fight. The only casualties have been among the professionals —the men who know the risks and accept them. No innocent bystanders have been hurt. I want to keep it that way. Anyone who monkeys around with this without knowing the score is in for trouble—whether he's wearing a police uniform or not.'

'But it needn't be handled at that level,' she said. 'Let the politicians handle it—the diplomats.'

I sighed and leaned back in my chair. 'When I first came to this country someone told me that there are three things which an Icelander can't explain—not even to another Icelander: the Icelandic political system, the Icelandic economic system, and the Icelandic drinking laws. We're not worried about alcohol right now, but politics and economics are right at the top of my list of worries.'

Elin said, 'I don't really know what you're talking about.'

'I'm talking about that refrigerator,' I said. 'And that electric coffee-grinder.' My finger stabbed out again. 'And the electric kettle and the transistor radio. They're all imported and to afford imports you have to export—fish, mutton, wool. The herring shoals have moved a thousand miles away, leaving your inshore herring fleet high and dry. Aren't things bad enough without making them worse?'

Sigurlin wrinkled her brow. 'What do you mean?'

'There are three nations involved—Britain, America and Russia. Supposing a thing like this is handled at diplomatic level with an exchange of Notes saying: "Stop fighting your battles on Icelandic territory." Do you really think a thing like that could be kept secret? Every country has political wild men—and I'm sure Iceland is no exception—and they'd all jump on the bandwagon.'

I stood up. 'The anti-Americans would shout about the Base at Keflavik; the anti-communists would have a good handle to grab hold of; and you'd probably restart the Fishing War with Britain because I know a lot of Icelanders who aren't satisfied with the settlement of 1961.'

I swung around to face Sigurlin. 'During the Fishing War your trawlers were denied entry to British ports, so you built up a fair trade with Russia, which you still have. What do you think of Russia as a trading partner?'

'I think they're very good,' she said instantly. 'They've done a lot for us.'

I said deliberately, 'If your government is placed in the position of having to take official notice of what's going on then that good relationship might be endangered. Do you want that to happen?'

Her face was a study in consternation. I said grimly, 'If this lark ever comes into the open it'll be the biggest *cause célèbre* to hit Iceland since Sam Phelps tried to set up Jorgen Jorgensen as king back in 1809.'

Elin and Sigurlin looked at each other helplessly. 'He's right,' said Sigurlin.

I knew I was right. Under the placid level of Icelandic society were forces not safe to tamper with. Old animosities still linger among the longer-memoried and it wouldn't take much to stir them up. I said, 'The less the politicians know, the better it will be for everybody. I like this country, damn it; and I don't want the mud stirred up.' I took Elin's hand. 'I'll try to get this thing cleaned up soon. I think I know a way.'

'Let them have the package,' she said urgently. 'Please, Alan; let them have it.'

'I'm going to,' I said. 'But in my own way.'

There was a lot to think about. The Volkswagen, for instance. It wouldn't take Kennikin long to check the registration and find out where it came from. That meant he'd probably be dropping in before the day was over. 'Sigurlin,' I said. 'Can you take a pony and join Gunnar?'

She was startled. 'But why . . .?' She took the point. 'The Volkswagen?'

'Yes; you might have unwelcome visitors. You'd be better out of the way.'

'I had a message from Gunnar last night, just after you left. He's staying out another three days.'

'That's good,' I said. 'In three days everything should be over.'

'Where are you going?'

'Don't ask,' I warned. 'You know too much already. Just get yourself in a place where there's no one to ask questions.' I snapped my fingers. 'I'll shift the Land-Rover too. I'm abandoning it, but it had better not be found here.'

'You can park it in the stables.'

'That's a thought. I'm going to move some things from the Land-Rover into the Volvo. I'll be back in a few minutes.'

I went into the garage and took out the electronic gadget, the two rifles and all the ammunition. The guns I wrapped in a big piece of sacking which I found and they went into the boot. Elin came out, and said, 'Where *are* we going?'

'Not we,' I said. 'Me.'

'I'm coming with you.'

'You're going with Sigurlin.'

That familiar stubborn, mulish look came on to her face. 'I liked what you said in there,' she said. 'About not wanting to cause trouble for my country. But it is my country and I can fight for it as well as anyone else.'

I nearly laughed aloud. 'Elin,' I said. 'What do you know about fighting?'

'As much as any other Icelander,' she said evenly.

She had something there. 'You don't know what's going on,' I said.

'Do you?'

'I'm beginning to catch on. I've just about proved that Slade is a Russian agent—and I loaded Kennikin just like a gun and pointed him at Slade. When they meet he's likely to go off, and I wouldn't like to be in Slade's position when it happens. Kennikin believes in direct action.'

'What happened last night? Was it bad?'

I slammed the boot closed. 'It wasn't the happiest night of my life,' I said shortly. 'You'd better get some things together. I want this house unoccupied within the hour.' I took out a map and spread it out.

'Where are you going?' Elin was very persistent.

'Reykjavik,' I said. 'But I want to go to Keflavik first.'

'That's the wrong way round,' she pointed out. 'You'll get to Reykjavik first—unless you go south through Hveragerdi.'

'That's the problem,' I said slowly, and frowned as I

looked at the map. The web of roads I had visualized existed all right but not as extensively as I had imagined. I didn't know about the Department's supposed manpower shortage, but Kennikin certainly wasn't suffering that way; I had counted ten different men with Kennikin at one time or another.

And the map showed that the whole of the Reykjanes Peninsula could be sealed off from the east by placing men at two points—Thingvellir and Hveragerdi. If I went through either of those towns at a normal slow speed I'd be spotted; if I went through hell-for-leather I'd attract an equivalent amount of attention. And the radio-telephone which had worked for me once would now work against me, and I'd have the whole lot of them down on me.

'Christ!' I said. 'This is bloody impossible.'

Elin grinned at me cheerfully. 'I know an easy way,' she said too casually. 'One that Kennikin won't think of.'

I looked at her suspiciously. 'How?'

'By sea.' She laid her finger on the map. 'If we go to Vik I know an old friend who will take us to Keflavik in his boat.'

I regarded the map dubiously. 'It's a long way to Vik, and it's in the wrong direction.'

'All the better,' she said. 'Kennikin won't expect you to go there.'

The more I studied the map, the better it looked. 'Not bad,' I said.

Elin said innocently, 'Of course, I'll have to come with you to introduce you to my friend.'

She'd done it again.

II

It was an odd way to get to Reykjavik because I pointed the Volvo in the opposite direction and put my foot down. It was with relief that I crossed the bridge over the Thjòrsà River because that was a bottleneck I was sure Kennikin would cover, but we got across without incident and I breathed again.

Even so, after we passed Hella I had a belated attack of nerves and left the main road to join the network of bumpy tracks in Landeyjasandur, feeling that anyone who

154

could find me in that maze would have to have extra-sensory perception.

At midday Elin said decisively, 'Coffee.'

'What have you got? A magic wand?'

'I've got a vacuum flask—and bread—and pickled herring. I raided Sigurlin's kitchen.'

'Now I'm glad you came,' I said. 'I never thought of that.' I pulled the car to a halt.

'Men aren't as practical as women,' said Elin.

As we ate I examined the map to check where we were. We had just crossed a small river and the farmstead we had passed was called Bergthórshvoll. It was with wonder that I realized we were in the land of Njal's Saga. Not far away was Hlidarendi, where Gunnar Hamundarsson was betrayed by Hallgerd, his wife, and had gone down fighting to the end. Skarp-Hedin had stalked over this land with death on his face and his war-axe raised high, tormented by the devils of revenge. And here, at Bergthórshvoll, Njal and his wife, Bergthóra, had been burned to death with their entire family.

All that had happened a thousand years ago and I reflected, with some gloom, that the essential nature of man had not changed much since. Like Gunnar and Skarp-Hedin I travelled the land in imminent danger of ambush by my enemies and, like them, I was equally prepared to lay an ambush if the opportunity arose. There was another similarity; I am a Celt and Njal had a Celtic name, nordicised from Neil. I hoped the Saga of Burnt Njal would not be echoed by the Saga of Burnt Stewart.

I aroused myself from these depressing thoughts, and said, 'Who is your friend in Vik?'

Valtýr Baldvinsson, one of Bjarni's old school friends. He's a marine biologist studying the coastal ecology. He wants to find out the extent of the changes when Katla erupts.'

I knew about Katla. 'Hence the boat,' I said. 'And what makes you think he'll run us to Keflavik?'

Elin tossed her head. 'He will if I ask him to.'

I grinned. 'Who is this fascinating woman with a fatal power over men? Can it be none other than Mata Hari, girl spy?'

She turned pink but her voice was equable as she said, 'You'll like Valtýr.'

And I did. He was a square man who, but for his

colouring, looked as though he had been rough-hewn from a pillar of Icelandic basalt. His torso was square and so was his head, and his hands had stubby, spatulate fingers which appeared to be too clumsy for the delicate work he was doing when we found him in his laboratory. He looked up from the slide he was mounting and gave a great shout. 'Elin! What are you doing here?'

'Just passing by. This is Alan Stewart from Scotland.'

My hand was enveloped in a big paw. 'Good to meet you,' he said, and I had the instant feeling he meant it.

He turned to Elin. 'You're lucky to have caught me here. I'm leaving tomorrow.'

Elin raised her eyebrows. 'Oh! Where for?'

'At last they've decided to put a new engine into that relic of a longship they've given me instead of a boat. I'm taking her round to Reykjavik.'

Elin glanced at me and I nodded. In the course of events you have to be lucky sometimes. I had been wondering how Elin was going to cajole him into taking us to Keflavik without arousing too many suspicions, but now the chance had fallen right into our laps.

She smiled brilliantly. 'Would you like a couple of passengers? I told Alan I hoped you could take us to have a look at Surtsey, but we wouldn't mind going on to Keflavik. Alan has to meet someone there in a couple of days.'

'I'd be glad to have company,' Valtýr said jovially. 'It's a fair distance and I'd like someone to spell me at the wheel. How's your father?'

'He's well,' said Elin.

'And Bjarni? Has Kristin given him that son yet?'

Elin laughed. 'Not yet—but soon. And how do you know it won't be a daughter?'

'It will be a boy!' he said with certainty. 'Are you on holiday, Alan?' he asked in English.

I replied in Icelandic, 'In a manner of speaking. I come here every year.'

He looked startled, and then grinned. 'We don't have many enthusiasts like you,' he said.

I looked around the laboratory; it appeared to be a conventional biological set-up with the usual rows of bottles containing chemicals, the balance, the two microscopes and the array of specimens behind glass. An odour of formalin was prevalent. 'What are you doing here?' I asked.

He took me by the arm and led me to the window. With a large gesture he said, 'Out there is the sea with a lot of fish in it. It's hazy now but in good weather you can see Vestmannaeyjar where there is a big fishing fleet. Now come over here.'

He led me to a window on the other side of the room and pointed up toward Mýrdalsjökull. 'Up there is the ice and, under the ice, a big bastard called Katla. You know Katla?'

'Everybody in Iceland knows of Katla,' I said.

He nodded. 'Good! I've been studying the sea off this coast and all the animals in it, big and small—and the plants too. When Katla erupts sixty cubic kilometres of ice will be melted into fresh water and it will come into the sea here; as much fresh water as comes out of all the rivers of Iceland in a year will come into the sea in one week and in this one place. It will be bad for the fish and the animals and the plants because they aren't accustomed to so much fresh water all at once. I want to find out how badly they will be hit and how long they take to recover.'

I said, 'But you have to wait until Katla erupts. You might wait a long time.'

He laughed hugely. 'I've been here five years—I might be here another ten, but I don't think so. The big bastard is overdue already.' He thumped me on the arm. 'Could blow up tomorrow—then we don't go to Keflavik.'

'I won't lose any sleep over it,' I said drily.

He called across the laboratory, 'Elin, in your honour I'll take the day off.' He took three big strides, picked her up and hugged her until she squealed for mercy.

I didn't pay much attention to that because my eyes were attracted to the headline of a newspaper which lay on the bench. It was the morning newspaper from Reykjavik and the headline on the front page blared: GUN BATTLE AT GEYSIR.

I read the story rapidly. Apparently a war had broken out at Geysir to judge from this account, and everything short of light artillery had been brought into play by persons unknown. There were a few eye-witness reports, all highly inaccurate, and it seemed that a Russian tourist, one Igor Volkov, was now in hospital after having come too close to Strokkur. Mr Volkov had no bullet wounds. The Soviet Ambassador had complained to the Icelandic Minister of Foreign Affairs about this unprovoked assault on a Soviet citizen.

I opened the paper to see if there was a leading article on the subject and, of course, there was. In frigid and austere tones the leader writer inquired of the Soviet Ambassador the reason why the aforesaid Soviet citizen, Igor Volkov, was armed to the teeth at the time, since there was no record of his having declared any weapons to the Customs authorities when he entered the country.

I grimaced. Between us, Kennikin and I were in a fair way to putting a crimp into Icelandic-Soviet relations.

III

We left Vik rather late the next morning and I wasn't in a good mood because I had a thick head. Valtýr had proved to be a giant among drinkers and, since I was suffering from lack of sleep, my efforts to keep up with him had been disastrous. He put me to bed, laughing boisterously, and woke up himself as fresh as a daisy while I had a taste in my mouth as though I had been drinking the formalin from his specimen jars.

My mood wasn't improved when I telephoned London to speak to Taggart only to find he was absent from his office. The bland official voice declined to tell me where he was but offered to pass on a message, an invitation which I, in my turn, declined to accept. The curious actions of Case had led me to wonder who in the Department was trustworthy, and I wouldn't speak to anyone but Taggart.

Valtýr's boat was anchored in a creek, a short distance from the open beach, and we went out to it in a dinghy. He looked curiously at the two long, sackcloth-covered parcels I took aboard but made no comment, while I hoped they did not look too much like what they actually were. I wasn't going to leave the rifles behind because I had an idea I might need them.

The boat was about twenty-five feet overall, with a tiny cabin which had sitting headroom and a skimpy wooden canopy to protect the man at the wheel from the elements. I had checked the map to find the sea distance from Vik to Keflavik and the boat seemed none too large. I said, 'How long will it take?'

'About twenty hours,' said Valtýr, and added cheerfully, 'If the bastard engine keeps going. If not, it takes forever. You get seasick?'

'I don't know,' I said. 'I've never had the chance to find out.'

'You have the chance now.' He bellowed with laughter.

We left the creek and the boat lifted alarmingly to the ocean swells and a fresh breeze streamed Elin's hair. 'It's clearer today,' said Valtýr. He pointed over the bows. 'You can see Vestmannaeyjar.'

I looked towards the group of islands and played the part which Elin had assigned me. 'Where is Surtsey from here?'

'About twenty kilometres to the south-west of Heimaey —the big island. You won't see much of it yet.'

We plunged on, the little boat dipping into the deep swells and occasionally burying her bows in the water and shaking free a shower of spray when she came up. I'm not any kind of a seaman and it didn't look too safe to me, but Valtýr took it calmly enough, and so did Elin. The engine, which appeared to be a toy diesel about big enough to go with a Meccano set, chugged away, aided by a crack from Valtýr's boot when it faltered, which it did too often for my liking. I could see why he was pleased at the prospect of having a new one.

It took six hours to get to Sursey, and Valtýr circled the island, staying close to shore, while I asked the appropriate questions. He said, 'I can't land you, you know.'

Surtsey, which came up thunderously and in flames from the bottom of the sea, is strictly for scientists interested in finding out how life gains hold in a sterile environment. Naturally they don't want tourists clumping about and bringing in seeds on their boots. 'That's all right,' I said. 'I didn't expect to go ashore.'

Suddenly he chuckled. 'Remember the Fishing War?'

I nodded. The so-called Fishing War was a dispute between Iceland and Britain about off-shore fishing limits, and there was a lot of bad blood between the two fishing fleets. Eventually it had been settled, with the Icelanders making their main point of a twelve-mile limit.

Valtýr laughed, and said, 'Surtsey came up and pushed

our fishing limit thirty kilometres farther south. An English skipper I met told me it was a dirty trick—as though we'd done it deliberately. So I told him what a geologist told me; in a million years our fishing limit will be pushed as far south as Scotland.' He laughed uproariously.

When we left Surtsey I abandoned my pretended interest and went below to lie down. I was in need of sleep and my stomach had started to do flip-flops so that I was thankful to stretch out, and I fell asleep as though someone had hit me on the head.

IV

My sleep was long and deep because when I was awakened by Elin she said, 'We're nearly there.'

I yawned. 'Where?'

'Valtýr is putting us ashore at Keflavik.'

I sat up and nearly cracked my head on a beam. Overhead a jet plane whined and when I went aft into the open I saw that the shore was quite close and a plane was just dipping in to land. I stretched, and said, 'What time is it?'

'Eight o'clock,' said Valtýr. 'You slept well.'

'I needed it after a session with you,' I said, and he grinned.

We tied up at eight-thirty, Elin jumped ashore and I handed her the wrapped rifles. 'Thanks for the ride, Valtýr.'

He waved away my thanks. 'Any time. Maybe I can arrange to take you ashore on Surtsey—it's interesting. How long are you staying?'

'For the rest of the summer,' I said. 'But I don't know where I'll be.'

'Keep in touch,' he said.

We stood on the dockside and watched him leave, and then Elin said, 'What are we doing here?'

'I want to see Lee Nordinger. It's a bit chancy, but I want to know what this gadget is. Will Bjarni be here, do you think?'

'I doubt it,' said Elin. 'He usually flies out of Reykjavik Airport.'

'After breakfast I want you to go to the Icelandair office at the airport here,' I said. 'Find out where Bjarni is, and stay there until I come.' I rubbed my cheek and felt unshaven bristles. 'And stay off the public concourse. Kenni-kin is sure to have Keflavik Airport staked out and I don't want you seen.'

'Breakfast first,' she said. 'I know a good café here.'

When I walked into Nordlinger's office and dumped the rifles in a corner he looked at me with some astonishment, noting the sagging of my pockets under the weight of the rifle ammunition, my bristly chin and general uncouth-ness. His eyes flicked towards the corner. 'Pretty heavy for fishing tackle,' he commented. 'You look beat, Alan.'

'I've been travelling in rough country,' I said, and sat down. 'I'd like to borrow a razor, and I'd like you to look at something.'

He slid open a drawer of his desk and drew out a battery-powered shaver which he pushed across to me. 'The washroom's two doors along the corridor,' he said. 'What do you want me to look at?'

I hesitated. I couldn't very well ask Nordlinger to keep his mouth shut no matter what he found. That would be asking him to betray the basic tenets of his profession, which he certainly wouldn't do. I decided to plunge and take a chance, so I dug the metal box from my pocket, took off the tape which held the lid on, and shook out the gadget. I laid it before him. 'What's that, Lee?'

He looked at it for a long time without touching it, then he said, 'What do you want to know about it?'

'Practically everything,' I said. 'But to begin with—what nationality is it?'

He picked it up and turned it around. If anyone could tell me anything about it, it was Commander Lee Nord-linger. He was an electronics officer at Keflavik Base and ran the radar and radio systems, both ground-based and airborne. From what I'd heard he was damned good at his job.

'It's almost certainly American,' he said. He poked his finger at it. 'I recognize some of the components—these resistors, for instance, are standard and are of American manufacture.' He turned it around again. 'And the input is standard American voltage and at fifty cycles.'

'All right,' I said. 'Now—what is it?'

'That I can't tell you right now. For God's sake, you bring in a lump of miscellaneous circuitry and expect me to identify it at first crack of the whip. I may be good but I'm not that good.'

'Then can you tell me what it's not?' I asked patiently.

'It's no teenager's transistor radio, that's for sure,' he said, and frowned. 'Come to that, it's like nothing I've ever seen before.' He tapped the odd-shaped piece of metal in the middle of the assembly. 'I've never seen one of these. for example.'

'Can you run a test on it?'

'Sure.' He uncoiled his lean length from behind the desk. 'Let's run a current through it and see if it plays "The Star-Spangled Banner." '

'Can I come along?'

'Why not?' said Nordlinger lightly. 'Let's go to the shop.' As we walked along the corridor he said, 'Where did you get it?'

'It was given to me,' I said uncommunicatively.

He gave me a speculative glance but said no more. We went through swing doors at the end of the corridor and into a large room which had long benches loaded with electronic gear. Lee signalled to a petty officer who came over. 'Hi, Chief; I have something here I want to run a few tests on. Have you a test bench free?'

'Sure, Commander.' The petty officer looked about the room. 'Take number five; I guess we won't be using that for a while.'

I looked at the test bench; it was full of knobs and dials and screens which meant less than nothing. Nordlinger sat down. 'Pull up a chair and we'll see what happens.' He attached clips to the terminals on the gadget, then paused. 'We already know certain things about it. It isn't part of an airplane; they don't use such a heavy voltage. And it probably isn't from a ship for roughly the same reason. So that leaves ground-based equipment. It's designed to plug into the normal electricity system on the North American continent—it could have been built in Canada. A lot of Canadian firms use American manufactured components.'

I jogged him along. 'Could it come from a TV set?'

'Not from any TV I've seen.' He snapped switches. 'A hundred ten volts—fifty cycles. Now, there's no amperage given so we have to be careful. We'll start real low.' He twisted a knob delicately and a fine needle on a dial barely quivered against the pin.

He looked down at the gadget. 'There's a current going through now but not enough to give a fly a heart attack.'

162

He paused, and looked up. 'To begin with, this thing is crazy; an alternating current with these components isn't standard. Now, let's see—first we have what seems to be three amplification stages, and that makes very little sense.'

He took a probe attached to a lead. 'If we touch the probe here we should get a sine wave on the oscilloscope . . .' He looked up. '. . . which we do. Now we see what happens at this lead going into this funny-shaped metal ginkus.'

He gently jabbed the probe and the green trace on the oscilloscope jumped and settled into a new configuration. 'A square wave,' said Nordlinger. 'This circuit up to here is functioning as a chopper—which is pretty damn funny in itself for reasons I won't go into right now. Now let's see what happens at the lead going *out* of the ginkus and into this mess of boards.'

He touched down the probe and the oscilloscope trace jumped again before it settled down. Nordlinger whistled. 'Just look at that spaghetti, will you?' The green line was twisted into a fantastic waveform which jumped rhythmically and changed form with each jump. 'You'd need a hell of a lot of Fourier analysis to sort that out,' said Nordlinger. 'But whatever else it is, it's pulsed by this metal dohickey.'

'What do you make of it?'

'Not a damn thing,' he said. 'Now I'm going to try the output stage; on past form this should fairly tie knots into that oscilloscope—maybe it'll blow up.' He lowered the probe and we looked expectantly at the screen.

I said, 'What are you waiting for?'

'I'm waiting for nothing.' Nordlinger looked at the screen blankly. 'There's no output.'

'Is that bad?'

He looked at me oddly. In a gentle voice he said, 'It's impossible.'

I said, 'Maybe there's something broken in there.'

'You don't get it,' said Nordlinger. 'A circuit is just what it says—a circle. You break the circle anywhere you get no current flow anywhere.' He applied the probe again. 'Here there's a current of a pulsed and extremely complex form.' Again the screen jumped into life. 'And here, in the same circuit, what do we get?'

I looked at the blank screen. 'Nothing?'

'Nothing,' he said firmly. He hesitated. 'Or, to put it more precisely, nothing that can show on this test rig.' He tapped the gadget. 'Mind if I take this thing away for a while?'

'Why?'

'I'd like to put it through some rather more rigorous tests. We have another shop.' He cleared his throat and appeared to be a little embarrassed. 'Uh . . . you won't be allowed in there.'

'Oh—secret stuff.' That would be in one of the areas to which Fleet's pass would give access. 'All right, Lee; you put the gadget through its paces and I'll go and shave. I'll wait for you in your office.'

'Wait a minute,' he said. 'Where did you get it, Alan?'

I said, 'You tell me what it does and I'll tell you where it came from.'

He grinned. 'It's a deal.'

I left him disconnecting the gadget from the test rig and went back to his office where I picked up the electric shaver. Fifteen minutes later I felt a lot better after having got rid of the hair. I waited in Nordlinger's office for a long time—over an hour and a half—before he came back.

He came in carrying the gadget as though it was a stick of dynamite and laid it gently on his desk. 'I'll have to ask you where you got this,' he said briefly.

'Not until you tell me what it does,' I said.

He sat behind his desk and looked at the complex of metal and plastic with something like loathing in his eyes. 'It does nothing,' he said flatly. 'Absolutely nothing.'

'Come off it,' I said. 'It must do *something*.'

'Nothing!' he repeated. 'There is no measurable output.' He leaned forward and said softly, 'Alan, out there I have instruments that can measure any damn part of the electromagnetic spectrum from radio waves of such low frequency you wouldn't believe possible right up to cosmic radiation—and there's nothing coming out of this contraption.'

'As I said before—maybe something has broken.'

'That cat won't jump; I tested everything.' He pushed at it and it moved sideways on the desk. 'There are three things I don't like about this. Firstly, there are components in here that are not remotely like anything I've seen before, components of which I don't even understand the function. I'm supposed to be pretty good at my job, and that, in itself, is enough to disturb me. Secondly, it's obviously incomplete—it's just part of a bigger complex—and yet I doubt if I would understand it even if I had everything. Thirdly—and this is the serious one—it shouldn't work.'

'But it isn't working,' I said.

He waved his hand distractedly. 'Perhaps I put it wrong. There should be an output of some kind. Good Christ, you can't keep pushing electricity into a machine—juice that gets used up—without getting something out. That's impossible.'

I said, 'Maybe it's coming out in the form of heat.'

He shook his head sadly. 'I got mad and went to extreme measures. I pushed a thousand watts of current through it in the end. If the energy output was in heat then the goddamn thing would have glowed like an electric heater. But no—it stayed as cool as ever.'

'A bloody sight cooler than you're behaving,' I said.

He threw up his hands in exasperation. 'Alan, if you were a mathematician and one day you came across an equation in which two and two made five without giving a nonsensical result then you'd feel exactly as I do. It's as though a physicist were confronted by a perpetual motion machine which works.'

'Hold on,' I said. 'A perpetual motion machine gets something for nothing—energy usually. This is the other way round.'

'It makes no difference,' he said. 'Energy can neither be created nor destroyed.' As I opened my mouth he said quickly, 'And don't start talking about atomic energy. Matter can be regarded as frozen, concentrated energy.' He looked at the gadget with grim eyes. 'This thing is destroying energy.'

Destroying energy! I rolled the concept around my cerebrum to see what I could make of it. The answer came up fast—nothing much. I said, 'Let's not go overboard. Let's see what we have. You put an input into it and you get out . . .'

'Nothing,' said Nordlinger.

'Nothing you can measure,' I corrected. 'You may have some good instrumentation here, Lee, but I don't think you've got the whole works. I'll bet that there's some genius somewhere who not only knows what's coming out of there but has an equally involved gadget that can measure it.'

'Then I'd like to know what it is,' he said. 'Because it's right outside my experience.'

I said, 'Lee, you're a technician, not a scientist. You'll admit that?'

'Sure; I'm an engineer from way back.'

'That's why you have a crew-cut—but this was designed by a long-hair.' I grinned. 'Or an egghead.'

'I'd still like to know where you got it.'

'You'd better be more interested in where it's going. Have you got a safe—a really secure one?'

'Sure.' He did a double-take. 'You want *me* to keep *this*?'

'For forty-eight hours,' I said. 'If I don't claim it in that time you'd better give it to your superior officer together with all your forebodings, and let him take care of it.'

Nordlinger looked at me with a cold eye. 'I don't know but what I shouldn't give it to him right now. Forty-eight hours might mean my neck.'

'You part with it now and it will be my neck,' I said grimly.

He picked up the gadget. 'This is American and it doesn't belong here at Keflavik. I'd like to know where it does belong.'

'You're right about it not belonging here,' I said. 'But I'm betting it's Russian—and they want it back.'

'For God's sake!' he said. 'It's full of American components.'

'Maybe the Russians learned a lesson from Macnamara on cost-effectiveness. Maybe they're shopping in the best market. I don't give two bloody hoots if the components were made in the Congo—I still want you to hold on to it.'

He laid the gadget on his desk again very carefully. 'Okay—but I'll split the difference; I'll give you twenty-four hours. And even then you don't get it back without a full explanation.'

'Then I'll have to be satisfied with that,' I said. 'Providing you lend me your car. I left the Land-Rover in Laugarvatn.'

'You've got a goddamn nerve.' Nordlinger put his hand in his pocket and tossed the car key on the desk.

'You'll find it in the car park near the gate—the blue Chevrolet.'

'I know it.' I put on my jacket and went to the corner to pick up the rifles. 'Lee, do you know a man called Fleet?'

He thought for a moment. 'No.'

'Or McCarthy?'

'The CPO you met in the shop is McCarthy.'

'Not the same one,' I said. 'I'll be seeing you, Lee. We'll go fishing sometime.'

'Stay out of jail.'

I paused at the door. 'What makes you say a thing like that?'

His hand closed over the gadget. 'Anyone who walks around with a thing like this ought to be in jail,' he said feelingly.

I laughed, and left him staring at it. Nordlinger's sense of what was right had been offended. He was an engineer, not a scientist, and an engineer usually works to the rule book—that long list of verities tested through the centuries. He tends to forget that the rule book was originally compiled by scientists, men who see nothing strange in broken rules other than an opportunity to probe a little deeper into the inexplicable universe. Any man who can make the successful transition from Newtonian to quantum physics without breaking his stride can believe anything any day of the week and twice as much on Sundays. Lee Nordlinger was not one of these men, but I'd bet the man who designed the gadget was.

I found the car and put the rifles and the ammunition into the boot. I was still wearing Jack Case's pistol in the shoulder holster and so now there was nothing to spoil the set of my coat. Not that I was any more presentable; there were scorch marks on the front from the burning peat of Kennikin's fire, and a torn sleeve from where a bullet had come a shade too close at Geysir. It was stained with mud and so were my trousers, and I was looking more and more like a tramp—but a clean-shaven tramp.

I climbed into the car and trickled in the direction of the International Airport, thinking of what Nordlinger hadn't been able to tell me about the gadget. According to Lee it was an impossible object and that made it scientifically important—so important that men had died and had their legs blown off and had been cooked in boiling water because of it.

And one thing made me shiver. By Kennikin's last words just before I escaped from the house at Thingvallavatn he had made it quite clear that I was now more important than the gadget. He had been prepared to kill me without first laying his hands on it and, for all he knew, once I was dead the gadget would have been gone forever with me.

I had Nordlinger's evidence that the gadget was of outstanding scientific importance, so what was it about me that made me even more important than that? It's not often in this drear, technological world that a single man becomes of more importance than a scientific breakthrough. Maybe we were returning to sanity at last, but I didn't think so.

There was a side entrance to the Icelandair office which one could use without going through the public concourse, so I parked the car and went in. I bumped pleasantly into a hostess, and asked, 'Is Elin Ragnarsdottir around?'

'Elin? She's in the waiting-room.'

I walked into the waiting-room and found her alone. She jumped up quickly. 'Alan, you've been so long!'

'It took longer than I expected.' Her face was strained and there seemed to be a sense of urgency about her. 'You didn't have trouble?'

'No trouble—not for me. Here's the newspaper.'

I took it from her. 'Then what's the matter?'

'I think you'd better . . . you'd better read the paper.' She turned away.

I shook it open and saw a photograph on the front page, a life-size reproduction of my *sgian dubh*. Underneath, the black headline screamed: HAVE YOU SEEN THIS KNIFE?

The knife had been found embedded in the heart of a man sitting in a car parked in the driveway of a house in Laugarvatn. The man had been identified as a British tourist called John Case. The house and the Volkswagen in which Case had been found belonged to Gunnar Arnarsson who was absent, being in charge of a pony-trekking expedition. The house had been broken into and apparently searched. In the absence of Gunnar Arnarsson and his wife, Sigurlin Asgeirsdottir, it was impossible to tell if anything had been stolen. Both were expected to be contacted by the police.

The knife was so unusual in form that the police had requested the newspaper to publish a photograph of it. Anyone who had seen this knife or a similar knife was requested to call at his nearest police station. There was a boxed paragraph in which the knife was correctly identified as a Scottish *sgian dubh*, and after that the paragraph degenerated into pseudo-historical blather.

The police were also trying to find a grey Volvo registered in Reykjavik; anyone having seen it was requested to communicate with the police at once. The registration number was given.

I looked at Elin. 'It's a mess, isn't it?' I said quietly.

'It *is* the man you went to see at Geysir?'

'Yes.' I thought of how I had mistrusted Jack Case and left him unconscious near Kennikin's house. Perhaps he had not been untrustworthy at all because I had no illusions about who had killed him. Kennikin had the *sgian dubh* and Kennikin had the Volkswagen—and probably Kennikin had stumbled across Case in his search for me.

But why had Case been killed?

'This is dreadful,' said Elin. 'Another man killed.' Her voice was filled with despair.

'I didn't kill him,' I said baldly.

She picked up the paper. 'How did the police know about the Volvo?'

'Standard procedure,' I said. 'As soon as Case was identified the police would dig into whatever he'd been doing since he entered the country. They'd soon find he hired a car—and it wasn't the Volkswagen he was found in.'

I was glad the Volvo was tucked away out of sight in Valtýr's garage in Vik. 'When is Valtýr going back to Vik?' I asked.

'Tomorrow,' said Elin.

It seemed as though everything was closing in on me. Lee Nordlinger had given me a twenty-four hour ultimatum; it was too much to hope that Valtýr wouldn't check on the Volvo as soon as he got back to Vik—he might even go to the Reykjavik police if he felt certain it was the car they were searching for. And when the police laid hands on Sigurlin then the balloon would certainly go up—I couldn't see her keeping silent in the face of a corpse parked in her home.

169

Elin touched my arm. 'What are you going to do?'

'I don't know,' I said. 'Right now I just want to sit and think.'

I began to piece the fragments together and gradually they made some kind of sense which hinged around Kennikin's sudden switch of attitude after he had captured me. At first he had been all for extracting the gadget from me and he was looking forward with unwholesome delight to the operation. But then he lost interest in the gadget and announced that my death was the more important, and that was just after he had received a telephone call.

I ticked off the sequence of events. At Geysir I had told Case of my suspicions of Slade, and Case had agreed to pass them on to Taggart. No matter what happened Slade would then be thoroughly investigated. But I had seen Slade talking to Case just before Kennikin took me. Suppose that Case had aroused Slade's suspicions in some way? Slade was a clever man—a handler of men— and maybe Case had shown his hand.

What would Slade do? He would contact Kennikin to find if I had been captured. He would insist that his cover next to Taggart should remain unbroken at all costs and that this was more important than the gadget. He would say, 'Kill the bastard!' That was why Kennikin had switched.

And it would be just as important to kill Jack Case before he talked to Taggart.

I had played right into Slade's hands and left Case for Kennikin to find, and Kennikin had stabbed him with my knife. Kennikin had traced where the Volkswagen had come from and gone looking for me, and he had left the body of Case. Terrorist tactics.

It all tied together except for one loose end which worried me. Why, when I had been jumped at Geysir by Kennikin's mob, had Jack Case run out on me? He hadn't lifted a finger to help; he hadn't fired a shot in my defence even though he was armed. I knew Jack Case and that was very unlike him, and that, together with his apparent chumminess with Slade, had been the basis of my mistrust of him. It worried me very much.

But it was all past history and I had the future to face and decisions to make. I said, 'Did you check on Bjarni?'

Elin nodded listlessly. 'He's on the Reykjavik-Höfn run.

He'll be in Reykjavik this afternoon.'

'I want him over here,' I said. 'And you're to stick in this office until he comes. You're not to move out of it even for meals. You can have those sent up. And most emphatically you're not to go out into the concourse of the airport; there are too many eyes down there looking for you and me.'

'But I can't stay here forever,' she protested.

'Only until Bjarni comes. Then you can tell him anything you think fit—you can even tell him the truth. Then you're to tell him what he must do.'

She frowned. 'And that is?'

'He's got to get you on a plane and out of here, and he has to do it discreetly without going through normal channels. I don't care if he has to dress you up as a hostess and smuggle you abroad as one of the crew, but you mustn't go down into the concourse as an ordinary passenger.'

'But I don't think he could do that.'

'Christ!' I said. 'If he can smuggle in crates of Carlsberg from Greenland he can smuggle you out. Come to think of it, going to Greenland might not be such a bad idea; you could stay in Narsassuaq until all this blows over. Not even Slade, clever though he is, would think of looking there.'

'I don't want to go.'

'You're going,' I said. 'I want you from underfoot. If you think things have been rough for the last few days then compared to the next twenty-four hours they'll seem like an idyllic holiday. I want you out of it, Elin, and, by God, you'll obey me.'

'So you think I'm useless,' she said bitterly.

'No, I don't; and you've proved it during the last few days. Everything you've done in that time has been against your better judgment, but you've stuck by me. You've been shot and you've been shot at, but you still helped out.'

'Because I love you,' she said.

'I know—and I love you. That's why I want you out of here. I don't want you killed.'

'And what about you?' she demanded.

'I'm different,' I said. 'I'm a professional. I know what to do and how to do it; you don't.'

'Case was a professional too—and he's dead. So was Graham, or whatever his name really was. And that man,

Volkov, was hurt at Geysir—and he was a professional. You said yourself that the only people hurt so far have been the professionals. I don't want you hurt, Alan.'

'I also said that no innocent bystanders have been hurt,' I said. 'You're an innocent bystander—and I want to keep it that way.'

I had to do something to impress the gravity of the situation upon her. I looked around the room to check its emptiness, then quickly took off my jacket and unslung Case's shoulder holster complete with gun. I held it in my hand and said, 'Do you know how to use this?'

Her eyes dilated. 'No!'

I pointed out the slide. 'If you pull this back a bullet is injected into the breech. You push over this lever, the safety catch, then you point it and pull the trigger. Every time you pull a bullet comes out, up to a maximum of eight. Got that?'

'I think so.'

'Repeat it.'

'I pull back the top of the gun, push over the safety catch and pull the trigger.'

'That's it. It would be better if you squeezed the trigger but this is no time for finesse.' I put the pistol back into the holster and pressed it into her reluctant hands. 'If anyone tries to make you do anything you don't want to do just point the gun and start shooting. You might not hit anyone but you'll cause some grey hairs.'

The one thing that scares a professional is a gun in the hands of an amateur. If another professional is shooting at you at least you know he's accurate and you have a chance of out-manœuvring him. An amateur can kill you by accident.

I said, 'Go into the loo and put on the holster under your jacket. When you come back I'll be gone.'

She accepted the finality of the situation along with the pistol. 'Where are you going?'

'The worm is turning,' I said. 'I'm tired of running, so I'm going hunting. Wish me luck.'

She came close to me and kissed me gently and there were unshed tears in her eyes and the gun in its holster was iron-hard between us. I patted her bottom and said, 'Get along with you,' and watched as she turned and walked away. When the door closed behind her I also left.

CHAPTER NINE

I

Nordlinger's Chevrolet was too long, too wide and too soft-sprung and I wouldn't have given a thank you for it in the *Óbyggdir*, but it was just what I needed to get into Reykjavik fast along the International Highway which is the only good bit of paved road in Iceland. I did the twenty-five miles to Hafnarfjördur at 80 mph and cursed when I was slowed down by the heavy traffic building up around Kopavogur. I had an appointment at midday in the souvenir shop of the Nordri Travel Agency and I didn't want to miss it.

The Nordri Travel Agency was in Hafnarstraeti. I parked the car in a side street near Naust and walked down the hill towards the centre of town. I had no intention at all of going into Nordri; why would I when Nordlinger had the gadget tucked away in his safe? I came into Hafnar-straeti and ducked into a bookshop opposite Nordri. There was a café above the shop with a flight of stairs leading directly to it so that one could read over a cup of coffee. I bought a newspaper as cover and went upstairs.

It was still before the midday rush so I got a seat at the window and ordered pancakes and coffee. I spread open the paper and then glanced through the window at the crowded street below and found that, as I had planned, I had a good view of the travel agency which was on the other side of the street. The thin gauze curtains didn't obstruct my view but made it impossible for anyone to recognize me from the street.

The street was fairly busy. The tourist season had begun and the first hardy travellers had already started to ran-sack the souvenir shops and carry home their loot. Camera-hung and map in hand they were easy to spot, yet I inspected every one of them because the man I was looking for would probably find it convenient to be mis-taken for a tourist.

This was a long shot based on the fact that everywhere I had gone in Iceland the opposition had shown up. I had followed instructions on arrival and gone the long way around to Reykjavik and Lindholm had been there. I had gone to earth in Asbyrgi and Graham had pitched up out of the blue. True, that was because of the radio bug planted on the Land-Rover, but it had happened. Fleet had lain in wait and had shot up the Land-Rover in a deliberate ambush, the purpose of which was still a mystery. Yet he, like Lindholm, had known *where* to wait. Kennikin had jumped me at Geysir and I'd got away from that awkward situation by the thickness of a gnat's whisker.

And now I was expected to call at the Nordri Travel Agency. It was a thin chance but it seemed logical to suppose that if past form was anything to go on then the place would be staked out. So I took a more than ordinary interest in those below who window-shopped assiduously, and I hoped that if Kennikin was laying for me I'd be able to recognize his man. He couldn't have brought a whole army to Iceland and, one way or another, I'd already laid eyes on a lot of his men.

Even so, it was a full half-hour before I spotted him, and that was because I was looking at him from an unfamiliar angle—from above. It is very hard to forget a face first seen past the cross hairs of a telescopic sight, yet it was only when he lifted his head that I recognized one of the men who had been with Kennikin on the other side of the Tungnaá River.

He was pottering about and looking into the window of the shop next to Nordri and appeared to be the perfect tourist complete with camera, street map and sheaf of picture postcards. I whistled up the waitress and paid my bill so that I could make a quick getaway, but reserved the table for a little longer by ordering another coffee.

He wouldn't be alone on a job like this and so I was interested in his relationship with the passers-by. As the minutes ticked on he appeared to become increasingly restless and consulted his watch frequently and, at one o'clock exactly, he made a decisive move. He lifted his hand and beckoned, and another man came into my line of sight and crossed the street towards him.

I gulped my coffee and went downstairs to lurk at the newspaper counter while observing my friends through the glass doors of the bookshop. They had been joined by a third man whom I recognized immediately—none other than Ilyich who had unwittingly provided me with the butane bomb. They nattered for a while and then Ilyich stuck out his arm and tapped his wrist-watch, shrugging expressively. They all set off up the street towards Posthusstraeti and I followed.

From the bit of action with the watch it seemed that they not only knew the rendezvous I was supposed to keep but the time I was to keep it. They had pulled off duty at one o'clock like workmen clocking off the job. It wouldn't have surprised me overmuch if they knew the passwords as well.

At the corner of Posthusstraeti two of them got into a parked car and drove away, but Ilyich turned smartly to the right across the street and headed at a quick clip towards the Hotel Borg, into which he disappeared like a rabbit diving into its hole. I hesitated for a moment and then drifted in after him.

He didn't stop to collect a key at the desk but went immediately upstairs to the second floor, with me on his heels. He walked along a corridor and knocked at a door, so I did a smart about-turn and went downstairs again where I sat at a table in the lounge from where I had a good view of the foyer. This meant another obligatory cup of coffee with which I was already awash, but that's the penalty of a trailing job. I spread my newspaper at arm's length and waited for Ilyich to appear again.

He wasn't away long—a matter of ten minutes—and when he came back I knew triumphantly that all my suspicions had been correct and that everything I had done in Iceland was justified. He came downstairs talking to someone—and that someone was Slade!

They came through the lounge on their way to the dining-room and Slade passed my table no farther away than six feet. It was to be expected that he would wait in his room for a report, positive or negative, and then head for the fleshpots. I shifted in my chair and watched where they would sit and, during the brouhaha of the seating ceremony. I left quickly and walked into the foyer and out of sight.

Two minutes later I was on the second floor and tapping at the same door Ilyich had knocked on, hoping that no one would answer. No one did and so, by a bit of trickery involving a plastic sheet from my wallet, I went inside.

That was something I had learned at school—the Department had trained me well.

I wasn't stupid enough to search Slade's luggage. If he was as smart as I thought he would have gimmicked it so that he could tell at a glance whether a suitcase had been opened. Standard operating procedure when on a job, and Slade had a double advantage—he'd been trained by both sides. But I did inspect the door of his wardrobe, checking to see if there were any fine hairs stuck down with dabs of saliva which would come free if the door was opened. There was nothing, so I opened the door, stepped inside, and settled down to wait in the darkness.

I waited a long time. That I expected, having seen the way Slade gourmandized, yet I wondered how he would take to the Icelandic cuisine which is idiosyncratic, to say the least. It takes an Icelander to appreciate *hakarl*—raw shark meat buried in sand for several months—or pickled whale blubber.

It was quarter to three when he came back and by that time my own stomach was protesting at the lack of attention; it had had plenty of coffee but very little solid food. Ilyich was with him and it came as no surprise that Slade spoke Russian like a native. Hell, he probably *was* a Russian, as had been Gordon Lonsdale, another of his stripe.

Ilyich said, 'Then there's nothing until tomorrow?'

'Not unless Vaslav comes up with something,' said Slade.

'I think it's a mistake,' said Ilyich. 'I don't think Stewartsen will go near the travel agency. Anyway, are we sure of that information?'

'We're sure,' said Slade shortly. 'And he'll be there within the next four days. We've all underestimated Stewart.'

I smiled in the darkness. It was nice to have an unsolicited testimonial. I missed what he said next, but Ilyich said, 'Of course, we don't do anything about the package he will carry. We let him get rid of it in the agency and then we follow him until we get him alone.'

'And then?'

'We kill him,' said Ilyich unemotionally.

'Yes,' said Slade. 'But there must be no body found. There has been too much publicity already; Kennikin was mad to have left the body of Case where he did.' There was a short silence and then he said musingly, 'I wonder what Stewart did with Philips?'

To this rhetorical question Ilyich made no answer, and Slade said, 'All right; you and the others are to be at the Nordri Agency at eleven tomorrow. As soon as you spot Stewart I must be notified by telephone immediately. Is that understood?'

'You will be informed,' said Ilyich. I heard the door open. 'Where is Kennikin?' he asked.

'What Kennikin does is no concern of yours,' said Slade sharply. 'You may go.'

The door slammed.

I waited and heard a rustle as of paper and a creak followed by a metallic click. I eased open the wardrobe door a crack and looked into the room with one eye. Slade was seated in an armchair with a newspaper on his knee and was applying a light to a fat cigar. He got the end glowing to his satisfaction and looked about for an ashtray. There was one on the dressing-table so he got up and moved his chair so that the ashtray would be conveniently to hand.

It was convenient for me too, because the action of moving the chair had turned his back to me. I took my pen from my pocket and opened the wardrobe door very slowly. The room was small and it only needed two steps to get behind him. I made no sound and it must have been the fractional change of the quality of the light in the room that made him begin to turn his head. I rammed the end of the pen in the roll of fat at the back of his neck and said, 'Stop right there or you'll be minus a head.'

Slade froze, and I snaked my other hand over his shoulder to the inside of his jacket where I found a pistol in a shoulder holster. Everyone seemed to be wearing guns these days and I was becoming exceptionally competent at disarming people.

'I don't want a move from you,' I said, and stepped back. I worked the action of the pistol to make sure it was loaded, and threw off the safety catch. 'Stand up.'

Obediently he stood, still clutching the newspaper. I said, 'Walk straight forward to the wall in front of you lean against it with your hands high and your arms held wide.'

I stepped back and watched him critically as he went

through the evolution. He knew what I was going to do; this was the safest way of searching a man. Being Slade, he tried to pull a fast one, so I said, 'Pull your feet out from the wall and lean harder.' That meant he would be off-balance to begin with if he tried anything—just enough to give me that extra fraction of a second that is all-important.

He shuffled his feet backwards and I saw the telltale quiver of his wrists as they took up the weight of his body. Then I searched him swiftly, tossing the contents of his pockets on to the bed. He carried no other weapon, unless you consider a hypodermic syringe a weapon, which I was inclined to do when I saw the wallet of ampoules that went with it. Green on the left for a six-hour certain knock-out; red on the right for death in thirty seconds equally certainly.

'Now bend your knees and come down that wall very slowly.' His knees sagged and I brought him into the position in which I had had Fleet—belly down and arms wide stretched. It would take a better man than Slade to jump me from that position; Fleet might have done it had I not rammed his rifle in the small of his back, but Slade was not as young and he had a bigger paunch.

He lay with his head on one side, his right cheek pressed to the carpet and his left eye glaring at me malevolently. He spoke for the first time. 'How do you know I won't have visitors this afternoon?'

'You're right to worry about that,' I said. 'If anyone comes through that door you're dead.' I smiled at him. 'It would be a pity if it was a chamber-maid, then you'd be dead for nothing.'

He said, 'What the devil do you think you're doing, Stewart? Have you gone out of your mind? I think you must have—I told Taggart so and he agrees with me. Now, put away that gun and let me stand up.'

'I must say you try,' I said admiringly. 'Nevertheless, if you move a muscle towards getting up I'll shoot you dead.' His only reaction to that was a rapid blinking of the one eye I could see.

Presently he said, 'You'll hang for this, Stewart. Treason is still a capital crime.'

'A pity,' I said. 'At least *you* won't hang, because what you are doing isn't treason—merely espionage. I don't think spies are hanged—not in peacetime, anyway. It would be treason if you were English, but you're not; you're a Russian.'

'You're out of your mind,' he said disgustedly. 'Me—a Russian!'

'You're as English as Gordon Lonsdale was Canadian.'

'Oh, wait until Taggart gets hold of you,' he said. 'He'll put you through the wringer.'

I said, 'What are you doing consorting with the opposition, Slade?'

He actually managed to summon up enough synthetic indignation to splutter. 'Dammit!' he said. 'It's my job. You did the same; you were Kennikin's right-hand man at one time. I'm just following orders—which is more than you are doing.'

'That's interesting,' I said. 'Your orders are very curious. Tell me more.'

'I'll tell nothing to a traitor,' he said virtuously.

I must say that at that moment I admired Slade for the first time. Lying in a most undignified position and with a gun at his head he wasn't giving an inch and was prepared to fight to the end. I had been in his position myself when I had got next to Kennikin in Sweden and I knew how nerve-abrading a life it was—never knowing from one day to another whether one's cover had been blown. Here he was, still trying to convince me that he was as pure as the latest brand of detergent, and I knew that if I let up on him for a fraction of a second so that he could get the upper hand I would be a dead man in that very second.

I said, 'Come off it, Slade. I heard you tell Ilyich to kill me. Don't tell me that was an order passed on from Taggart.'

'Yes,' he said, without the flicker of an eyelash. 'He thinks you've gone over. I can't say I blame him, either, considering the way you've been behaving.'

I almost burst out laughing at his effrontery. 'By God, but you're good!' I said. 'You lie there with your face hanging out and tell me that. I suppose Taggart also told you to ask the Russkies to do the job for him.'

Slade's exposed cheek wrinkled up into the rictus of a half smile. 'It's been done before,' he said. 'You killed Jimmy Birkby.'

Involuntarily my finger tightened on the trigger, and I had to take a deep breath before I relaxed. I tried to keep my voice even as I said, 'You've never been nearer death than now, Slade. You shouldn't have mentioned Birkby —that's a sore point. Let's not have any more comedy. You're finished and you know it quite well. You're going to tell me a lot of things I'm interested in, and you're going to tell it fast, so speak up.'

'You can go to hell,' he said sullenly.

'You're a great deal nearer hell right now,' I said. 'Let me put it this way. Personally, I don't give a damn if you're English or Russian, a spy or a traitor. I don't give a damn for patriotism either; I've got past that. With me this is purely personal—on a man-to-man basis, if you like. The foundation for most murders. Elin was nearly killed in Asbyrgi on your instruction, and I've just heard you tell a man to kill me. If I kill you right now it will be self-defence.'

Slade lifted his head a little and turned it so that he could look at me straight. 'But you won't do it,' he said.

'No?'

'No,' he said with certainty. 'I told you before—you're too soft-centred. You might kill me under different circumstances; if I were running away, for instance, or if we were shooting at each other. But you won't kill me while I'm lying here. You're an English gentleman.' He made it sound like a swearword.

'I wouldn't bet on it,' I said. 'Maybe Scots are different.'

'Not enough to matter,' he said indifferently.

I watched him look into the muzzle of the pistol without a quiver and I had to give the devil his due. Slade knew men and he had my measure as far as killing was concerned. He also knew that if he came for me I would shoot to kill. He was safe enough while lying defenceless, but action was another thing.

He smiled. 'You've already proved it. You shot Yuri in the leg—why not in the heart? By Kennikin's account you were shooting accurately enough across that river to have given every man a free shave without benefit of barber. You could have killed Yuri—but you didn't!'

'Maybe I wasn't feeling in the mood at the time. I killed Gregor.'

'In the heat of action. Your death or his. Any man can make that kind of decision.'

I had the uneasy feeling that the initiative was passing from me and I had to get it back. I said, 'You can't talk if you're dead—and you're going to talk. Let's begin by you telling me about the electronic gadget—what is it?'

He looked at me contemptuously and tightened his lips.

I glanced at the pistol I held. God knows why Slade carried it because it was a .32—a popgun just as heavy to lug about as a modern .38 but without the stopping power. But maybe he was a crack shot and could hit his target every time so that wouldn't matter much. What would matter when shooting in a populous place was that the muzzle blast was much less and so were the decibels. You could probably fire it in a busy street and no one would take much notice.

I looked him in the eye and then put a bullet into the back of his right hand. He jerked his hand convulsively and a strangled cry broke from his lips as the muzzle of the pistol centred on his head again. The noise of the shot hadn't even rattled the windows.

I said, 'I may not shoot to kill you but I'll cut you to pieces bit by bit if you don't behave yourself. I hear from Kennikin that I'm a fair hand at surgical operations too. There are worse things than getting yourself shot dead. Ask Kennikin some time.'

Blood oozed from the back of his hand and stained the carpet, but he lay still, staring at the gun in my hand. His tongue came out and licked dry lips. 'You bloody bastard!' he whispered.

The telephone rang.

We stared at each other for the time it took to ring four times. I walked around him, keeping clear of his legs, and I picked up the telephone whole and entire complete with base. I dumped it next to him, and said, 'You'll answer that, and you'll remember two things—I want to hear *both* ends of the conversation and that there are plenty of other parts of your fat anatomy. I can work on.' I jerked the gun. 'Pick it up.'

Awkwardly he picked up the handset with his left hand. 'Yes?'

I jerked the gun again and he held up the telephone so that I could hear the scratchy voice. 'This is Kennikin.'

'Be natural,' I whispered.

Slade licked his lips. 'What is it?' he asked hoarsely.

'What's the matter with your voice?' said Kennikin.

Slade grunted, his eye on the gun I held. 'I have a cold. What do you want?'

'I've got the girl.'

There was a silence and I could feel my heart thumping in my chest. Slade went pale as he watched my finger curl around the trigger and slowly take up the pressure. I breathed, 'Where from?'

Slade coughed nervously. 'Where did you find her?'

'At Keflavik Airport—hiding in the Icelandair office. We know her brother is a pilot, and I had the idea of looking for her there. We took her out without any trouble.'

That made it true. 'Where now?' I whispered into Slade's ear and put the gun to the nape of his neck.

He asked the question, and Kennikin said, 'In the usual place. Where can I expect you?'

'You'll be right out.' I pressed the muzzle harder into his fat and felt him shiver.

'I'll leave straight away,' said Slade, and I quickly cut the contact by depressing the telephone bar.

I jumped back fast in case he tried to start something, but he just lay there gazing at the telephone. I felt like screaming, but there was no time for that. I said, 'Slade, you were wrong—I *can* kill you. You know that now, don't you?'

For the first time I detected fear in him. His fat jowl developed a tremor and his lower lip shook so that he looked like a fat boy about to burst into tears. I said, 'Where's the usual place?'

He looked at me with hatred and said nothing. I was in a quandary; if I killed him I would have got nothing out of him, yet I didn't want to damage him too much because I wanted him fit to walk the streets of Reykjavik without occasioning undue attention. Still, he didn't know my problem, so I said, 'You'll still be alive when I've finished with you, but you'll wish you weren't.'

I put a bullet just by his left ear and he jerked violently. Again the noise of the shot was very small and I think he must have doctored the cartridges by taking out some of the powder to reduce the bang. It's an old trick when you want to shoot without drawing notice to yourself and, if done carefully and the gun is fired at not too great a range, the bullet is still lethal. It's much better than using a silencer which is a much overrated contraption and dangerous to the user. A silencer is good for one quiet shot—after that the steel wool packing becomes compressed and the back pressure builds up so high that the user is in danger of blowing off his own hand.

I said, 'I'm a good shot, but not all that good. I intended to put that bullet exactly where I did, but only you know the accuracy of this popgun. I'm inclined to think it throws to the left a bit, so if I try to clip your right ear you stand a fair chance of stopping one in the skull.'

I shifted the gun a little and took aim. He broke—his nerve gone completely. 'For God's sake, stop!' This sort of Russian roulette wasn't to his taste.

I sighted on his right ear. 'Where's the usual place?'

There was a sheen of sweat on his face. 'At Thingvalla-vatn.'

'The house to which I was taken after Geysir?'

'That's it.'

'You'd better be right,' I said. 'Because I have no time to waste in chasing about Southern Iceland.' I lowered the gun and Slade's expression changed to one of relief. 'Don't start cheering yet,' I advised. 'I hope you don't think I'm going to leave you here.'

I went to the stand at the bottom of the bed and flipped open the lid of his suitcase. I took out a clean shirt and tossed it to him. 'Rip some strips off that and bind up your hand. Stay on the floor and don't get any smart ideas such as throwing it at me.'

While he tore up the shirt awkwardly I rummaged about in the suitcase and came up with two clips of .32 ammunition. I dropped them into my pocket then went to the wardrobe and took out Slade's topcoat, the pockets of which I had already searched. 'Stand up facing the wall and put that on.'

I watched him carefully, alert for any trickery. I knew that if I made one false step he would take full advantage of it. A man who could worm his way into the heart of British Intelligence hadn't done it by being stupid. The mistakes he had made weren't such as would normally have discommoded him and he had done his damnedest to rectify them by eliminating me. If I weren't careful he could still pull it off.

I picked up his passport and his wallet from the bed and pocketed them, then threw his hat across the room so that it landed at his feet. 'We're going for a walk. You'll keep that bandaged hand in your coat pocket and you'll behave like the English gentleman you're not. One wrong move from you and I'll shoot you dead and take my chances, and I don't care if it has to be in the middle of Hafnar-straeti. I hope you realize that Kennikin did exactly the wrong thing in taking Elin.'

He spoke to the wall. 'Back in Scotland I warned you about that. I told you not to let her get involved.'

'Very thoughtful of you,' I said. 'But if anything happens to her you're a dead man. You may have been right about my inability to kill before, but I hope you're not counting on it now because one of Elin's nail parings is of more importance to me than the whole of your lousy body. You'd better believe that, Slade. I protect my own.'

I saw him shudder. 'I believe you,' he said quietly.

I really think he did. He knew he had encountered something more primitive than patriotism or the loyalty of a man to his group. This was much more fundamental, and while I might not have killed him because he was a spy I would kill without mercy any man who got between me and Elin.

'All right,' I said. 'Pick up your hat and let's go.'

I escorted him into the corridor, made him lock the door, and then took the key. I had one of his jackets draped over my arm to hide the gun, and I walked one pace behind him and to the right. We left the hotel and walked the streets of Reykjavik to where I had left Nordlinger's car. 'You'll get behind the wheel,' I said.

We performed an intricate ballet in getting into the car. While unlocking it and getting him settled I had to make sure that never for one moment could he take advantage and, at the same time, our antics had to look reasonably normal to the passers-by. At last I managed to get him seated and myself behind him in the rear.

'Now you'll drive,' I said.

'But my hand,' he protested. 'I don't think I can.'

'You'll do it. I don't care how much it hurts—but you'll do it. And never for one moment will you exceed thirty miles an hour. You won't even think of putting the car into a ditch or crashing it in any other way. And the reason you won't think of such things is because of this.' I touched his neck with the cold metal of the pistol.

'This will be behind you all the way. Just imagine that you're a prisoner and I'm one of Stalin's boys back in the bad old days. The approved method of execution was an unexpected bullet in the back of the head, wasn't it? But if you do anything naughty this is one bullet you can expect for sure. Now, take off, and do it carefully—my trigger finger is allergic to sudden jerks.'

I didn't have to tell him where to drive. He drove along the Tjarnargata with the duck-strewn waters of the Tjörnin lake on our left, past the University of Iceland, and so into Miklabraut and out of town. He drove in silence and once on the open road he obeyed orders and never let the speed drift above thirty miles an hour. I think this was less out of sheer obedience and more because changing gears hurt his hand.

After a while he said, 'What do you think you're going to gain by this, Stewart?'

I didn't answer him: I was busy turning out the contents of his wallet. There wasn't anything in it of interest —no plans for the latest guided missile or laser death ray that a master spy and double agent might have been expected to carry. I transferred the thick sheaf of currency and the credit cards to my own wallet; I could use the money—I was out of pocket on this operation—and should he escape he would find the shortage of funds a serious disability.

He tried again. 'Kennikin won't believe anything you say, you know. He won't be bluffed.'

'He'd better be,' I said. 'For your sake. But there'll be no bluff.'

'Your work will be cut out convincing Kennikin of that,' said Slade.

'You'd better not push that one too hard,' I said coldly. 'I might convince him by taking him your right hand— the one with the ring on the middle finger.'

That shut him up for a while and he concentrated on his driving. The Chevrolet bounced and rolled on its soft springing as the wheels went over the corrugated dips and rises of the road. We would have got a smoother ride had we travelled faster but, as it was, we climbed up and down every minuscule hill and valley. I dared not order him to speed up, much as I wanted to get to Elin; 30 mph gave me the leeway both to shoot Slade and get out safely should he deliberately run the car off the road.

Presently I said, 'I notice you've given up your protestations of innocence.'

'You wouldn't believe me no matter what I told you—

so why should I try?'

He had a point there. 'I'd just like to clear up a few things, though. How did you know I was going to meet Jack Case at Geysir?'

'When you make a call on open radio to London you can expect people to listen,' he said.

'You listened and you told Kennikin.'

He half-turned his head. 'How do you know it wasn't Kennikin who listened?'

'Keep your eyes on the road,' I said sharply.

'All right, Stewart,' he said. 'There's no point in fencing. I admit it all. You've been right all along the line. Not that it will do you much good; you'll never get out of Iceland.' He coughed. 'What gave me away?'

'Calvados,' I said.

'Calvados!' he repeated. He was at a loss. 'What the hell is that supposed to mean?'

'You knew that Kennikin drinks Calvados. No one else did, except me.'

'I see! That's why you asked Taggart about Kennikin's drinking habits. I was wondering about that.' His shoulders seemed to sag and he said musingly, 'It's the little things. You cover every possibility; you train for years, you get yourself a new identity—a new personality—and you think you're safe.' He shook his head slowly. 'And then it's a little thing like a bottle of Calvados that you saw a man drink years before. But surely that wasn't enough?'

'It started me thinking. There was something else, of course. Lindholm—who was conveniently in the right place at the right time—but that could have been coincidence. I didn't get around to suspecting you until you sent in Philips at Asbyrgi—that was a bad mistake. You ought to have sent Kennikin.'

'He wasn't immediately available.' Slade clicked his tongue. 'I ought to have gone in myself.'

I laughed gently. 'Then you'd be where Philips is now. Count your blessings, Slade.' I looked ahead through the windscreen and then leaned forward to check the position of his hands and feet to make sure he wasn't conning me—lulling me with conversation. 'I suppose there was a man called Slade once.'

'A boy,' said Slade. 'We found him in Finland during the war. He was fifteen then. His parents were British and had been killed in a bombing raid by our Stormoviks.

We took him into our care, and later there was a substitution—me.'

'Something like Gordon Lonsdale,' I said. 'I'm surprised you survived inspection in the turmoil after the Lonsdale case.'

'So am I,' he said bleakly.

'What happened to young Slade?'

'Siberia perhaps. But I don't think so.'

I didn't think so either. Young Master Slade would have been interrogated to a fare-thee-well and then dispatched to some anonymous hole in the ground.

I said, 'What's your name—the real Russian one, I mean?'

He laughed. 'You know, I've quite forgotten. I've been Slade for the better part of my life, for so long that my early life in Russia seems like something I once dreamed.'

'Come off it! No one forgets his name.'

'I think of myself as Slade,' he said. 'I think we'll stick to it.'

I watched his hand hovering over the button of the glove compartment. 'You'd better stick to driving,' I said drily. 'There's only one thing you'll find in the glove compartment and that's a quick, sweet death.'

Without hurrying too much he withdrew his hand and put it back where it belonged—on the wheel. I could see that his first fright was over and he was regaining confidence. More than ever I would have to watch him.

An hour after leaving Reykjavik we arrived at the turn-off to Lake Thingvallavatn and Kennikin's house. Watching Slade, I saw that he was about to ignore it, so I said, 'No funny business—you know the way.'

He hastily applied the brakes and swung off to the right and we bumped over a road that was even worse. As near as I could remember from the night drive I had taken with Kennikin along this same road the house was about five miles from the turn-off. I leaned forward and kept one eye on the odometer, one eye on the countryside to see if I could recognize anything, and the other on Slade. Having three eyes would be useful to a man in my position, but I had to make do with two.

I spotted the house in the distance or, at least, what I thought was the house, although I could not be entirely sure since I had previously only seen it in darkness. I laid the gun against Slade's neck. 'You drive past it,' I said. 'You don't speed up and you don't slow down—you just keep the same pace until I tell you to stop.'

As we went past the drive that led to the house I glanced sideways at it. It was about four hundred yards off the road and I was certain this was the place. I was absolutely sure when I spotted the lava flow ahead and to the left where I had encountered Jack Case. I tapped Slade's shoulder. 'In a little while you'll see a level place to the left where they've been scooping out lava for road-making. Pull in there.'

I kicked the side of the door and swore loudly as though I had hurt myself. All I wanted to do was to make noise enough to cover the sound of my taking the clip out of the pistol and working the slide to eject the round in the breech. That would leave me unarmed and it wouldn't do for Slade to know it. I was going to hit him very hard with the butt of the pistol and to do that with a loaded gun was to ask for a self-inflicted gut shot.

He pulled off the road and even before the car rolled to a halt I let him have it, striking sideways in a chopping motion at the base of his neck. He moaned and fell forward and his feet slipped on the foot pedals. For one alarming moment the car bucked and lurched but then the engine stalled and it came to a standstill.

I dipped into my pocket and put a full clip into the pistol and jacked a round into the breech before I examined Slade at close quarters. What I had done to him was in a fair way towards breaking his neck, but I found that his head lolled forward because I had merely knocked him cold. I made sure of that by taking the hand which had a bullet hole through the palm and squeezing it hard. He didn't move a muscle.

I suppose I should have killed him. The knowledge in his head culled from his years in the Department was a deadly danger, and my duty as a member of the Department was to see that the knowledge was permanently erased. I didn't even think of it. I needed Slade as one hostage to set against another and I had no intention of exchanging dead hostages.

E. M. Forster once said that if he had to choose between betraying his country and betraying his friend then he hoped he would have the guts to betray his country. Elin was more than my friend—she was my life—and if the only way I could get her was to give up Slade then I would do so.

I got out of the car and opened the boot. The sacking which was wrapped around the rifles came in handy for tearing into strips and binding Slade hand and foot. I then put him in the boot and slammed the lid on him.

The Remington carbine I had taken from Philips I hid in a crevice of the lava close to the car, together with its ammunition, but Fleet's piece of light artillery I slung over my shoulder as I walked towards the house. It was very likely that I would need it.

II

The last time I had been anywhere near this house it had been dark and I had plunged away not knowing the lie of the land. Now, in the daylight, I found I could get to within a hundred yards of the front door without breaking cover. The ground was broken and three big lava flows had bled across the landscape during some long-gone eruption and had hardened and solidified while in full spate to form jagged ridges full of crevices and holes. The ever-present moss grew thickly, covering the spiky lava with soft vegetable cushions. The going was slow and it took me half an hour to get as close to the house as I dared.

I lay on the moss and studied it. It was Kennikin's hide-away, all right, because a window was broken in the room where I had been kept captive and there were no curtains at that window. The last time I had seen them they had been going up in flames.

A car stood outside the front door and I noticed that the air over the bonnet shimmered a little. That meant that the engine was still hot and someone had just arrived. Although my own journey had been slow, Kennikin had farther to travel from Keflavik—there was a good chance that whatever he intended to do to Elin to get her to tell him where I was had not yet begun. And, possibly, he would wait for Slade before starting. For Elin's sake I hoped so.

I loosened a big slab of moss and pushed Fleet's rifle out of sight beneath it, together with the ammunition for it. I had brought it along as insurance—it was useless in the boot of the car, anyway. It would also be useless in the house too, but now it was tucked away within a fast sprint of the front door.

I withdrew and began a painful retreat across the lava beds until I reached the driveway, and the walk towards the house was the longest distance I have ever walked, psychologically if not physically. I felt as a condemned man probably feels on his way to the scaffold. I was walking quite openly to the front door of the house and if anyone was keeping a watch I hoped his curiosity would get the better of him enough to ask *why* I was coming instead of shooting me down ten paces from the threshold.

I crunched my way to the car and casually put out my hand. I had been right; the engine was still warm. There was a flicker of movement at one of the windows so I carried on and walked to the door. I pressed the bell-push and heard the genteel peal of chimes inside the house.

Nothing happened for a while but soon I heard boots crushing loose lava chips and I looked sideways to see a man coming around the corner of the house to my left. I looked to the right and saw another, and both were strolling towards me with intent expressions on their faces.

I smiled at them and jabbed the bell-push again and the chimes jingled softly just as in any house in the stock-broker belt. The door opened and Kennikin stood there. He had a gun in his hand.

'I'm the man from the Prudential,' I said pleasantly. 'How's your insurance, Vaslav?'

CHAPTER TEN

I

Kennikin looked at me expressionlessly and his pistol was pointing at my heart. 'Why shouldn't I kill you now?'

'That's what I've come to talk to you about,' I said. 'It really would be a bad thing if you did.' I heard footsteps behind me as the outflankers moved in for the kill. 'Aren't you interested to know why I'm here? Why I walked up and rang the bell?'

'It did cross my mind that it was strange,' said Kennikin. 'You won't object to a slight search?'

'Not at all,' I said, and felt heavy hands on me. They took Slade's gun and the clips of ammunition. 'This is most inhospitable,' I said. 'Keeping me at the door like this. Besides, what will the neighbours think?'

'We have no neighbours for some considerable distance,' said Kennikin, and looked at me with a puzzled expression. 'You're very cool, Stewartsen. I think you must have gone mad. But come in.'

'Thanks,' I said, and followed him into the familiar room where we had talked before. I glanced at the burnt patches on the carpet and said, 'Heard any good explosions lately?'

'That was very clever,' said Kennikin. He waved his pistol. 'Sit down in the same chair. You will observe there is no fire.' He sat down opposite me. 'Before you say anything I must tell you that we have the girl, Elin Ragnarsdottir.'

I stretched out my legs. 'What on earth do you want her for?'

'We were going to use her to get you,' he said. 'But it seems that is no longer necessary.'

'Then there's no need to keep her. You can let her go.'

Kennikin smiled. 'You're really funny, Stewartsen. It's a pity the English music hall has gone into eclipse; you could make quite a good living as a comedian.'

'You ought to hear me wow them in the working men's clubs,' I said. 'That should appeal to a good Marxist such

191

as yourself. But I wasn't being funny, Vaslav. She is going to walk out of this house unharmed, and you are going to let her go.'

He narrowed his eyes. 'You'd better elaborate on that.'

'I walked in here on my own feet,' I said. 'You don't think I'd do that unless I could trump your ace. You see, I've got Slade. Tit for tat.' His eyes opened wide, and I said, 'But I forget—you don't know a man called Slade. You told me so yourself, and we all know that Vaslav Viktorovich Kennikin is an honourable man who doesn't stoop to fibs.'

'Even supposing I did know this Slade, what proof have you of this? Your word?'

I put my hand to my breast pocket and stopped sharply as his gun came up. 'Not to worry,' I said. 'But do you mind if I dig for a bit of evidence?' I took the jerk of the gun as assent and extracted Slade's passport from my pocket and tossed it to him.

He stooped to where it had fallen and picked it up, flicking open the pages with one hand. He studied the photograph intently and then snapped the passport closed. 'This is a passport made out in the name of Slade. It is no proof of possession of the man. To hold a passport is meaningless; I, myself, possess many passports in many names. In any case, I know of no Slade. The name means nothing to me.'

I laughed. 'It's so unlike you to talk to yourself. I know for a fact that not two hours ago you spoke to a non-existent man at the Hotel Borg in Reykjavik. This is what you said, and this is what he said.' I recited the telephone conversation verbatim. 'Of course, I could have been wrong about what Slade said, since he doesn't exist.'

Kennikin's face tightened. 'You have dangerous knowledge.'

'I have more than that—I have Slade. I had him even as he spoke to you. My gun was in his fat neck.'

'And where is he now?'

'For Christ's sake, Vaslav!' I said. 'You're talking to me, not some muscle-bound, half-witted ape like Ilyich.'

He shrugged. 'I had to try.'

I grinned. 'You'll have to do a bloody sight better than that. I can tell you this, though—if you go looking for him, by the time you find him he'll be cold meat. Those are my orders.'

Kennikin pulled at his lower lip, thinking deeply. 'Orders you have received—or orders you have given?'

I leaned forward, preparing to lie heroically. 'Let's make no mistake about this, Vaslav. Those are orders I've given. If you, or anyone who even smells like you, gets close to Slade, then Slade dies. Those are the orders I have given and they'll be followed, you may depend upon it.'

At all costs I had to drive out of his mind any suggestion that I had been given orders. The only man who could give me orders was Taggart, and if he had issued such orders then the game was blown as far as Slade was concerned. If Kennikin believed for one minute that Taggart had penetrated Slade's cover then he'd cut his losses by killing me and Elin, and get the hell back to Russia as fast as he could move.

I buttressed the argument by saying, 'I may be rapped over the knuckles when the Department catches up with me, but until then those orders stand—Slade will catch a bullet if you go near him.'

Kennikin smiled grimly. 'And who will pull the trigger? You've said you're working independently of Taggart, and I know you're alone.'

I said, 'Don't sell the Icelanders short, Vaslav. I know them very well and I have a lot of friends here—and so does Elin Ragnarsdottir. They don't like what you've been doing in their country and they don't like one of their own being put in danger.'

I leaned back in the chair. 'Look at it this way. This is a biggish country with a small population. Everyone knows everyone else. Damn it, everyone is related to everyone else if you push it back far enough—and the Icelanders do. I've never known a people, other than the Scots, who are so genealogically minded. So everyone cares what happens to Elin Ragnarsdottir. This isn't a mass society where people don't even know their next-door neighbour. By taking Elin Ragnarsdottir you've laid yourself wide open.'

Kennikin looked thoughtful. I hoped I had given him something to chew over for a long time, but I didn't have the time so I pushed him. 'I want the girl down here in this room—intact and in one piece. If any harm has come to her then you've made a big mistake.'

He regarded me keenly, and said, 'It's obvious you haven't informed the Icelandic authorities. If you had, the police would be here.'

'You're so right,' I said. 'I haven't, and for good reasons. Firstly, it would cause an international brouhaha, which would be lamentable. Secondly, and more important, all the authorities could do would be to deport Slade. My friends are tougher-minded—they'll kill him if necessary.' I leaned over and jabbed Kennikin in the knee with a hard forefinger. 'And *then* they'll blow you off to the police, and you'll be up to your neck in uniforms and diplomats.' I straightened up. 'I want to see the girl, and I want to see her now.'

'You talk straight,' he said. 'But, then, you always did . . .' His voice tailed away, and he whispered, '. . . until you betrayed me.'

'I don't see you have any options,' I said. 'And just to screw it tighter I'll tell you something else. There's a time limit. If my friends don't get the word from Elin's own lips within three hours then Slade gets what's coming to him.'

I could see Kennikin visibly debating it with himself. He had to make a choice and a damned thin one it was. He said, 'Your Icelandic friends—do they know who Slade is?'

'You mean that he's in Russian Intelligence?' I said. 'Or in British Intelligence, for that matter?' I shook my head. 'All they know is that he's a hostage for Elin. I didn't tell them anything else about him. They think you're a crowd of gangsters and, by God, they're not far wrong!'

That clinched it. He thought he had me isolated, that only Elin and I knew the truth that Slade was a double agent. Given that premise which, God knows, was true enough since my Icelandic friends were pure invention, then he could do a deal. He was faced with the choice of sacrificing Slade, who had been laboriously built up over many years into a superlative Trojan Horse, for a no-account Icelandic girl. The choice was obvious. He would be no worse off than before he had taken her, and his weasel mind would already be working out ways of double-crossing me.

He sighed. 'At least you can see the girl.' He signalled to the man standing behind him who left the room.

I said, 'You've really queered this one, Vaslav. I don't think Bakayev is going to be too cheerful about it. It'll be Siberia for sure this time, if not worse—and all because of Slade. It's funny, isn't it? You spent four years in

Ashkhabad because of Slade, and now what do you have to look forward to?'

There was a look almost of pain in his eyes. 'Is it true —what you said about Slade and Sweden?'

'Yes, Vaslav,' I said. 'It was Slade who cut the ground from under you there.'

He shook his head irritably. 'There's one thing I don't understand,' he said. 'You say you are willing to trade Slade for the girl. Why should a member of your Department do that?'

'I swear to God you don't listen to me. I'm not a member of the Department—I quit four years ago.'

He pondered. 'Even so—where are your loyalties?'

'My loyalties are my business.' I said curtly.

'The world well lost for a woman?' he asked mockingly.

'I've been cured of that way of thinking—and you were the doctor.'

'Now, you're not still harping on that,' I said. 'If you hadn't jumped when you should have fallen flat you'd have been killed decently.'

The door opened and Elin came in under escort. I was about to get up but subsided again as Kennikin lifted his pistol warningly. 'Hello, Elin; you'll forgive me if I don't get up.'

Her face was pale and when she saw me it acquired a bleak look. 'You, too!'

'I'm here by choice,' I said. 'Are you all right? They didn't hurt you?'

'Not more than was necessary,' she said. 'Just some arm twisting.' She put her hand to her wounded shoulder.

I smiled at her. 'I've come to collect you. We'll be leaving soon.'

'That's a matter of opinion,' said Kennikin. 'How do you expect to do it?'

'In the normal way—through the front door,' I said.

'Just like that!' Kennikin smiled. 'And what about Slade?'

'He'll be returned unharmed.'

'My dear Alan! Not long ago you accused *me* of being unrealistic. You'll have to work out a better exchange mechanism than that.'

I grinned at him. 'I didn't think you'd fall for it but, as you said, one has to try. I daresay we can work out something equitable.'

'Such as?'

I rubbed my chin. 'Such as sending Elin away. She'll contact our friends and then you exchange Slade for me. The arrangements can be made by telephone.'

'That sounds logical,' said Kennikin. 'But I'm not sure it's reasonable. Two for one, Alan?'

'It's a pity you can't ask Slade if it's reasonable or not.'

'You make a point.' Kennikin moved restlessly. He was trying to find the flaws in it. 'We get Slade back unharmed?'

I smiled apologetically. 'Er . . . well—not entirely. He's been leaking blood through a hole, but it's minor and not fatal. And he might have a headache—but why should you care about that?'

'Why, indeed?' Kennikin stood up. 'I think I can go along with you on this, but I'd like to think about it a little more.'

'Not for too long,' I said warningly. 'Remember the time limit.'

Elin said, 'Have you really captured Slade?'

I stared at her, trying to pass an unspoken message and hoping to God she didn't let me down. 'Yes. Our friends are taking care of him—Valtýr is in charge.'

'Valtýr!' She nodded. 'He's big enough to handle anyone.'

I switched my eyes back to Kennikin and tried not to show too much relief at the way Elin had played that one. 'Buck it up, Vaslav,' I said. 'Time's a-wasting.'

He came to the decision quickly. 'Very well, it shall be as you say.' He looked at his watch. 'I also shall lay down a time limit. If there is no telephone call within two hours then you will die regardless of what may happen to Slade.' He swung on his heel and faced Elin. 'Remember that, Elin Ragnarsdottir.'

'There's just one thing,' I said. 'I'll have to talk to Elin before she leaves to tell her where to find Valtýr. She doesn't know, you see.'

'Then you'll do it in my hearing.'

I gave him a pained look. 'Don't be an idiot. You'd know as much as I do, and that might be unwise. You'd know where Slade is and you might be tempted to get him out. And where would that leave me?' I stood up cautiously. 'I talk to Elin privately or not at all. It's another stalemate, Vaslav, but I'm sure you understand that I have to look out for my own skin.'

'Yes, I'm sure you do,' he said contemptuously. He gestured with the gun. 'You may talk in the corner, but I remain in the room.'

'Fair enough.' I jerked my head at Elin and we walked over to the corner. I stood with my back to Kennikin because, for all I knew, lip-reading in six languages might have been one of his minor talents.

Elin whispered, 'Have you really got Slade?'

'Yes, but Valtýr doesn't know about it, nor anyone else. I've sold Kennikin a credible story but not the true one. But I *have* got Slade.'

She put her hand to my chest. 'They took me so quickly,' she said. 'I couldn't do anything. I was afraid, Alan.'

'That doesn't matter now,' I said. 'You're going to walk out of here, and this is how you do it. You . . .'

'But you are staying.' There was pain in her eyes.

'I won't be staying long if you do as I say. Listen carefully. You'll leave here, walk up to the road and turn left. About half a mile along you'll come to a big dreamboat of an American car. Whatever you do, don't open the boot. Just climb into it and go like a bat out of hell to Keflavik. Got that?'

She nodded. 'What do I do there?'

'See Lee Nordlinger. Raise a storm and demand to see a CIA agent. Lee and everyone else will deny having such an article on the premises, but if you persist long enough they'll dig one up. You can tell Lee it's about the gadget he tested; that might help. Tell the CIA man the whole story and then tell him to open the boot of the car.' I grinned wryly. 'But don't call it the boot or he won't know what the hell you're talking about. Call it the trunk.'

'So what is in there?'

'Slade,' I said.

She stared at me. 'He's *here*! Just outside this house!'

'It was all I could do at short notice,' I said. 'I had to act quickly.'

'But what about you?'

'Get the CIA man to make the telephone call. You'll have just on two hours from the time you leave here, so you'll have to be bloody persuasive. If you can't do it in time or if the CIA man won't be persuaded, then make the call yourself and spin Kennikin some kind of yarn.

Set up a meeting to exchange me for Slade. It might be phoney but it will buy me time.'

'What if the Americans won't believe me?'

'Tell them you know about Fleet and McCarthy. Tell them you'll give it to the Icelandic newspapers. That should produce some kind of reaction. Oh, yes; and tell them that all your friends know exactly where you are —just as insurance.' I was trying to cover all the possibilities.

She closed her eyes briefly as she memorized her instructions. When she opened them, she asked, 'Is Slade alive?'

'Of course he is. I told Kennikin the truth about that. He's damaged but alive.'

She said, 'I was thinking the CIA might believe Slade rather than me. He might even know the CIA people at Keflavik.'

'I know,' I said. 'But we have to take that risk. That's why you must tell the whole story before producing Slade. Get your oar in first. If you pitch it really hot they won't just let him walk out.'

She didn't seem too happy about that, and neither was I, but it was the best we could do. I said, 'Make it fast, but not so fast that you have an accident in that car.' I put my hand under her chin and tipped her head up. 'Everything will be all right. You'll see.'

She blinked rapidly. 'There's something you must know. That gun you gave me—I've still got it.'

It was my turn to blink. *'What!'*

'They didn't search me. I have it on me—in the holster under this anorak.'

I looked at her. Her anorak was admittedly very loose and no sign of the gun was visible. Someone had slipped. It was unlikely that an Icelandic girl would be armed, but even so it was bad workmanship. No wonder Kennikin went off pop periodically about the quality of his team. Elin said, 'Can I pass it to you safely?'

'Not a chance,' I said regretfully, aware of Kennikin at my back. He would be watching like a hawk, and a Smith & Wesson .38 pistol isn't something you can palm in your hand like a playing-card. 'You'd better keep it. Who knows, you might need it.'

I put my hand on her good shoulder and drew her towards me. Her lips were cold and hard under mine, and she trembled slightly. I drew back my head, and said, 'You'd better go,' and turned to face Kennikin.

'Very touching,' he said.

'There's one thing,' I said. 'Your time limit is too short. Two hours isn't enough.'

'It will have to do,' he said uncompromisingly.

'Be reasonable, Vaslav. She has to drive through Reykjavik. The day is getting on and by the time she reaches town it will be just after five o'clock—right in the middle of the rush hour when people are going home. You wouldn't want to lose Slade because of a traffic jam, would you?'

'You're not thinking of Slade,' he said. 'You're thinking of yourself. You're thinking of the bullet in your head.'

'Maybe I am, but you'd better think of Slade because if I'm dead then so is he.'

He nodded shortly. 'Three hours,' he said. 'Not a minute more.'

Kennikin was a logical man and susceptible to a reasoned argument. I had won Elin another hour in which to convince the top brass at Keflavik. 'She goes alone,' I said. 'No one follows her.'

'That is understood.'

'Then give her the telephone number she is to call. It would be a pity if she walked out without it.'

Kennikin took out a notebook and scribbled down a number, then ripped out the sheet and gave it to her. 'No tricks,' he said. 'Especially no police. If there is an undue number of strangers around here, then he dies. You'd better know that I mean it.'

In a colourless voice she said, 'I understand. There will be no tricks.'

She looked at me and there was something in her eyes that made my heart turn over, and then Kennikin took her by the elbow and led her to the door. A minute later I saw her through the window, walking away from the house up towards the road.

Kennikin returned. 'We'll put you somewhere safe,' he said, and jerked his head at the man who held a gun on me. I was led upstairs and into an empty room. Kennikin surveyed the bare walls and shook his head sadly. 'They did these things so much better in medieval times,' he said.

I was in no mood for light conversation but I played

along with him. I had the idea that, perhaps, he wouldn't mind at all if Slade didn't show up. Then he would be able to get down to the delightful business of killing me—slowly. And I had put the idea into his mind; I had tried to antagonize him towards Slade. Maybe it hadn't been such a good idea.

I said, 'What do you mean?'

'In those days they built with stone.' He strode to the window and thumped on the exterior wall. It responded with a wooden hollowness. 'This place is built like an eggshell.'

That was true enough. The chalets around Thingvallavatn are holiday cottages, not designed for permanent occupancy. A timber frame, skinned on each side with thin planking and with a filling of foamed polystyrene for insulation, finished off with a skim of plaster maybe half an inch thick on the interior to make the place look nice. The nearest thing to a permanent tent.

Kennikin went to the opposite wall and rapped on it with his knuckles. It echoed even more hollowly. 'You could get through this partition wall in fifteen minutes, using nothing more than your hands. Therefore this man will stay in here with you.'

'You needn't worry,' I said sourly. 'I'm not Superman.'

'You don't need to be Superman to tangle the feet of the incompetents I've been given for this operation,' said Kennikin, equally sourly. 'You've proved that already. But I think the orders I give now will penetrate the thickest head.' He turned to the man with the gun. 'Stewartsen will sit in that corner. You will stand in front of the door. Do you understand?'

'Yes.'

'If he moves, shoot him. Understand?'

'Yes.'

'If he speaks, shoot him. Understand?'

'Yes.'

'If he does anything else at all, shoot him. Understand?'

'Yes,' said the man with the gun stolidly.

Kennikin's orders weren't leaving much room for manœuvre. He said musingly, 'Now, have I forgotten anything? Oh, yes! You said that Slade had a hole in him—right?'

'Not much of one,' I said. 'Just in the hand.'

He nodded, and said to the guard, 'When you shoot him,

don't kill him. Shoot him in the stomach.' He turned on his heel and left the room. The door slammed behind him.

II

I looked at the guard and the guard looked right back at me. His gun was trained on my belly and didn't deviate a hair's-breadth. With his other hand he gestured wordlessly towards the corner, so I backed into it until my shoulder-blades touched and then bent my knees until I was squatting on my heels.

He looked at me expressionlessly. 'Sit!' he said economically.

I sat. He wasn't going to be bluffed. He stood in front of the door about fifteen feet away and he was impregnable. He had the look of a man who would obey orders to the letter; if I rushed him I'd catch a bullet and I couldn't even con him into doing anything stupid. It was going to be a long three hours.

Kennikin had been right. Left alone in the room and I'd have gone through the partition wall, and it wouldn't have taken me any fifteen minutes either. True, once through the wall I would still be in the house, but I'd be in an unexpected place, and surprise, as all generals know, wins battles. Now that Elin was gone I was prepared to do anything to get away, and Kennikin knew it.

I looked at the window. All I could see was a small patch of blue sky and a fleecy cloud drifting by. The time oozed on, maybe half an hour, and I heard the crunch of tyres as a car drew up outside. I didn't know how many men had been in the house when I arrived, although I knew of three, but now there were more and the odds had lengthened.

I turned my wrist slowly and drew back the cuff of my jacket to look at my watch, hoping to God that the guard would not interpret that as an unnatural action. I kept my eye on him and he looked back at me blankly, so I lowered my gaze to see what time it was. It had not been half an hour—only fifteen minutes had passed. It was going to be a longer three hours than I had thought.

Five minutes after that there was a tap at the door and I heard the raised voice of Kennikin. 'I'm coming in.'

The guard stepped to one side as the door opened. Kennikin came in and said, 'I see you've been a good boy.' There was something in the way he said it that made me uneasy. He was too damned cheerful.

'I'd like to go over what you told me again,' he said. 'According to you, Slade is being kept with friends of yours—Icelandic friends—I think you said. These friends will kill him unless they get you in exchange. I think that was the argument. Am I right?'

'Yes,' I said.

He smiled. 'Your girl-friend is waiting downstairs. Shall we join her?' He waved largely. 'You can get up—you will not be shot.'

I stood up stiffly, and wondered what the hell had gone wrong. I was escorted downstairs and found Elin standing in front of the empty fireplace flanked by Ilyich. Her face was pale as she whispered, 'I'm sorry, Alan.'

'You must think I'm stupid,' said Kennikin. 'You don't suppose I thought you had walked here? You tramped up to the front door and immediately I wondered where you had left your car. You had to have a car because this is no country for walking, so I sent a man to look for it even before you rang the bell.'

'You always were logical,' I said.

He was enjoying himself. 'And what do you suppose my man found? A large American car complete with key. He had not been there long when this young lady came up in a very great hurry, so he brought her—and the car—back here. You see, he was unaware of the agreement we had reached. We can't blame him for that, can we?'

'Of course not,' I said flatly. *But had he opened the boot? 'I don't see that this makes any difference.'*

'No, you wouldn't. But my man had standing orders. He knew we were looking for a small package containing electronic equipment, and so he searched the car. He didn't find the package.'

Kennikin stopped and looked at me expectantly. He was really relishing this. I said, 'Do you mind if I sit down? And for God's sake, give me a cigarette—I've run out.'

'My dear Alan—but of course,' he said solicitously. 'Take your usual chair.' He produced his cigarette case and carefully lit my cigarette. 'Mr Slade is very angry with you. He doesn't like you at all.'

'Where is he?'

'In the kitchen having his hand bound up. You're a very good diagnostician, Alan; he *does* have a headache.'

My stomach felt as though it had a ball of lead in it. I drew on the cigarette, and said, 'All right; where do we go from here?'

'We carry on from where we left off the night we came here from Geysir. Nothing has changed.'

He was wrong—Elin was here. I said, 'So now you shoot me.'

'Perhaps. Slade wants to talk to you first.' He looked up. 'Ah, here he is.'

Slade looked bad. His face was grey and he staggered slightly as he walked in. When he came closer I saw that his eyes had a curiously unfocused appearance and I guessed he was still suffering from concussion. Someone had bound up his hand neatly with clean gauze bandages, but his clothes were rumpled and stained and his hair stood on end. As he was a man who usually cared very much for outward appearances, I guessed he was probably very disturbed.

I was right, and I found out how much he was disturbed pretty damned quick.

He walked up and looked down at me, and gestured with his left hand. 'Pick him up and take him over there—to the wall.'

I was grabbed before I could move. Someone put a hammer lock on me from behind and I was dragged from the chair and hustled across the room. As I was slammed against the wall, Slade said, 'Where's my gun?'

Kennikin shrugged. 'How should I know?'

'You must have taken it from Stewart.'

'Oh, that one.' Kennikin pulled it from his pocket. 'Is this it?'

Slade took the pistol and walked over to me. 'Hold his right hand against the wall,' he said, and held up his bandaged hand before my eyes. 'You did that, Stewart, so you know what's going to happen now.'

A hard hand pinned my wrist to the wall and Slade raised his gun. I had just sense enough and time enough to stop making a fist and to spread my fingers so he wouldn't shoot through them before he pulled the trigger and I took the bullet in the palm of my hand. Curiously enough, after the first stabbing shock it didn't hurt.

All I felt was a dead numbness from shoulder to finger-tip. It would hurt soon enough as the shock wore off, but it didn't hurt then.

My head swam and I heard Elin scream, but the cry seemed to come from a long way away. When I opened my eyes I saw Slade looking at me unsmilingly. He said curtly, 'Take him back to his chair.' It had been a purely vindictive act of revenge and now it was over and he was back to business as usual.

I was dumped back into the chair and I raised my head to see Elin leaning against the chimney piece with tears streaming down her face. Then Slade moved between us and I lost sight of her.

'You know too much, Stewart,' he said. 'So you must die—you know that.'

'I know you'll do your best,' I said dully. I now knew why Slade had cracked in the hotel room because the same thing was happening to me. I found I couldn't string two consecutive thoughts together to make sense and I had a blinding headache. The penetration of a bullet into flesh has that effect.

Slade said, 'Who knows about me—apart from the girl?'

'No one,' I said. 'What about the girl?'

He shrugged. 'You'll be buried in the same grave.' He turned to Kennikin. 'He might be telling the truth. He's been on the run and he hasn't had a chance to let anyone know.'

'He might have written a letter,' said Kennikin doubtfully.

'That's a risk I'll take. I don't think Taggart has any suspicions. He might be annoyed because I've dropped out of sight but that will be all. I'll be a good boy and take the next plane back to London.' He lifted his wounded hand and grinned tightly at Kennikin. 'And I'll blame this on you. I've been wounded trying to save this fool.' He reached out and kicked my leg.

'What about the electronic equipment?'

'What about it?'

Kennikin took out his cigarette case and selected a cigarette. 'It seems a pity not to complete the operation as planned. Stewartsen knows where it is, and I can get the information from him.'

'So you could,' said Slade thoughtfully. He looked down at me. 'Where is it, Stewart?'

'It's where you won't find it.'

'That car wasn't searched,' said Kennikin. 'When you were found in the boot everything else was forgotten.' He snapped out orders and his two men left the room. 'If it's in the car they'll find it.'

'I don't think it's in the car,' said Slade.

'I didn't think *you* were in the car,' said Kennikin waspishly. 'I wouldn't be at all surprised to find it there.'

'You may be right,' said Slade. His voice indicated that he didn't think so. He bent over me. 'You're going to die, Stewart—you may depend upon it. But there are many ways of dying. Tell us where the package is and you'll die cleanly and quickly. If not, I'll let Kennikin work on you.'

I kept my mouth firmly shut because I knew that if I opened it he would see the tremulous lower lip that is a sign of fear.

He stood aside. 'Very well. You can have him, Kennikin.' A vindictive note entered his voice. 'The best way to do it is to shoot him to pieces slowly. He threatened to do it to me.'

Kennikin stepped in front of me, gun in hand. 'Well, Alan; we come to the end of the road, you and I. Where is the radar equipment?'

Even then when facing his gun I noted that new piece of information. *Radar equipment*. I screwed up my face and managed a smile. 'Got another cigarette, Vaslav?'

No answering smile crossed his face. His eyes were bleak and his mouth was set in grim lines. He had the face of an executioner. 'There is no time for tradition— we are done with that foolery.'

I looked past him. Elin was still standing there, forgotten, and there was an expression of desperation on her face. But her hand was inside her anorak and coming out slowly, grasping something. The jolting realization came that she still had the gun!

That was enough to bring me to my senses fast. When all hope is gone and there is nothing more to look forward to than death one sinks into a morass of fatalism as I had done. But given the faintest hint that all is not lost and then a man can act—and my action now was to talk and talk fast.

I turned my head and spoke to Slade. I had to attract his attention to me so he would not even think of looking at Elin. 'Can't you stop him?' I pleaded.

'You can stop him. All you have to do is to tell him what we want to know.'

'I don't know about that,' I said. 'I'll still die, anyway.'

'But easier,' said Slade. 'Quickly and without pain.'

I looked back to Kennikin and, over his shoulder, saw that Elin had now withdrawn the pistol and it was in plain sight. She was fiddling with it and I hoped to God she remembered the sequence of actions she would have to go through before it would fire.

'Vaslav,' I said. 'You wouldn't do this to an old mate. Not you.'

His pistol centred on my belly and then dropped lower. 'You don't have to guess to know where I'm going to put the first bullet,' he said. His voice was deadly quiet. 'I'm just following Slade's orders—and my own inclination.'

'Tell us,' urged Slade, leaning forward.

I heard the snap of metal as Elin pulled back the slide of the pistol. So did Kennikin and he began to turn. Elin held the pistol in both hands and at arm's length and as Kennikin began his turn she fired and kept on firing.

I distinctly heard the impact of the first bullet in Kennikin's back. His hand tightened convulsively around his gun and it exploded in my face, the bullet burying itself in the arm of the chair next to my elbow. By then I was moving. I dived for Slade head first and rammed him in the paunch. My skull was harder than his belly and the breath came out of him in a great whoosh and he folded up and lay gasping on the floor.

I rolled over, aware that Elin was still shooting and that bullets were still whanging across the room. 'Stop!' I yelled.

I scooped up Slade's popgun and came up under Elin's elbow, grabbing her by the wrist. 'For Christ's sake, stop!'

I think she had shot off the whole magazine. The opposite wall was pock-marked and Kennikin lay in front of the chair in which I had been sitting. He lay face upwards gazing sightlessly at the ceiling. Elin had hit him twice more which was hardly surprising, considering she had been shooting at a range of less than six feet. Come to think of it, I was fortunate she hadn't put a bullet into me. There was a ragged red spot dead centre in Kennikin's forehead to prove he'd had the vitality to turn around and try to shoot back. Another bullet had caught him in the angle of the jaw and had blown off the bottom half of his face.

He was very dead.

I didn't stop to ruminate about how in the midst of life we are in death. I dragged Elin behind me and headed for the door. The boys outside might be prepared for the odd shot, especially after Slade's little demonstration, but the barrage Elin had laid down would be a matter for urgent investigation and that had to be discouraged.

At the door I let go of Elin's wrist with my left hand and swapped it for the gun I held in my wounded right hand. With a hole through the palm I couldn't possibly use a gun in that hand, even one with as little recoil as Slade's gimmicked weapon. I'm a lousy pistol shot at the best of times and even worse when shooting left-handed; but one of the nice things about gun battles is that the man you're shooting at doesn't ask you for a proficiency certificate before he decides to duck.

I glanced at Elin. She was obviously in a state of shock. No one can shoot a man to death without undergoing an emotional upheaval—especially for the first time, especially when a civilian, especially when a woman. I put a snap in my voice. 'You'll do exactly as I say without question. You'll follow me and you'll run like hell without any hesitation.'

She choked back a rasping sob and nodded breathlessly, so I went out of the front door, and I went out shooting. Even as we went someone took a crack at us from the *inside* of the house and a bullet clipped the architrave by my ear. But I had no time to worry about that because the pair who had been sent to search the Chevrolet were heading right at me.

I shot at them and kept on squeezing the trigger and they vanished from view, diving right and left, and we belted between them. There was a tinkle of glass as somebody decided it was quicker to smash a window than to open it, and then the bullets came after us. I dropped Slade's gun and again grasped Elin by the wrist and forced her to follow me in a zigzag. Behind I could hear the heavy thud of boots as someone chased us.

Then Elin was hit. The bullet pushed her forward into a stumble but, as her knees gave in, I managed to put my arm around her to hold her up. We were then ten yards from the edge of the lava flow where I had hidden the rifle, and how we managed to travel that short distance I still don't know. Elin could still use her legs and that helped, and we scrambled up towards the top of the flow, over the mossy humps, until I stooped and laid my hands on the butt of Fleet's rifle.

I was jacking a round into the breech even before I got it clear of the moss. Elin fell to the ground as I swung around holding the rifle in my left hand. Even with a hole in the palm of my right hand I could still pull the trigger, and I did so to some effect.

The magazine contained the mixed load I had carefully put into it—steel-jacketed and soft-nosed bullets. The first one that came out was jacketed; it hit the leading pursuer in the chest and went through him as though he wasn't there. He came on for four more paces before his heart realized it had a hole in it and it was time to quit beating, then he dropped on the spot, nearly at my feet, with a surprised look on his face.

By that time I had shot the man just behind him, and that was spectacular. A man hit by a big, soft-nosed bullet driven by a magnum charge at a range of twenty yards isn't as much killed as disintegrated, and this character came apart at the seams. The bullet hit him in the sternum and then started to expand, lifted him clear off the ground and throwing him back four feet before lifting his spine out and splattering it over the landscape.

Everything was suddenly quiet. The deep-throated bellow of Fleet's gun had told everyone concerned that something new had been added to the game and they held their fire while they figured what was going on. I saw Slade by the door of the house, his hand clutched to his belly. I lifted the rifle again and took a shot at him, too quickly and with shaking hands. I missed him but gave him a hell of a fright because he ducked back in haste and there was no one to be seen.

Then a bullet nearly parted my hair and from the sound of the report I knew someone in the house also had a rifle. I got down off the skyline and reached for Elin. She was lying on the moss, her face screwed up with pain and trying to control her laboured breathing. Her hand was at her side and, when she withdrew it, it was red with blood.

I said, 'Does it hurt much?'

'When I breathe,' she said with a gasp. 'Only then.'

That was a bad sign, yet from the apparent position of the wound she had not been hit in the lung. There wasn't anything I could do there and then. For the next few minutes I'd be busy making sure we stayed alive for the next few minutes. There's not much point in worrying about dying of septicaemia in the next week when you might have your head blown off in the next thirty seconds.

I scrabbled for the box of ammunition, took the magazine from the rifle and reloaded it. The numbness had left my hand and it was now beginning to really hurt. Even the experimental flexing of my trigger finger sent a shock up my arm as though I'd grabbed a live wire, and I didn't know if I could do much more shooting. But it's surprising what you can do when you're pushed to it.

I poked my head carefully around a slab of lava and took a look at the house. Nobody and nothing moved. Just to my front lay the bodies of the men I had shot, one lying as though peacefully asleep and the other dreadfully shattered. In front of the house were the two cars; Kennikin's car appearing to be quite normal, but Nordlinger's Chevrolet was a bit of a wreck—they had ripped the seats out in the search for the package and the two nearer doors gaped open. I'd be running up quite a bill for damage to people's cars.

Those cars were less than a hundred yards away and, dearly as I wanted one of them, I knew it was hopeless to try. I also knew we couldn't leave on foot. Apart from the fact that walking on the lava beds is a sport which even the Icelanders aren't keen on, there was Elin to consider. I couldn't leave her, and if we made a break for it we'd be picked up within fifteen minutes.

Which left only one thing—since neither the Mounties nor the US Cavalry were going to show up on the horizon in the time-honoured manner, I had to fight a pitched battle against an unknown number of men securely ensconced in that house—and win.

I studied the house. Kennikin hadn't thought much of it as a prison. 'Built like an eggshell,' he had said. A couple of planks thick, a half-inch of plaster and a few inches of foamed polystyrene. Most people would regard a house as bullet-proof, but I laugh every time I see a Western film when the hero takes refuge in a clapboard hut and the baddies carefully shoot at the windows.

Even a 9 mm bullet from a Luger will penetrate nine

inches of pine board from very close range, and that's a pee-wee bullet compared to the .44 fired by the Western Colt. A few well placed shots would whittle away the shack from around our hero.

I looked at the house and wondered how those flimsy walls would stand up against the awesome power of Fleet's rifle. The soft-nosed bullets mightn't do much—they would tend to splash on impact; but the jacketed bullets should have a hell of a lot of penetrative power. It was time to find out, but first I had to locate that rifleman.

I withdrew my head and looked at Elin. She seemed better now that she had her breathing under control. 'How are you feeling now?'

'My God!' she said. 'How do you think I feel?'

I grinned at her with some relief. That spurt of temper showed she had improved. 'Everything will get better from now on.'

'They can hardly get worse.'

'Thanks for what you did in there,' I said. 'It was very brave.' Considering the attitude she had previously shown towards killing it was much more than that.

She shivered. 'It was horrible!' she said in a low voice. 'I shall see it as long as I live.'

'You won't,' I said with certainty. 'The mind has a knack of forgetting things like that. That's why wars are so long and frequent. But just so you don't have to do it again, you can do something for me.'

'If I can.'

I pointed to a lump of lava above her head. 'Can you push that over the edge when I tell you to? But don't expose yourself or you'll get a bullet.'

She looked up at the lava fragment. 'I'll try.'

'Don't do it until I say.' I pushed the rifle ahead of me and looked at the house. Still nothing moved and I wondered what Slade was up to. 'Right,' I said. 'Shove it over.'

There was a clatter as the rock moved and rolled down the slope of the lava flow. A rifle spoke and a bullet sang overhead and then another, better aimed, struck rock splinters a little to the left. Whoever was shooting knew his work, but I had him spotted. He was in an upstairs room and, by the shadowy movement I had seen, he was kneeling at the window with his head barely showing.

I took aim, not at the window but at the wall below it and a little to the left. I squeezed the trigger and, through the scope, saw the wood of the wall planking splinter under the impact. There was a faint cry and a shift of light at the window, and then I saw the man in full sight standing with his hands to his chest. He staggered backwards and vanished.

I had been right—Fleet's rifle would shoot through walls.

I shifted sights to the downstairs rooms and methodically put a bullet into the wall alongside every window on the ground floor, just where it would be natural for a man to wait in cover. Every time I squeezed the trigger the torn sinews in my hand shrieked in protest and I relieved my feelings by bellowing at the top of my voice.

I felt Elin tug at my trouser leg. 'What's the matter?' she said worriedly.

'Don't hinder the man on the job,' I said, and dropped back. I took out the empty magazine. 'Fill that up—it's difficult for me.' These periods with an empty gun worried me and I wished Fleet had had a spare clip. To be jumped on by somebody now would be slightly disastrous.

I saw that Elin was coping with reloading the clip with the right bullets and took a look at the house again. Someone was wailing over there and there were confused shouts. I had no doubt that the house was now filled with a considerable amount of consternation; the idea that a bullet can rip through a wall and hit the man behind it is highly unsettling for the man behind the wall.

'Here,' said Elin, and passed me the full clip of five rounds. I slotted it into the gun and poked it forward again just in time to see a man break from the front door and take cover behind the Chevrolet. I could see his feet through the telescopic sight. The door nearer to me was swung wide open and, with a mental apology to Lee Nordlinger, I put a bullet through the car and through the metal of the opposite door. The feet moved and the man came into view and I saw it was Ilyich. His hand was at his neck and blood spurted from between his fingers. He tottered a few more steps then dropped, rolled over and lay still.

It was becoming very difficult for me to work the bolt action with my ruined hand. I said to Elin, 'Can you crawl over here beside me?' She came up on my right side, and I said, 'Lift up that lever, pull it back, and ram it forward again. But keep your head down while you're doing it.'

She operated the bolt while I held the rifle firm with my

left hand, and she cried out as the empty brass case jumped out into her face unexpectedly. In this dot-and-carry-one manner I put another three rounds into selected points of the house where I thought they would do most damage. When Elin put the last round into the breech I took out the magazine and told her to fill it again.

I felt happier with that one round in the breech as an insurance against emergency, and I settled down to observe the house and to compile an interim report. I had killed three men for certain, wounded another—the rifleman upstairs—and possibly yet another, judging from the moaning still coming from the house. That was five—six if Kennikin was included. I doubted if there were many more, but that didn't mean that more weren't on their way—someone could have used a telephone.

I wondered if it was Slade who was doing the wailing. I knew his voice but it was difficult to tell from that inarticulate and unstructured sound. I glanced down at Elin. 'Hurry up!' I said.

She was fiddling desperately. 'One of them is stuck.'

'Do your best.' Again I peered around the rock in front of me and my eye was caught by a movement beyond the house. Someone was doing what they all ought to have done at the start of this action—getting away from the back of the house. It was only because of the sheer unexpectedness of the gun power I wielded that they hadn't done it before—and it was dangerous because I could be outflanked.

I racked up the telescopic sight to a greater magnification and looked at the distant figure. It was Slade and he was apparently unhurt except for his bandaged hand. He was leaping like a bloody chamois from hummock to hummock at a breakneck speed, his coat tails flying in the breeze and his arms outstretched to preserve his balance. By the convenient range-finder system built into the sight I estimated that he was a little under three hundred yards away and moving farther every second.

I took a deep breath and let it out slowly to steady myself and then took aim carefully. I was in considerable pain and had difficulty in controlling the wavering sight. Three times I almost squeezed off the shot and three times I relaxed the pressure on the trigger because the sight had drifted off target.

My father bought me my first rifle when I was twelve and, wisely, he chose a .22 single-shot. When a boy hunts rabbits and hares and knows that he has only one shot at his disposal then he also knows that the first and only shot must count, and no finer training in good shooting habits is possible. Now, again, I had only one shot available and I was back to my boyhood again, but it was no rabbit I was shooting—more like a tiger.

It was difficult to concentrate and I felt dizzy and a wash of greyness passed momentarily in front of my eyes. I blinked and it cleared away and Slade stood out preternaturally clearly in the glass. He had begun to move away at an angle and I led him in the sight and let him run into the aiming point. There was a roaring of blood in my ears and the dizziness came again.

My finger painfully took up the final pressure and the butt of the rifle jolted my shoulder and Slade's nemesis streaked towards him at 2,000 miles an hour. The distant figure jerked like a marionette with suddenly cut strings, toppled over, and disappeared from sight.

I rolled over as the roaring in my ears increased. The dizziness built up again and the recurring waves of greyness turned to black. I saw the sun glowing redly through the darkness and then I passed out, the last thing I heard being Elin's voice crying my name.

III

'It was a deception operation,' said Taggart.

I was lying in a hospital bed in Keflavik and there was a guard on the door, not so much to keep me imprisoned as to shield me from prying eyes. I was a potential *cause célèbre*, a *casus belli* and all those other foreign phrases which the leader writers of *The Times* trot out so readily in moments of crisis, and all attempts were being made to keep the situation potential and to prevent it from becoming actual. All parties concerned wanted the whole thing hushed up, and if the Icelandic government knew what had been going on they were damned careful not to say so.

Taggart was with another man, an American, whom he introduced as Arthur Ryan. I recognized Ryan; the last time I had seen him was through the sights of Fleet's rifle—he had been standing beside a helicopter on the other side of Búdarháls ridge.

It was the second time they had come to see me. The first time I was drowsy with dope and not very coherent, but still coherent enough to ask two questions.

'How's Elin?'

'She's all right,' said Taggart soothingly. 'In better shape than you are, as a matter of fact.' He told me that the bullet had been a ricochet and had the force taken out of it; it had just penetrated the flesh and lodged between two ribs. 'She's as right as rain,' said Taggart heartily.

I looked at him with dislike but I was too wobbly to push it then. I said, 'How did I get here?'

Taggart glanced at Ryan who took a pipe from his pocket, looked at it uncertainly, and then put it away again. He said in a slow voice, 'That's quite a girl you have, Mr Stewart.'

'What happened?'

'Well, when you passed out she didn't know what to do. She thought about it a bit, then she loaded the rifle and started to put even more holes into that house.'

I thought of Elin's attitude towards killing. 'Did she hit anyone?'

'I guess not,' said Ryan. 'I think you did most of the damage. She shot off all the ammunition—and there was a hell of a lot of it—and then she waited a while to see what would happen. Nothing did, so she stood up and walked into the house. I think that was a very brave thing to do, Mr Stewart.'

I thought so too.

Ryan said, 'She found the telephone and rang the Base, here, and contacted Commander Nordlinger. She was very forceful and got him really stirred up. He got even more stirred up when the phone went dead.' He grimaced. 'It's not surprising she fainted—that place was like a slaughterhouse. Five dead and two badly wounded.'

'Three wounded,' said Taggart. 'We found Slade afterwards.'

Soon after that they went away because I was in no shape for serious conversation, but twenty-four hours later they were back and Taggart was talking about deception.

'When can I see Elin?' I said abruptly.

'This afternoon,' said Taggart. 'She's quite all right, you know.'

I looked at him stonily. 'She'd better be.'

He gave an embarrassed cough. 'Don't you want to know what it was all about?'

'Yes,' I said. 'I would. I'd certainly like to know why the Department did its damnedest to get me killed.' I switched my eyes to Ryan. 'Even to the extent of getting the co-operation of the CIA.'

'As I say, it was a deception operation, a scheme cooked up by a couple of American scientists.' Taggart rubbed his chin. 'Have you ever considered *The Times* crossword puzzle?'

'For God's sake!' I said. 'No, I haven't.'

Taggart smiled. 'Let us assume it takes some maniacal genius eight hours to compile it; then it has to be set up in type, a block made, and printed in the paper. This involves quite a few people for a short time. Let us say that a total of forty man-hours is used up in this way—one working man-week.'

'So?'

'So consider the consumer end of the operation. Let's assume that ten thousand readers of *The Times* apply their brain power to working out the damned thing—and that each one takes an hour. That's ten thousand hours— five man-years. You see the implication? One man-week of labour has tied up five man-years of brain power in totally unproductive activity.' He looked at Ryan. 'I think you can take it from there.'

Ryan had a low, even voice. 'There are a lot of discoveries made in the physical sciences which have no immediate application, or any conceivable application, for that matter. One example is silly putty. Have you ever seen the stuff?'

'I've heard of it,' I said, wondering what they were getting at. 'I've never seen it.'

'It's funny stuff,' said Ryan. 'You can mould it like putty, but if you leave it alone it flows like water. Furthermore, if you hit it with a hammer it shatters like glass. You'd think that a substance with such diverse properties would be useful, but so far no one has thought of a single goddamn thing to do with it.'

'I believe they're now putting it into the middle of golf

balls,' offered Taggart.

'Yeah, a real technological breakthrough,' said Ryan ironically. 'In electronics there are quite a few effects like that. The electret, for example, carries a permanent electric charge like a magnet carries a magnetic field. That idea has been around for forty years and only now has a use been found for it. When the scientists began to kick the quantum theory around they came up with any number of odd effects—the tunnel diode, the Josephson effects, and a lot more—some of them usable and some not. A fair number of these discoveries have been made in laboratories working on defence contracts and they're not generally known.'

He shifted uneasily in his chair. 'Mind if I smoke?'

'Go ahead.'

Thankfully he took out his pipe and began to fill it. 'One scientist, a guy called Davies, surveyed the field and came up with an idea. As a scientist he's not very bright—certainly not of the first rank—but his idea was bright enough even if he merely intended it as a practical joke. He figured it was possible to put together an electronic package, utilizing a number of these mysterious but unusable effects, which would baffle a really big brain. In fact, he did put together such a package, and it took five top research men at Caltech six weeks to discover they'd been fooled.'

I began to get the drift. 'The deception operation.'

Ryan nodded. 'One of the men who was fooled was a Dr Atholl, and he saw possibilities in it. He wrote a letter to someone important and in due course the letter was passed on to us. One of the sentences in that letter is outstanding—Dr Atholl said this was a concrete example of the aphorism: "Any fool can ask a question which the wisest of men cannot answer." Davies's original package was relatively unsophisticated, but what we finally came up with was really complex—and it was designed to do precisely nothing.'

I thought of how Lee Nordlinger had been baffled and began to smile. 'What are you laughing at?' asked Taggart.

'Nothing much. Carry on.'

Taggart said, 'You see the principle, Stewart; it's just like *The Times* crossword. The design of the package didn't take much brain power—three scientists worked on it for a year. But if we could get it into the hands of the Russians it could tie up some of their finest minds for a hell of a long time. And the joke is that the problem was fundamentally unsolvable—there was no answer.'

'But we had a problem,' said Ryan. 'How to get it into the hands of the Russians. We started by feeding them a line by a series of carefully controlled leaks. The word was that American scientists had invented a new form of radar with fascinating properties. It had over the horizon capability, it showed a detailed picture and not just a green blob on a screen, and it wasn't affected by ground-level clutter and so could detect a low-level air attack. Any nation would sell its Premier's daughter into white slavery for a gadget like that, and the Russians began to bite.'

He pointed out of the window. 'You see that funny antenna out there—that's supposed to be it. The radar is supposed to be having a field test here at Keflavik, and we've had jet fighters skimming the waves for five hundred miles around here for the last six weeks just to add to the plausibility. And that's when we brought you British in.'

Taggart said, 'We sold another story to the Russians. Our American friends were keeping this radar to themselves and we were annoyed about it, so annoyed that we decided to have a look at it ourselves. In fact, one of our agents was sent to pinch a bit of it—an important bit.' He flicked a finger at me. 'You, of course.'

I swallowed. 'You mean I was intended to let the Russians have it!'

'That's right,' said Taggart blandly. 'And you were hand-picked. Slade pointed out—and I agreed—that you were probably not a good agent any more, but you had the advantage, for our purposes, of being known to the Russians as a good agent. Everything was set up and then you fooled everybody—us and the Russians. In fact, you were a devil of a lot better than anyone supposed.'

I felt the outrage beginning to build up, and said deliberately, 'You lousy, amoral son of a bitch! Why didn't you let me in on it? It would have saved a hell of a lot of trouble.'

He shook his head. 'It had to look authentic.'

'By God!' I said. 'You sold me—just as Bakayev sold

Kennikin in Sweden.' I grinned tightly. 'It must have complicated things when Slade turned out to be a *Russian* agent.'

Taggart glanced sideways at Ryan and appeared to be embarrassed. 'Our American friends are a bit acid about that. It wrecked the operation.' He sighed, and said plaintively, 'Counter-espionage work is the very devil. If we don't catch any spies then everybody is happy; but when we do our job and catch a spy then there's a scream to high heaven that we *haven't* been doing our job.'

'You break my heart,' I said. '*You* didn't catch Slade.'

He changed the subject quickly. 'Well, there Slade was —in charge of the operation.'

'Yeah,' said Ryan. 'In charge on *both* sides. What a sweet position to be in. He must have thought he couldn't lose.' He leaned forward. 'You see, once the Russians knew about the operation they decided they had no objection to grabbing the package if they thought it would fool us into believing they'd been fooled. A sort of double blind thing.'

I looked at Taggart with distaste. 'What a bastard you are,' I said. 'You must have known that Kennikin would do his best to kill me.'

'Oh, no!' he said earnestly. 'I didn't know about Kennikin. I think Bakayev must have realized they were wasting a good man so they decided to rehabilitate him by sending him on this operation. Perhaps Slade had something to do with it too.'

'He would!' I said bitterly. 'And because I was supposed to be a pushover they gave Kennikin a scratch team. He was complaining about that.' I looked up. 'And what about Jack Case?' I demanded.

Taggart didn't bat an eyelid. 'He had my orders to steer you to the Russians—that's why he didn't help you at Geysir. But when he talked to Slade you had already filled him up with your suspicions. He must have tried to pump Slade, but Slade is a clever man and realized it. That was the end of Case. Slade was doing everything to make sure his cover wasn't blown and in the end you were more important to him than that damned package.'

'Write off Jack Case,' I said sourly. 'He was a good man. When did you catch on to Slade?'

'I was slow there,' said Taggart. 'When you telephoned me I thought you'd done your nut, but after I sent Case here I found I couldn't get hold of Slade. He'd made himself unobtainable. That's against all procedure so I began to look into his record. When I found he'd been in Finland as a boy and that his parents were killed during the war I remembered that you'd mentioned Lonsdale and I wondered if the same trick hadn't been played.' He grimaced. 'But when Case's body was discovered with your pet knife in it, I didn't know what the hell to think.' He nudged Ryan. 'The knife.'

'What! Oh, yes—the knife.' Ryan put his hand into his breast pocket and produced the *sgian dubh*. 'We managed to get it from the police. I guess you'd like to have it back.' He held it out. 'It's a real cute knife; I like that jewel in the hilt.'

I took it. A Polynesian would have said it had *mana*; my own distant ancestors would have named it and called it *Weazand Slitter* or *Blood Drinker*, but to me it was just my grandfather's knife and his grandfather's before him. I laid it gently on the bedside table.

I said to Ryan. 'Your people shot at me. What was the idea of that?'

'Hell!' he said. 'You'd gone crazy and the whole operation was in danger. We were floating about in a chopper above that goddamn wilderness and we saw you, and we saw the Russians chasing you, and we reckoned you had a good chance of getting clear away. So we dropped a guy to stop you in your tracks. And we couldn't be too obvious about it because it had to look good to the Russians. We didn't know then that the whole operation was a bust, anyway.'

Neither Taggart nor Ryan had a grain of morality, but I didn't expect it. I said, 'You're lucky to be alive. The last time I saw you was through the sights of Fleet's rifle.'

'Jesus!' he said. 'I'm glad I didn't know it at the time. Talking about Fleet; you busted him up but good—but he'll survive.' He rubbed his nose. 'Fleet is sort of married to that rifle of his. He'd like to have it back.'

I shook my head. 'I've got to get something out of this deal. If Fleet is man enough let him come and get it.'

Ryan scowled. 'I'll doubt if he will. We've all had a bellyful of you.'

There was just one more thing. I said, 'So Slade is still alive.'

'Yes,' said Ryan. 'You shot him through the pelvis. If he ever walks again he'll need steel pins through his hips.'

'The only walking Slade will do for the next forty years is in the exercise yard of a prison,' said Taggart. He stood up. 'All this comes under the Official Secrets Act, Stewart. Everything has to be hushed. Slade is in England already; he was flown across yesterday in an American aircraft. He'll stand trial as soon as he comes out of hospital but the proceedings will be in camera. You'll keep quiet, and so will that girl-friend of yours. The sooner you turn her into a British subject the better I'll be pleased. I'd like to have some control over her.'

'Christ Almighty!' I said wearily. 'You can't even act as Cupid without an ulterior motive.'

Ryan joined Taggart at the door. He turned, and said, 'I think Sir David owes you a lot, Mr Stewart; a lot more than thanks, anyway—which I notice he hasn't proffered.' He looked at Taggart from the corner of his eye, and I thought there was no love lost between them.

Taggart was impervious; he didn't turn a hair. 'Oh, yes,' he said casually. 'I dare say something can be arranged. A medal, perhaps—if you like such trinkets.'

I found that my voice was shaking. 'All I want is your permanent absence,' I said. 'I'll keep quiet for just as long as you stay away from us, but if you, or any of the boys from the Department, come within shouting distance, I'll blow the gaff.'

'You won't be disturbed again,' he said, and they went out. A moment later he popped his head around the door. 'I'll send in some grapes.'

I V

Elin and I were flown to Scotland by courtesy of the CIA and the US Navy in a plane laid on by Ryan, and we were married in Glasgow by a special licence provided by Taggart. Both of us were still in bandages.

I took Elin back to the glen under Sgurr Dearg. She liked the scenery, especially the trees—the marvellous un-Icelandic trees—but she didn't think much of the cottage. It was small and it depressed her and I wasn't at all surprised; what suits a bachelor is not good for a married man.

'I'm not going to live in the big house,' I said. 'We'd rattle around in there and, anyway, I usually rent it to Americans who come for the shooting. We'll let a gillie have the cottage and we'll build our own house a little farther up the glen, by the river.'

So we did.

I still have Fleet's rifle. I don't keep it over the fireplace as a trophy but decently in the gun cabinet along with all the other working tools. I use it sometimes when the deer herd needs culling, but not often. It doesn't give the deer much of a chance.

Desmond Bagley

'Mr Bagley is nowadays incomparable.' *Sunday Times*

THE ENEMY 85p
THE FREEDOM TRAP 85p
THE GOLDEN KEEL 85p
HIGH CITADEL 85p
LANDSLIDE 85p
RUNNING BLIND 85p
THE SNOW TIGER 85p
THE SPOILERS 85p
THE TIGHTROPE MEN 85p
THE VIVERO LETTER 85p
WYATT'S HURRICANE 85p

Fontana Paperbacks

James Jones

FROM HERE TO ETERNITY £1.75
The world famous novel of the men of the U.S. Army
stationed at Pearl Harbour in the months immediately before
America's entry into World War II. 'One reads every page
persuaded that it is a remarkable, a very remarkable book
indeed.' *Listener*

A TOUCH OF DANGER 95p
A superb first thriller by the author of *From Here to Eternity*
set on an Aegean island where the sun and sex are corrupted by
violence and drugs. 'A believable private eye at last—not too
tough, not too lucky—and a plot built with loving care.'
John Braine, Daily Express

GO TO THE WIDOW-MAKER £1.50
A superb novel about the war between the sexes, set in the
world of rich men and those who cater to them. In Jones's
tale of dangerous living, love is for men and women are for
sex. 'Jones is the Hemingway of our time . . . There is savage
poetry in his descriptions of spear-fishing and treasure-
hunting.' *Spectator*

THE MERRY MONTH OF MAY £1.00
Paris in the spring of 1968: students on the rampage and their
effect on a wealthy American family living in Paris. 'Very
gripping . . . a novel of our time which takes the reader into
the heart of the Revolution. The atmosphere is splendidly
conveyed.' *Financial Times*

Fontana Paperbacks

Fontana Paperbacks

Fontana is a leading paperback publisher of fiction and non-fiction, with authors ranging from Alistair MacLean, Agatha Christie and Desmond Bagley to Solzhenitsyn and Pasternak, from Gerald Durrell and Joy Adamson to the famous Modern Masters series.

In addition to a wide-ranging collection of internationally popular writers of fiction, Fontana also has an outstanding reputation for history, natural history, military history, psychology, psychiatry, politics, economics, religion and the social sciences.

All Fontana books are available at your bookshop or newsagent; or can be ordered direct. Just fill in the form and list the titles you want.

FONTANA BOOKS, Cash Sales Department, G.P.O. Box 29, Douglas, Isle of Man, British Isles. Please send purchase price, plus 8p per book. Customers outside the U.K. send purchase price, plus 10p per book. Cheque, postal or money order. No currency.

NAME (Block letters)

ADDRESS